CW01647503

It's Only Rock and Roll

Berni Stevens

Book 2 – Izzy

Books in series:
Izzy's Christmas Star
It's Only Rock and Roll

Choc Lit

Where heroes are like chocolate – irresistible!

Published 2022 by Choc Lit Limited
Penrose House, Crawley Drive, Camberley, Surrey GU15 2AB, UK
www.choc-lit.com

EPUB: 978-1-78189-089-9
PRINT: 978-1-78189-046-2

For Bob, because drummers are always at the back!

Acknowledgements

The crazy world of the rock musician has long held a fascination for me. Not that I've ever experienced the high-flying world that Izzy does in this book. It was more the club and pub circuit gigs that I experienced as an art student, which were far more problematic, with vans breaking down, venues double-booked and a lot of hanging around while the band packed up their own gear – no roadies for those guys! Our area of Sussex spawned a lot of famous musicians and the music scene at the time was pretty vibrant and a lot of fun. But it was also really hard work, and I have to acknowledge and salute all those musicians for the dedication to their profession. All those who made the "big time" deserved it, but so did the ones who didn't quite make the dizzy heights of international fame. Thank you all for the music!

Many thanks to the wonderful Choc Lit Tasting Panel, for their support and comments as always: Zoe Rippon, Dimitra Evangelou, Karen Mace, Jenny Kinsman, Janice Butler, Lynda Adcock, Michele Rollins, Alan Roberton, Deborah Warren, Sharon Walsh, Fran Stevens and Lorna Baker.

And I'm always appreciative of the massive amount of hard work my lovely editor does for my books, and the wonderful support from the Choc Lit team and my fellow authors. We are like a family, and I love being a part of it. I also have to thank the bloggers, the tweeters and everyone who has reviewed, retweeted, shared or commented on social media in favour of my books. Thank you all so much.

Chapter One

Izzy tore her fascinated gaze away from two diminutive girls, whose sole intention appeared to be to cause grievous bodily harm to each other before anyone stopped them, and turned to watch the beautiful bride mingling with her guests at the reception instead. Best to feign ignorance of the melee just in case somebody, somewhere, thought *she* could be the responsible enough adult to dive in and prise the, now *screaming,* girls apart.

Jo looked sensational. There was no other word for it. She was wearing the dress she'd finally chosen after umpteen shopping trips with Izzy, countless try-ons in zillions of cramped changing rooms all over the West End, the East End and practically every other end of London. But now Jo just kind of … *glowed*. Of course, it could simply be the effect being newly married had on her. Izzy wondered whether she would glow too, if there was ever a break in *someone's* busy schedule at some point in the next decade or two. *That's if he ever even asks me.* Her thoughts were bordering on the churlish, given where she was – she knew that. But even though she didn't feel exactly ready for the gigantic leap into wedded bliss quite yet – not even with the most drop-dead gorgeous man on the planet— although … what if he really *did* ask her, then perhaps? But no, definitely *no* – not yet. The big event for her this summer would be graduating from uni – she was still reeling from getting a first. How very cool was that? A first! *But what if he* did *ask?* Did guys like Seth even *want* to get married? The very idea seemed ludicrous.

And he had tried it once before …

Izzy continued to watch Jo moving effortlessly through the throng of well-wishers like a graceful model, neatly avoiding the chaos caused by cherubic bridesmaid number three, who was now hanging on like grim death to the ponytail of the little *non*-bridesmaid who was dressed in bright pink. It looked like things could get ugly – or ugli*er*. She really hoped someone would come and claim them soon.

Jo really did make the most beautiful bride; in fact, the role of bride could have been made just for her and nobody else. Were all brides like that? Izzy moved forward to join her, the groom and both sets of parents, as they chatted to guests. She suddenly felt hungry; breakfast seemed a very long time ago. She wondered whether she'd have to "meet and greet" everyone in the room before lunch. There was a good chance she'd faint.

Izzy sighed; she didn't think she'd ever achieve the poise and confidence to carry off the whole bride thing when she thought about it. For much of her spare time she was dressed in her fluorescent-coloured dance kit. Not exactly the stuff fairy-tale brides were made of – well, maybe a luridly-dressed, Zumba-teaching kind of bride, and she wasn't sure how well *that* would go down with anyone, let alone Mr Cool. She felt relieved as she watched harassed-looking mothers rush to the rescue now, carting off their wailing children in opposite directions. That was one problem solved, thank goodness. Finding herself alone for the moment, she wandered over to the side of the large reception room and sat down gratefully in the nearest chair. Her shoes were gorgeous, but the heels were a lot higher than Izzy usually wore. *Good one, Izzy*, she thought idly. What on earth could she have been thinking, buying shoes like these, when she knew perfectly well she'd be on her feet most of the day?

An elegant elderly lady immediately engaged Izzy in a conversation about geraniums. Izzy knew nothing about geraniums, other than they usually came in bright colours and smelt horrible. But she smiled and nodded in what she hoped were all the right places. Another elderly lady joined in the geranium conversation, and Izzy allowed her mind to wander again.

She tried to picture Seth dressed as a bridegroom, and failed miserably. Seth was … well … *Seth*. Tall, hunky rock star Seth, customarily dressed in jeans and T-shirt, yet still managing to pull off a sexy, cool look without apparently even trying. She missed him. She'd known what she was getting into, of course; she'd realised he'd be away on tour for at least half the year and in the studio for the other half. *Busy man*. But god, how she missed him. Right on cue, her phone buzzed. She struggled to get it out of the dainty blue bag, glanced at it, and then smiled. The guy must be psychic.

'Hey.' She took a quick slurp of champagne and nearly choked when he spoke.

'Hey yourself.'

The sound of his voice was like warm chocolate oozing down the phone, almost melting her ears. How had he known she'd be missing him even more today?

'So … how do you look all dressed up as a bridesmaid?' She could hear the unmistakable laughter in his voice now.

'I'll have you know I look completely amazing.' Which was a bit far from the truth. Actually, it was a hell of a long way away from the truth. Izzy felt certain she looked like a short blue meringue, but she wasn't going to tell *him* that. Not Mr Super Cool who'd still look sexy in a bin liner.

'I'll be the judge of that. Send me a picture.'

Uh-oh – she'd been rumbled. Izzy grimaced. 'Seriously?'

'Of *course*, seriously. Otherwise, I'll have to rat you out to everyone I know.'

Izzy giggled. She couldn't help it. 'How do I know you won't post it on Instagram?'

'You don't.'

'Never going to happen then.'

'Fair enough. When's graduation?'

Izzy breathed a sigh of relief. *A change of subject.* 'June fifteenth.'

'I'll be there.'

'I don't expect—' she began, flustered.

'I know that,' he interrupted. 'I'll be there.'

A warm glow filled Izzy at his words. She knew he'd try to be there, but she also knew anything in the world could prevent it. She really should check the band's website and see where he was meant to be. Something had held her back from doing just that. Perhaps part of her hadn't wanted to face up to the fact that he might be on the other side of the world on June fifteenth.

He wouldn't mean to let her down, of course he wouldn't, but the decisions weren't always his to make. Tickets would have been sold almost a year in advance. If memory served, he should be somewhere in Australia at the moment, so who knew where he'd be in the middle of June? It was only a few weeks away now ...

'How's it all going?' she said instead.

'Pretty good. The album's gone down well here, so the gigs are all sold out.'

'Busy then …'

'I miss you, Iz.'

There was no mistaking the sincerity in his voice, even from so far away. The glow inside Izzy reignited.

'I miss you too.'

'You'd better.' His deep laugh floated down the phone.

Izzy sighed, wishing she could be with him. He had offered to fly her out to Sydney or Melbourne, but she didn't dare disappear this close to graduation. She'd even stayed in London most of the time, telling her parents she had to be professional about the whole graduation ceremony and everything that went with it. There were the year photos to have done, tables to book for various meals and celebrations, parents and annoying younger brothers to find accommodation for. *And a fabulous dress to discover that isn't a blue meringue.* She was thinking something slinky and black … understated, yet chic …

'After graduation, you'll need a holiday.' He broke into her frenzied thoughts.

'Which means …?' She took a deep breath, knowing exactly what it meant.

'A trip to a quiet, far-flung beach with your favourite rock singer.'

'Oh, is Dave Grohl likely to be on a quiet, far-flung beach at the end of June?'

'Careful.'

Izzy peered into the reception, 'I have to go back in,' she said. 'Looks like food's coming.'

They said their goodbyes, and Izzy made her way towards the top table.

Most people were sitting down at the tables – at last – so it really did look like lunch would be soon. In spite of everything, Izzy was definitely looking forward to the celebratory meal now, although she wondered whether she could actually *eat* anything at all whilst wearing the blue meringue.

Jo was already at her place next to the groom, and she still looked sensational. And so very *glowy*. She caught Izzy's eye and grinned. Marriage certainly seemed to agree with her.

Seth put the phone back in his pocket and stared out at the night view of a floodlit Sydney Opera House. He wished Izzy was with him. He never thought he'd miss anyone as much as he missed her. He loved being away on tour, totally loved every second. Music was his life. But he really wanted Izzy there too. It was so difficult to be away from her. Across the other side of the world away as well. He hated hotels too, even plush ones with views of the Sydney Opera House. He never felt able to relax properly in hotels; they were either too bland and impersonal, which made the rooms feel cold and unwelcoming, or they were garish and bright, which just made them impossible to relax in. Chucking more money at the type of hotel he stayed in didn't seem to help much either. Perhaps it was just him. He missed his huge Tudor farmhouse in Sussex; the silence and solitude there suited him down to the ground. No invasive reporters and photographers, no gaggle of fans clamouring to be noticed by him. Just the welcoming peace and quiet. He missed his comfortable apartment in London too. But what it all boiled down to, if he was honest, was what he missed most of all: Izzy's company. His beautiful red-haired Izzy. With her irrepressible sense of fun in any situation, and the fact she hadn't known who the hell he was when they'd first met. He'd loved that – in fact he still loved that.

Someone knocked on his door. He ignored whoever it was. They'd clear off eventually.

'Seth?' Zach's voice sounded a bit muffled through the door. 'You in there, man?'

'Hold on.' Seth padded barefoot across the thick carpet to open the door.

Zach, sound engineer and best mate, was standing outside with a big grin on his face, his wiry ginger hair exploding in all different directions, as he clutched a bunch of cold bottled beers to his chest.

'Help you with those?' Seth raised his eyebrows hopefully.

'Please.'

Seth took hold of some of the beers and led the way back inside his suite.

'To what do I owe the honour?' Seth asked once they were sitting in the lounge area with the beer bottles freshly opened.

'Thought you might be feeling in need of a few beers.'

Seth appraised the bottle he was drinking from and raised it in salute to Zach. 'You know me so well.'

'Spoken to Izzy?'

'Just now.' Seth nodded. 'She's at Jo's wedding.'

'And that makes you hacked off because …?'

Seth sighed. 'I should be there. I mean, what kind of bloke am I if she has to go around solo for most of the year?'

'And the real reason is …?'

Seth narrowed his eyes at Zach. 'Stop being so bloody intuitive.'

Zach shrugged.

‘What if she meets some other guy? A Joe Normal type of guy who can give her a twenty-four-seven kind of relationship?’

‘Ah.’

‘That’s it? *Ah*?’

‘Mate … Izzy is totally and completely in love with you. You don’t have to be a genius to work that out.’

‘Until some other guy turns up.’

‘The other guy you’ve just made up in your head?’

‘Well, he’ll be around somewhere.’

‘Even if he is, do you think she’d be interested?’

Seth pushed a hand through his mane of tangled curls, and then twisted the heavy silver cuff Izzy had bought him around on his wrist until he could see the embossed gryphon. ‘I couldn’t say.’

‘Well, I can.’ Zach leaned forward. ‘But do you want to know what I *really* think?’

Seth eyed him somewhat dubiously. ‘Why do I get the feeling I’m not going to want to hear this?’

Zach grinned. ‘I think you should probably just marry her.’

Izzy kind of enjoyed the reception. The food had been fabulous, so at least she wasn’t starving any more and also no longer in any danger of fainting. She’d had a slight problem getting through to the best man that she really wasn’t available, not even remotely interested, and was, in fact, very much attached to someone else – even if he wasn’t around at the moment. It had taken a while. It seemed this particular best man wasn’t exactly used to being turned down. She felt pretty sure Seth would be amused by this, but then started to wonder whether he’d actually be a bit put out instead, because *he* couldn’t be there with her. She hadn't a clue whether he'd actually be jealous, and she'd only ever seen him annoyed once or twice, but perhaps it would be better to simply keep the best man to herself, so to speak. She didn't want to make the incident appear more important than it was by talking about it.

Then she wondered again whether she could phone Seth. It had been hours since they'd talked after all. The lunch had consisted of several courses, and had even had tiny dishes of lemon sorbet between each course. Izzy had been more than happy to do every course justice, but when the meal ended, her mind drifted back to a certain rock god once again. *Could* she phone him? Would he be asleep? Writing music? She started working out the time in Sydney. Were they ten or eleven hours ahead? Did that mean it was tomorrow there already? But whatever the time difference, it would definitely be late – past midnight. Seth wasn't your normal kind of rock star and he might just be asleep. He tended to avoid the after-show parties. Although Zach was there, so they might be having a few beers. She really didn't want to come across as the clingy, pathetic girlfriend who couldn't go a few hours without ringing him. She *could* text him though, couldn't she? Yes, definitely she could text. She *should* text – it was the right thing to do. Wasn't it? She'd wait until the speeches were finished, of course. Rude not to. Anyway, the best man, in spite of his faults, was being very funny.

When the speeches ended, and had been enthusiastically applauded, conversation and laughter broke out around the room again; people were now standing up and moving around. Izzy felt it was probably okay to make a call now the formal stuff was out of the way. No doubt there were whole books on wedding etiquette out there somewhere that would argue the point, but if other people were wandering about, and the bride and groom had left the top table too, Izzy felt it was acceptable for her to move around as well.

She fished her phone out of the silly little bag again, standing up at the same time. 'Whose idea *was* this bag?' she muttered to herself. Yes, it was made out of the same material as the dress, so it matched. But all she could fit in it (at a push) was her phone and a lipstick, and that was no mean feat. There wasn't even room left for a small comb.

Hey Mister Music Man, are you asleep?

If I said yes, would you believe me? His answer pinged back straight away.

Izzy grinned to herself. *Of course*, she typed in her reply.

I hope you're fighting off the queues of rampant men like I told you to?

I am, and finding it surprisingly easy.

Music to my ears – hold on, I'll call.

Her phone buzzed. 'Hey.' She smiled down the phone as if he could see. She had a quick, guilty glance round the room to check guests were still wandering about, and felt relieved to see they were. In fact, the bride and groom were now happily whirling around the dance floor to an old Abba song. Personally, Izzy would have preferred leaping about to Scarlet Gryphon if she were the bride. Although that might be pretty weird for Seth, she realised.

'What's the time with you?' she continued, as she walked towards the French windows; wide open now in order to let in the glorious warm weather, and let the guests out. Several of those in attendance had clearly leapt at the chance and were already strolling around the lawns, drinks in hand.

‘No idea.’ He laughed. ‘Zach and I just had a bunch of beers and I’m nicely fuzzy now.’

Izzy laughed. ‘I’m trying to imagine you fuzzy and failing.’

‘So who’s been after my girl today?’

‘Well, it was quite difficult to convince the best man I was spoken for.’ The words were out before Izzy remembered she’d made the decision not to tell him. She’d never been very good at hiding anything. She could have bitten her tongue.

‘And is he devastatingly handsome and rich?’ His voice was careful, or was that only her imagination?

‘Trust me, you can hold your own.’ *More than hold his own*, she thought, wishing she’d simply stuck to her original plan of not mentioning anything.

‘Good to know.’

Izzy snagged a glass of champagne from a passing waiter and wandered outside to sit on the terrace in the sunshine. A change of subject was needed.

‘How long will you be in Sydney?’

‘Three more nights, then on to Melbourne.’

‘Have you played there before?’

‘A few times, yes.’

Izzy looked around at the expansive manicured grounds of the hotel, watching bees buzz in and out of the vivid flowers in the huge stone urns on the terrace. It really had been the most perfect day for Jo’s wedding – almost as hot as a day in mid-summer. But she still couldn’t help but wish that Seth was here with her, even if she did have trouble picturing him among the suited and booted.

‘Where have you gone, Iz?’ His melodious voice brought her back to the moment.

'Sorry. I came outside to sit in the sunshine and be alone with you.'

'Not still being bothered by the best man then?'

Izzy was really beginning to wish she hadn't told him about the incident now. Her first decision had been the right one. *Stupid Izzy*. Live and learn.

She peered inside at the reception, quickly spotting the man in question. It seemed he'd managed to corner the only other adult bridesmaid, who appeared a lot more receptive to his dubious charms than Izzy had been.

'Oh, he's over me already,' she said with a laugh. 'There are only two other bridesmaids, and the third and youngest is just four years old. He's working on the second.'

'Man's insatiable,' commented Seth.

'Dense I'd have said,' returned Izzy.

'You're a tough cookie, Isabelle Grant.'

'True.'

'So … three weeks until the fifteenth of June …'

'Seth, I know it's going to be difficult for you—' Izzy began.

'Anna's on the case. I'll be there.'

A flurry from a vision in white heralded Jo's appearance. 'We're going to cut the cake, Iz,' she called.

'Is that Jo?' Seth asked. 'Put her on.'

Obligingly, Izzy passed the phone across to Jo, who laughed at whatever Seth said and flushed prettily at the last thing he said. 'Definitely,' she said, before handing the phone back to Izzy.

'Go help cut cake,' he encouraged when Izzy put the phone back to her ear. 'I'll see you soon.'

'Look after my rock god,' said Izzy.

She followed Jo back into the room, feeling suddenly bereft and more than a little bit lonely.

Chapter Two

The weeks before graduation passed in a whirl of parties, numerous drunken selfies with friends and packing up her stuff from halls, which helped Izzy realise – and not for the first time – what Seth's normal daily life must be like.

She'd booked everything she was supposed to book for her parents and Ben. The hotel was booked, the restaurant for the graduation day evening meal was booked – she'd actually booked for five, but was starting to wonder whether to change it to four. She still couldn't imagine how Seth would be able to make it, even though he continued to insist he'd be there. If she asked him every time he rang or messaged, she could see all too clearly how it could get boring. But how would Anna ever fix it? In the middle of a world tour? Izzy knew Anna was one of the best PAs in the business, but even so … and then there was the added stress of finding something suitable, yet fabulous, to wear. Not that she could ask Seth's opinion about that when he was busy with the tour.

She realised that the worst thing to do would be to actually look forward to Seth turning up. That way lay huge disappointment and the possible ruination of the most important day of her life so far. Plus, she couldn't help but wonder how on earth he'd be able to just casually turn up without a cavalcade of reporters and photographers following him. Would it spoil the day for the other students? She really didn't want to be responsible for that. Izzy badly needed Jo's help. What was she *thinking,* going off on honeymoon when she so desperately needed her?

Trying to find the perfect dress really wasn't helping to soothe her queasy nerves. She'd gone through dress after dress on very many rails of dresses in countless department stores, wondering why there were *so* many dresses with violently coloured patterns, and whose bright idea it had been to put them all on the same rail. The effect was lurid enough to give her a migraine.

Then, of course, Izzy's thoughts inevitably went back to Seth and the tour. He'd probably be in Japan or somewhere on graduation day anyway, and she was panicking needlessly about reporters and fans. She really should check the website. *Or just ask him,* a nagging voice said in her head. *Next time he calls, just ask him if he's really coming.* Good advice from herself to herself. Which she had no intention of taking.

With only two days to go before graduation, Izzy was still trawling through rails of dresses in various different stores, and discarding them all for one reason or another. She was beginning to lose both hope and interest, and realised now how Jo must have felt when she was searching for her wedding dress. She flicked a few more dresses along yet another rail. Still too many patterns, she hated patterns, *what was it with patterns?* Surely there must be something plain and classy somewhere ... and then ... *there it was!* The perfect dress. Just when she'd almost given up hope and decided she'd simply wear black trousers instead. A gorgeous little black number popped up, beautifully cut and *so* classy. Although it was with some trepidation that she carried it off to the changing rooms. What if it didn't fit – or simply looked awful?

Twirling in front of the full length mirror a few minutes later, she breathed a heartfelt sigh of relief. It fitted perfectly. She *loved* this dress. It made her look really elegant and instantly taller. Thank goodness. At long last: outfit – *sorted.*

Izzy joined the queue to pay, feeling dizzy with relief and more than a little bit pleased with herself. This was the best dress *ever*!

Back outside on the pavement, she headed towards the tube station. It was just getting busy with the start of the rush hour as she hurried into Tottenham Court Road station, but she felt too elated by her successful shopping expedition to care. She'd be back in Finchley soon, and she might just try the dress on again.

The sense of elation continued as Izzy walked towards Seth's road. She wondered whether there'd be any lingering fans outside today. The few she'd encountered so far seemed surprisingly friendly and always called out to her.

But, if she was honest with herself, she still felt a little weird staying in Seth's London flat without him, even though he'd insisted. He'd said, quite reasonably, that his flat was just sitting there empty whilst she didn't have a place to stay after leaving halls, and that had ultimately been too convincing an argument to ignore. She hadn't really fancied travelling up to town from Sussex every other day anyway. She would have felt happier if Kathleen, his housekeeper, had been around, but she was away on holiday.

Turning the corner into Seth's road, she spotted the familiar gaggle of fans outside, hoping for a glimpse of their idol. A couple of girls took her photo on their phones. *Seriously?* She gave them a friendly wave anyway.

'Where's Seth?' one of them called.

'Australia,' Izzy replied.

'Bummer.' The other girl sighed in typical teenage fashion.

Tapping in the entry code on the pad next to the huge double oak doors, Izzy headed for the lift furthest away in the foyer. Seth's private lift. She smiled as she remembered the first time she'd come here and how she'd teased him about the private lift. He'd probably lived like this for a long time now, but to Izzy it was a whole new world. This last year had felt like a Cinderella story – and she'd somehow nabbed the prince.

She let herself into the quiet flat with the spare keys Seth had given her before he'd left to go on tour. '*Use the place, Iz.*' She could still hear his encouraging voice in her head. '*Please.*'

But it still felt *weird.*

She drifted upstairs to the bedroom … *his* bedroom.

When Izzy had first arrived at the flat a week ago, she'd been tempted to sleep in the spare room, but quickly discovered it was full of guitars, amps, mic stands and other musician-type stuff. *Shouldn't this all be kept in a studio? Or down in Sussex in his home studio?* The guest double bed had been completely swamped by a mountainous heap of Seth's clothes too, which appeared to have been picked up from a dry-cleaners by someone, as they were all covered by the same protective plastic. Izzy wondered whether she should hang them up … but thought better of it when she'd seen the obstacle course of music paraphernalia between the bed and the wardrobe. So Seth's room it was: the huge master bedroom that Izzy's room in halls could have fitted in at least six times.

Izzy automatically made a beeline for the gorgeous en suite bathroom. She was getting used to the bathroom at least. A girl could always make herself at home in a snazzy bathroom, couldn't she? The bath itself stood on clawed feet near the window, and if it could have beckoned her in with a claw she felt sure it would have. But, nevertheless, after finding, and buying, the perfect dress, a celebration bath sounded good to Izzy right now. The shower standing separately in its own gleaming cubicle didn't feel quite as inviting as a soak in the deep tub with a generous dollop of bubbles.

She wondered what time it was in Australia now. *Is he even still in Australia?* Graduation was only the day after tomorrow now, and there hadn't been a word from him for a couple of days, which was unusual. He must be travelling; it was the only answer. But was he travelling home to her or just travelling onwards to somewhere else on the tour?

One of the perks of being Seth Roberts of Scarlet Gryphon was the speed with which he was escorted through customs at Heathrow, and then having the luxury of Dave waiting for him in the usual place to help with his luggage and whisk him away to the posh part of Finchley. He spotted his driver straight away and raised a hand in greeting.

'How's it going?' Dave's laconic greeting sounded like music to Seth's tired ears.

'Good to be back,' said Seth. 'Even if it is only for a week.'

He sank into the back seat of the Audi with a sigh of relief and closed his eyes. He really hoped Izzy would be at his flat. She'd said she was staying there … but would she be out partying? He smiled as he remembered her end-of-term hangover last Christmas. What did they call that particular celebration? "Drink the bar dry". That was it, and Izzy had certainly done her very best to help with that.

He remembered going to pick her up the next day from halls, and the look of abject horror on her face when he let himself into her room. To him, of course, she still looked like his beautiful Izzy, albeit with very strange hair and bleary eyes. He couldn't wait to see her again. It felt like a really long time since he had.

Seth must have dozed off, because suddenly the car drew up outside the mansion block and he came to with a start.

'Lights are on,' observed Dave.

'Burglars,' quipped Seth, heaving himself out of the car. 'Thanks man, appreciate it.'

Dave's deep chuckle made him smile. 'Need a hand up with your case?'

'Nah, I'm good, thanks.' Seth took his case from Dave. 'See ya soon.'

He felt a huge sense of relief when he spotted the distinct lack of fans outside his place. Normally he didn't mind, and would spend a few minutes with them having selfies taken and chatting. But tonight he just wanted Izzy.

Izzy sank down into the hot water, submerged up to her neck in Seth's fragrant bath bubbles. They smelt tangy and sexy – like him. She closed her eyes to picture him, sighing blissfully. This really was the life. She could have brought a book in, but no, it would probably have felt too much like hard work to read words and sentences in the bath. She'd done nothing *but* read for months and months. Possibly years …

She hummed a Scarlet Gryphon song quietly, and continued to enjoy the wallowing. This was so much better than the pathetic, lukewarm trickle she'd endured for three years from the showers at uni, and infinitely more peaceful than the family bathroom in Sussex. No annoying younger brother hammering on the door because he couldn't be bothered to use the downstairs loo and interrupt his latest Xbox game for too long. *Bliss.* Nobody here but her …

'Anything I can help you with?' A familiar deep voice from the doorway made her eyes fly open in shock.

Seth's tall frame leaned nonchalantly against the open door frame, thumbs hooked through the belt loops of his faded jeans. He was grinning his usual mischievous grin, his amazing blue eyes sparkled and his feet were bare. A sight for sore eyes.

'Where're your shoes?' Izzy managed to gasp eventually. 'Did you leave them on the plane?'

Seth sauntered into the bathroom, pulling off his T-shirt as he got nearer, and then casually stepped into the bath, jeans and all. 'Is that the best you can do?' he said.

Chapter Three

Seth slept for ten hours straight. At one point Izzy actually poked him to make sure he was still breathing. That didn't go down too well. She still couldn't believe he was really here, in London, for her graduation.

Over a late breakfast, lunch, or maybe early dinner – Izzy wasn't sure which – he patted his chest as he proclaimed he was Seth Roberts and, as such, could be wherever he wanted to be. Then he feigned horror at her lack of confidence, both in him and Anna.

Izzy narrowed her eyes at him. 'So how many strings *did* Anna have to pull?'

Seth laughed. 'Quite a few. I think the official line is I had a family emergency and had to rush back for a week.'

'A week …' It didn't sound very long to Izzy, but then she realised she was lucky he was here at all. 'I can't believe you're here! I think I must be dreaming.'

Seth raised his eyebrows. 'I could offer to pinch you to make up for all the poking.'

'I poked you once because you didn't appear to be breathing.'

'So you always have my best interests at heart?'

'Absolutely.'

'Good – then you'll make sure you're ready to fly back with me when I leave.'

'In a *week* …?'

Seth looked serious for once. He took hold of her hand in both of his. 'Please Iz, I need you with me.'

Her heart melted. 'I'll be ready.'

The look on his face was worth the abject panic which filled her at that moment. Her active brain was already sifting through everything she'd need to sort out beforehand. *Where the hell is my passport? Do I need a visa?*

'Make sure you have all you need for a holiday too.'

'No pressure then.'

He leaned across the table and ran a finger gently down her cheek. 'And whatever you forget, I'll buy when we get there.'

'Wherever *there* is …?'

'You'll have to wait and see.' He sat up again and the grin was back. 'Are you wearing your bridesmaid's dress to graduate in?'

Izzy burst out laughing. 'I never want to see that dress again.'

'You said you looked really good in it.'

'I lied.'

'And yet still the best man fancied you.'

Oh, him again ... lesson definitely *learned, Iz.*

'The best man would have fancied any female with a pulse.'

'Don't put yourself down, Iz. I think you rocked the blue taffeta thingy.'

'How do you know it was blue taffeta …?'

'Jo sent a picture …' Seth laughed at the look on Izzy's face.

'Oh, she is *so* dead.'

'Those little puffy sleeves were a particularly nice touch.'

Izzy picked up the nearest cushion and threw it at Seth's head. He caught it deftly and waggled it back at her. 'I have two sisters – remember? I'm very good at catching and ducking things chucked at me. I've had *years* of practice.'

It was the morning of graduation and Izzy had just put *the* dress on. '*Oh no, Isabelle – not another black dress.*' Izzy's mum hadn't been overly impressed when she'd been told over the phone. Izzy reminded her that the graduation gown was black and would therefore look much smarter with something black underneath. *'Like a barrister*,' her father had said helpfully. Ben had snorted derisively at the thought of his sister as any kind of lawyer. '*More like a bat*,' was his comment.

But Izzy adored the dress. She did a bit of a twirl in front of Seth's wardrobe mirror, and loved the way the expensive material moved as she moved. *Will* he *like it?* she wondered. Would he say if he didn't? She didn't think he would; he'd had plenty of practice with sisters after all, like he'd said. But she still hoped he'd like it …

'Well, it's a definite improvement on the blue taffeta.' His voice startled her out of her frantic thoughts and back to reality. She turned to face him. 'Thanks – I think.'

He came closer and wrapped strong arms around her. 'Gorgeous,' he said against her hair. 'Mmmm … have you been at my bubbles again?'

She giggled. 'No, I had a shower – and before you ask, I used my own shower gel.'

'You smell good enough to eat.'

'Perhaps I can graduate before you do?'

He released her, took a box from his flight bag on the floor and handed it to her. 'Graduation present.'

Izzy opened the box; inside was a silver pendant shaped like two teardrops melded together, with a pattern of tiny silver stars in one tear and larger drops of raised silver in the other. It hung on a delicate silver chain – she'd never seen anything quite like it.

'It's … *amazing*, Seth! Thank you so much. I love it.'

He took the pendant from the box and fastened it around her neck before standing back to admire it. 'Looks awesome,' he said. 'Aborigine design, apparently, and I just loved the shape of it. It suits you.' He grinned. 'I knew it would.'

Izzy stood on tiptoe and wound her arms around his neck. 'Then you're a very clever man, Seth Roberts.'

'I am.' He twirled a strand of her hair around his finger and pulled her in closer for a kiss. 'What time do we need to leave?'

'Leave?' She was still reeling from the kiss. 'Damn, I should have called for a cab. I said I'd pick the folks up from their hotel … what *is* the time?'

'Ten-ish. What time do you want to pick them up?'

'Eleven latest. I have to go and pick up a gown, and then get official photos done.'

'And the ceremony is at …?' Seth's quiet questions calmed Izzy down. '*Breathe,* Izzy.'

She wrinkled her nose at him. 'It's at two.'

'Good.' Seth pulled his phone out of his pocket. 'Where's the hotel?'

'Woodside Park Road. You aren't sending Dave?'

'He won't mind at all, and he gets well paid. He can pick the folks up and drop them at the coffee shop nearest to uni, then come back for us and we'll go wherever you need to get your gown from, then we'll meet the folks and go get your photos done.'

Izzy felt impressed. 'Either you've been learning from Anna, or she's been learning from you.'

Seth gave her a look that made her laugh. 'Got a name for the hotel?'

'Alderley Park.'

Seth rang Dave and gave him the hotel name and address.

Whilst he continued talking to the driver, Izzy went back to checking herself out in the mirror. The pendant gleamed brightly against the black, the different facets of silver catching the light whenever she moved. She felt a million dollars and more than slightly nervous.

For the first time, she noticed Seth had added what appeared to be an expensive black suit jacket over his customary blue jeans. He wore a plain white T-shirt under the jacket; she suspected a proper collared shirt *plus* a jacket would have been more than he could take, and Izzy couldn't begin to imagine he'd ever wear the matching trousers to the jacket – or even have bought them. He looked completely scrumptious and cool as a cucumber – if cucumbers were ever sexy rock gods.

Still talking on the phone, Seth wandered into the bathroom, coming back out seconds later with his hair pulled back in a short ponytail. Izzy drew in a breath. If possible, he looked even more devastating than before. He finished the call and put the phone in his jacket pocket. He spotted Izzy watching him.

'Problem?'

'No … I've just never seen your hair tied back like that.'

'It works well as a bit of a disguise.' He laughed when she didn't say anything. 'Do you hate it?'

'If I did that with my hair I'd look like a brat from St Trinian's.'

Seth raised his eyebrows. 'There's a thought that's going to stay with me. I'm imagining you in the uniform …'

Dave was his efficient self as always. He'd picked everyone up from the right places, duly delivered them to the right places, and ferried Seth and Izzy to and from the gown place, then back to the place at uni where the official photographs were being taken, even fetching the family so they could be in the photos.

Seth had joined Izzy in a photograph too, for which she'd love him forever; she knew he must be heartily sick of being photographed.

The photographer fiddled with his camera and then looked up. 'I bet you hear this all the time, mate,' he commented. 'But you don't half look like that bloke from Scarlet Gryphon. Dead ringer – different hair, of course.'

Izzy bit back a smile as her mum shot a warning look at Ben.

Seth smiled. 'Yeah, I get that a lot. But he's better looking.'

'You're taller.'

'Yeah – way taller.'

Photos finished, Izzy took her receipt and tucked it safely in her bag. Thanking the photographer, they all hurried out before Ben told the photographer – and the rest of the world – that actually Seth really *was* Seth.

After leisurely sandwiches in a quiet pub Izzy knew, she left them to join the other graduates before the ceremony, and Seth followed her family up the stairs in the Great Hall to the seats reserved for them. He looked around him. *What a place*. He thought it would make a good music venue and wondered what the acoustics were like. The ceilings were high, maybe too high, and then suddenly he realised Beth, Izzy's mum, was speaking to him.

'Sorry, Beth?' He gave her a friendly smile and leaned down to hear what she was saying.

'I just wondered how you found Izzy,' she said again.

'It was easy, she's staying in my flat,' he quipped.

Beth laughed. 'You know what I mean.'

Seth nodded. 'Very nervous about today – especially this morning.'

'She's seemed a bit quieter than usual recently, whenever we've spoken on the phone. Ever since Jo got married, in fact.'

Seth felt a lurch in his gut. Surely this wasn't going to be a "what are your intentions towards my daughter" speech? He hadn't a clue what he'd say if it was.

Why did everyone suddenly want to get him married off? Even Zach. He'd been there and done that once before, and look how well that turned out. He didn't feel exactly *anti* marriage as such, not any more anyway, not now he had Izzy. But he did wish everyone would give him a bit of space regarding the whole thing. He really wanted to get his own head around the thought first – on his own. Anyway, for all he knew, Izzy might run for the hills if he mentioned it. And he *certainly* didn't want that.

'Any idea why?' he said instead.

Beth appraised him with a look his own mother would have been proud of. 'Several,' she said. 'She and Jo have been close friends since school. Jo came to London first but Izzy didn't know what she wanted to do, so she worked in a local leisure centre for a few years until she finally decided she wanted something more.'

'So that's where the Zumba came from?'

'She's always loved dancing,' said Beth with a smile. 'And she's really good too. I would have liked her to go to dance college really.'

And preferably not get hooked up with a rock singer? wondered Seth.

At that moment, a short, portly man in a mortar board and gown fussed his way onto the stage below, and all conversation stopped.

'Good afternoon, everyone,' he said. 'Welcome to the graduation of our English Literature students.'

There was a polite round of applause.

Seth hoped there wouldn't be lots of lengthy speeches. He thought he might just drop off if there were. Jet lag from Australia was always a killer. He desperately wanted to put his sunglasses on to alleviate the glare from the lights but nothing said "Hey, look at me" more than someone wearing shades indoors. The leg room between the rows of seats wasn't made for someone his height either. He felt as if his knees were up around his ears.

Another round of applause signified the ceremony was about to begin. There was a queue of gowned graduates in the wings now. Seth squinted towards them, but he couldn't see Izzy. He hoped she felt okay. Then he started to wonder where Beth had been going with the conversation. He had no idea what he would have said if she'd just come out and asked him if he intended to marry Izzy. He loved her – a lot – that wasn't in any doubt … but was it enough for the moment?

Have I even told her I love her? Knowing him, probably not. The fears she'd meet a nice normal "nine-to-fiver" and opt for an ordinary life were very real to him. He was experienced enough in his own world to know it wasn't exactly conducive to sustaining long-term relationships. Cancelled dates, even holidays cut short by rearranged studio slots, happened all the time, and he and the rest of the band just had to suck it up. Most of the wives were in the business; in fact, two of them were backing singers with the band, and now Zach was in a relationship with Anna, Seth's much valued PA, so they already knew the score. Would Izzy travel with him or would she prefer to stay at home? And if she stayed at home, would she find someone else? Would he? It had been a while since Seth had even wanted to be involved in a lengthy, serious relationship, let alone thought about the "M" word. The last thing he wanted to do was compromise the harmony within the band during a world tour, like a *certain* bass player seemed intent on doing. Or at least the girlfriend of said bass player did.

'And gaining a first, Isabelle Grant.'

Seth hauled his phone out of his jacket pocket again and started to video Izzy walking across the stage. She looked so small down there, but very graceful. It was a new experience for him, watching someone else down on a stage as opposed to being the one performing. It was kind of a weird feeling too, if he was honest.

Switching from video mode to photos, he took several of her receiving the diploma. Even from here he could see her face was flushed, and he wanted to jump up and shout out how proud he was. He didn't, of course – that would be a very bad idea.

She left the stage and disappeared into the wings. *Will she come upstairs or stay down there?* he wondered.

Beth tapped him lightly on the arm, 'You could go down and see her now if you want to.'

'Is it okay to do that?'

Beth smiled. 'Yes, don't worry. I asked before we knew you'd be here. I would have gone myself otherwise.'

Seth kissed Beth's cheek lightly. If he had to choose a mother-in-law, she'd be a great one. Then he stood up quietly and slipped out and down the stairs. A few people gave him a second glance as if they were trying to remember where they'd seen him before. Whispered conversations followed him round the twisting corridor to the room at the back of the stage. He heard his name a couple of times and steeled himself not to react. Today was Izzy's day – as far as everyone else was concerned, he was Joe Bloggs.

The evening meal was perfect. Izzy had chosen a discreet French-style bistro where the food was amazing. Seth enjoyed watching Izzy interacting with her family, her eyes sparkling and the soft lights in the restaurant picking out the different shades of red in her amazing hair. She'd let it grow longer – past her shoulders now – and he loved it.

He felt relaxed and at home with the whole family, which was something he hadn't felt with any other family, except his own, for many years.

Actually, the band were his family most of the time, and like any family they argued. A lot of egos in one room made it tough sometimes. He'd been a long time on the road, he realised. Years of travelling from one country to the next, city to city. A hard life, but not one he wanted to give up any time soon. And yet it felt like there was always something or some*one* who was out to cause trouble. He immediately thought of Jonno's latest girlfriend, and hoped to god she wouldn't suddenly turn up in Australia. She certainly had the money to turn up wherever she fancied. If ever anyone was potentially trouble, it was Sophie something–*something*, whatever her no doubt double-barrelled name was, with a mega-rich, indulgent father who spoilt her rotten. She'd started flexing her muscles last year in London, and he thought he'd nipped it all in the bud, but instinct told him different. The girl was trouble, he felt it in his bones.

Then he found his mind wandering to the marriage thing again. He really didn't have a clue how Izzy felt about marriage; it had simply never come up. She'd only just graduated for heaven's sake, and even though she'd been a bit older compared to the other students in her year, she was still a few years younger than him. As far as he knew, she hadn't decided on a definite career path yet – although she had once mentioned an interest in journalism. Still, there was plenty of time for the serious stuff. There was no great rush to tie the knot – *was there?* Although he didn't want to *lose* her – not *ever* ... not now he'd found her ...

'You're quiet, Seth.' He came back to earth with a bump when he realised Izzy had been talking to him.

'Hell – I'm sorry, Iz, it's this damn jet lag,' he apologised. 'You'll understand when you fly back with me.' He grinned. 'Then I can poke *you*.'

At the same time, they both realised what he'd said and burst out laughing.

'What's funny?' asked Ben. 'Did you tell Izzy a joke?'

'Something like that,' agreed Seth. 'So Ms I've Got a First, what's the plan?'

'Plan?'

'Yes, what do you want to do with your First?'

'Good question … write … work in TV, maybe … I haven't really thought much about it.'

'No burning ambition?'

'Journalism is a possibility – I think I told you …' She patted his arm. 'But definitely not a music journo.'

He gave her a stern look. 'You'd get thrown off the tour bus if you were.'

'Really?'

He poured her more wine and topped up her parents' glasses before filling his own. 'Apparently, a well-known singer out on tour in the US discovered one of the girls on the tour bus was actually a journo for a music magazine and had her thrown off in the middle of nowhere.'

Izzy looked horrified. 'What? But that's insane. She could have been abducted or killed or both …'

Seth couldn't help grinning. 'Well – I doubt he's that much of a monster. And as the story goes, he got one of his people to send a car for her and take her back to the last town.'

'Who was it?'

'Actually, I'm not a hundred per cent sure. I only know the tour involved, and there were several bands on the same tour.'

'Well, frankly, I hope he never sells another album, whoever he is.'

'What's wrong with being a journalist?' Ben wanted to know.

Seth spent the next ten minutes explaining why musicians weren't overly keen on music journalists, telling him about the reporter who'd followed him and Izzy around when they first met.

'You must have seen the photo of us that was in the paper one time?'

'Izzy said they were plastered around her corridor in halls.' Ben laughed. 'Who'd want photos of Izzy everywhere?'

'Hey, I'm sitting right here.' Izzy shot her brother an indignant look.

Seth took hold of her hand and turned back to Ben. 'I would for one.'

'Well, you're bonkers.'

'Time we went back to the hotel, I think,' said Izzy's dad, clearly sensing the start of an argument and reaching inside his jacket for his wallet.

Seth stopped him. 'I'll get this, Tom,' he said. 'I've been AWOL for months, so it's the least I can do. Do you need a ride back?'

'Don't worry, we'll get a cab,' said Beth quickly. 'Your man's been ferrying us around all day. Let him have the evening off.' She leaned across and kissed Seth on the cheek. 'Thank you.'

Both parents hugged their daughter and left with a protesting Ben, who insisted he was thirteen, nearly fourteen, and *way* old enough to stay out with Izzy and Seth.

Seth watched them leave thoughtfully. 'Tough being that age, not quite grown up, but too old to be stuck with your parents on a night out.'

'I was far too busy to be a problem teenager, I think,' said Izzy with a laugh.

'Doing what exactly?' Seth turned to look at her with a smile. This sounded intriguing. 'Do tell.'

'Riding horses and dancing mostly.'

'Ah yes, that would keep you busy. I'd forgotten you can ride.'

'You were going to introduce me to your horses some time, weren't you?'

Seth made a face. 'True. It might have to be in the autumn now.'

Izzy looked down at the table to cover her disappointment, but Seth noticed and put his hand over hers. 'Fancy getting out of here?'

She nodded and he signalled to the waiter for the bill.

Yes, relationships were definitely still tricky, he thought. Especially for someone like him. It was one of the reasons he hadn't stayed with anyone for longer than a year since his divorce.

He knew he'd be straight back into the vibe of the tour almost from the moment he and Izzy touched down in Adelaide. Three more weeks of travel and gigs before they all took the halfway holiday break – three weeks of rehearsals, sound checks and concerts. None of which Izzy would really want to get involved in – or so he thought. He knew all too well how boring it could be for anyone not actually in the band or crew. Was it selfish of him to drag her to the other side of the world, when she could be doing whatever normal people did after finishing uni with a good grade? He hoped she didn't see it like that. He really did.

Chapter Four

Izzy woke late the next morning to find herself alone. She sat up in the huge bed and yawned. She could hear Seth talking to someone downstairs but couldn't hear anyone answering, so assumed he must be on the phone.

She lay back against the pillows again, basking in the sound of his voice and the fact he was only just downstairs. Only a few days and they'd be flying out to Australia together. She really hadn't managed to get her head around that fact, let alone get everything together she needed for a couple of months away. Then, of course, she'd have to travel back home on her own as the band headed off to Japan and Hong Kong. She'd told herself it was no big deal: students back-packed alone around the world all the time. Not a big deal at all. Except for her, it really *was* a big deal. She felt nervous about it but had no intention of letting on to anyone exactly *how* nervous. Seth flew back alone for her graduation after all. *Yes, but he flies all over the place all year round*, a nagging voice in her head told her. *It means diddly squat to him*. But it meant a lot to Izzy. She also didn't even want to start thinking about how many people he'd ticked off by flying home for her graduation.

Seth came in at that moment carrying two mugs. The fragrant smell of coffee wafted in with him, and he grinned at the expression on her face.

'You made coffee?' Izzy gave him a sceptical look.

'What? I can't be multi-talented and thoughtful too?'

'I'll ask again – you made *coffee*?'

'I cannot tell a lie – Kathleen made it.'

Izzy laughed. 'But you carried it here so beautifully.'

He bowed his head and passed a mug to her.

'I thought Kathleen was on holiday?'

'Back yesterday and straight back to work today.' Seth sat on the edge of the bed. 'She's very impressed with how tidy the place is too.'

Izzy sipped at the coffee. 'This is good … almost as good as coffee shop coffee.'

'Praise indeed.'

'Funny the people you meet in coffee shops.' She remembered sitting at his table in the crowded coffee shop last summer. Almost a year ago now. And she'd had no idea he was one of the most famous rock stars on the planet back then.

Seth turned to look at her, his expressive eyes glinting. 'It is,' he agreed. 'And it's even funnier the people who gatecrash your table …' He leaned forward and kissed her. 'Are you going to stay in there all day?'

'Says the man who slept for so long I thought he was dead.'

'And we're back to the poking.' Seth's mischievous grin was also back. He stood up. 'Get showered and ready for a slap-up brunch in Hampstead. Dave will be here in an hour.'

He sauntered towards the door and turned back to mouth 'one hour' before leaving the room and closing the door behind him. Shame he'd closed the door; Izzy had been admiring the rear view. Muttering 'one hour' to herself, she finished her coffee and wiggled reluctantly out from under the duvet.

Dave duly arrived exactly fifty minutes later, and Seth felt impressed to see Izzy actually appear, ready to go, at almost the same time. She looked gorgeous too. For someone who didn't appear to know much about his work or the way the "rock chicks" dressed, she looked every inch a rock chick in faded denim cut-offs, a black vest top and the silver pendant he'd bought her. She'd even tied a bright green bandana around her red hair and knotted it on top of her head, American-style. Definitely very fanciable.

He grinned at her. 'Perfect timing,' he said. 'Dave's here.'

Kathleen came into the room and smiled at Izzy. 'Don't you look a picture now?' she said. 'You need to get some colour in those cheeks though.' She turned to Seth. 'The girl needs a holiday, so she does. Been cleaning this place for weeks, I shouldn't wonder.'

'And she's going to get one,' Seth assured her. 'Eventually.'

Taking hold of Izzy's arm, he steered her towards the front door. 'You won't need a jacket,' he said when she hesitated by her leather jacket hanging on a peg. 'The sun's shining and you'd melt in that.'

Izzy didn't look too convinced.

The sun greeted them with a blast of bright warmth to prove Seth right, as they left the flat and made a dash for the car waiting for them.

'Fans warning,' muttered Seth, gripping Izzy's arm tighter. He opened the car door and she slid in quickly, moving up the seat to make room for him.

One of the girls noticed him just as he closed the car door. The cries of, 'Seth! Seth!' sounded louder as the fans ran towards the car.

'Let's go, Dave. Try not to run anybody over.'

'Do me best,' Dave replied, keeping an eye out for anyone stupid enough to get in the road. 'Hampstead, right?'

'Yep, as near Flask Walk as you can so we can make a dash for the pub.'

'We could have just cooked something,' Izzy pointed out.

Seth turned to look at her. 'We?'

She laughed. 'Well, I could have.'

'Not as much fun as running the gauntlet of the Finchley Fan Mafia.'

'I don't understand how you can be hungry after that huge meal last night.'

'Jet lag.'

'That's a bad excuse and doesn't last for ever.'

Seth took hold of her hand and laced their fingers together. It felt so good to be with Izzy again. He really *had* missed her.

Izzy had been to The Flask a few times but only for the occasional drink; she'd never eaten there. It was a quaint Victorian pub built on the original site of The Flask Tavern where folk had travelled from all over in order to buy the famous Hampstead mineral water. Apparently, if Izzy remembered correctly, Hampstead had been some kind of holiday destination in the 1700s – the equivalent of a spa town today. She tried to imagine Seth's face if someone attempted to palm him off with a glass of spa water instead of his favourite beer. That would definitely not be a wise thing to do. She turned to look at him and found him already looking at her.

'What?' She laughed.

'You had a sort of secret smile on your face, like you know something I don't.'

'I probably know a lot of things you don't, and vice versa.'

He brought her hand to his lips and kissed it. 'As always, you put me firmly in my place.'

In typical Seth style, he went for the eight-ounce steak with triple cooked chips, while Izzy plumped for the smoked salmon open sandwich with cucumber, watercress, crème fraiche and definitely no chips. He raised his eyebrows at her order but said nothing.

They chatted easily over the meal, with Izzy trying to find out where the holiday destination was. Seth, still as adept as ever at avoiding questions he had absolutely no intention of answering, fielded all her trick questions with his usual charm.

'You can be infuriating, do you know that?' she said, at last admitting defeat.

'So I'm told.' He grinned at her frustration. 'Iz, we'll be in Australia this time next week, I'll be working like a lunatic for two or three weeks to make up for spending a week here, and then we'll be off on holiday for two weeks before the Japanese leg of the tour.'

'And then ...?'

'I'll be home.'

'London or Sussex?'

'Both.'

Both sounded good to Izzy. She knew he'd still be working, of course – writing and maybe recording – but to have him in the same hemisphere for a few months would be wonderful.

'You can stay at my Sussex place if you like, when you're back from the holiday?' He offered it casually as if offering her a glass of wine.

Izzy bit her bottom lip. 'I'd rattle around there like a ... lonely frozen pea.'

Seth laughed aloud. 'Strange choice of words.'

'Well – you know what I mean.'

'The offer's there. There are four energetic horses who might need some exercise.'

'You don't have …' Izzy hesitated, then waved her hands about. '… a groom or someone to do that?'

Seth looked amused. 'I thought you liked riding.'

'I do.'

'Done deal then. I'll be sure to tell Ted to look after you, if and when you decide to go.'

'Ted?'

'He's the guy who looks after the horses.'

Izzy wasn't sure how she felt yet about going to stay in Seth's Tudor farmhouse without him – or riding his horses. It seemed a bit ... kind of intrusive somehow. Staying in the London flat was one thing – Kathleen was back from her holiday now after all and would be popping in and out most days – but the Sussex place was Seth's very private refuge, all high security and entry phones. It would be like staying at Balmoral – except the farmhouse was in Sussex, not Scotland, and the Queen wouldn't be there. Still, she had plenty of time to think about it. There was the little matter of flying off to Australia with Seth first, and then a secret holiday location to enjoy!

Chapter Five

On the day of their departure, Dave arrived exactly on time, as he usually did, to take them to the airport. Izzy still felt sure she'd forgotten something, but Seth assured her that, as long as she had her passport, nothing she'd forgotten would be a problem.

'Take good care of this one,' Kathleen said to Seth, making him grin. 'She's a bit special so she is.'

'And don't I know it?' he said, plonking a kiss on the housekeeper's cheek. 'You take care of yourself.'

Izzy hugged Kathleen. 'Enjoy the peace and quiet,' she said.

'Ah get away, the more noise the better for me.'

Dave expertly wheeled Izzy's cases out towards the lift, leaving Seth to bring his much smaller one himself.

'I don't think you can have left anything behind, judging by those cases.' Seth nodded towards them. 'Have we still got the silver, Kathleen?'

Kathleen laughed and pushed him towards the door. 'Get away, you daft thing,' she said. 'If there was ever any silver here, I've surely never seen it.'

'Ah, but you looked, didn't you?' Seth gave her a look of mock outrage, making her laugh again.

They made the car without anyone noticing Seth this time.

'"Under cover of the night",' commented Izzy. 'I feel like a spy.'

'Sounds like a Stones' track to me,' said Seth.

Dave pulled away from the kerb, and they were on their way. Izzy felt a little nauseous, which she hoped was simply excitement and not some dreaded lurgy.

Taking a deep breath, she turned to look at Seth. His profile was every bit as gorgeous as every other angle, outlined by the light from various street lamps as they drove by. Sensing her looking at him, he turned to face her then, his blue eyes taking on the shine from the lights.

'Are you okay?'

'Nervous.' Izzy smiled.

Seth frowned. 'Of what? Flying?'

'I'm not sure really … being away for so long, so far away …'

'With a big bad rock singer?'

'Well, that's probably my parents' version.'

'Nah, not your very cool, Bowie-loving mum.'

'Just my dad then.'

'There was a saying – apparently – whenever the Stones went to a particular place on tour: "Lock up your daughters, the Rolling Stones are in town".'

'I remember you telling me that – and now they say it about you?'

'They've never said it about me.' His face looked the picture of innocence as he draped an arm around her shoulders. 'I'm a virtual paragon.'

Dave's laugh from the driver's seat shot that theory to bits as far as Izzy was concerned, yet she couldn't stop a giggle from escaping. The very idea of Seth as any kind of paragon was hysterical.

He grinned and pulled her closer. 'Except when I'm hungry.'

Izzy laughed aloud at that. He was *always* hungry.

Their luggage had been taken away for checking in and loading, and they were shown directly to the first class lounge, which was a complete revelation to Izzy, who'd only ever travelled in economy class. There were curtains at the windows, huge comfortable-looking sofas and armchairs, several bars, restaurants, and, in one corner, even a large piano.

'Is that for you?' Izzy asked Seth as he steered her towards one of the bars.

'God, I hope not.' He pulled a face. 'I'll be put to work soon enough once we're in Adelaide.'

Izzy put a hand on his arm. 'I'm still so over the moon you made it back for my graduation.'

He smiled down at her. 'That's what makes it all worthwhile.' He leaned down to kiss her. 'Totally.'

'And I owe Anna big time.'

'We both do, and don't think she'll let us forget it either.'

Seth chose two comfy armchairs in a secluded corner and a waiter materialised almost immediately, electronic pad and stylus in hand, poised to take their order. Izzy went for a lime and soda, leaving Seth to order beer as usual.

'Do we stop over anywhere?' Izzy had visions of a romantic night in Singapore or Bangkok, but Seth shook his head.

'No, we have a direct flight to Sydney, where we change for an internal Qantas flight to Adelaide. I hate changing planes halfway, and luckily Anna knows that.'

The waiter reappeared with their drinks, a dish of olives and a basket of fragrant-smelling rosemary bread. Izzy hadn't felt at all hungry until the nibbles appeared, but she took a piece of bread anyway.

'Hungry?' Seth grabbed some olives.

'Not really – but this bread smells so good.'

Izzy had to restrain herself from staring around too often at the other people in the lounge. She realised she must be the only person in there who wasn't famous, or at least very rich. She leaned towards Seth. 'Is that …?'

'Jonathan Ross and his missus, yes.' Seth grinned and raised a hand in greeting to them as they went by. 'Forever asking me to go on his show.'

'And you don't because …?'

'The band as a whole don't do talk shows.'

'Why?'

'Not my scene at all, and I don't think it would be a cool thing for the band to do either.'

Personally, Izzy thought it would be fun, but clearly Seth had a thing against talk shows so she didn't comment.

Seth started to feel antsy after an hour and felt relieved when their flight was called. Long haul was bad enough without all the hanging around that went with it. He stood up and held a hand down to Izzy. 'Time to go,' he said. She looked nervous, and he still wondered why. He realised the next few weeks would be the longest they'd been together at any one time, and would definitely test their relationship. Perhaps it bothered her. He hoped it didn't and kept hold of hand as they walked towards the departure gate, resolving to try and pay her as much attention as possible. He knew he'd be so focused on rehearsals and the forthcoming gigs that there might be a tendency to forget Izzy was actually there with him. It could be difficult. Perhaps he should enlist Anna's help – although she'd be frantically busy too. Maybe he should get Izzy to help her? Would that be insulting? *Relationships were a bloody minefield*, he thought.

He really hoped Anna would be able to give him some advice if he needed it.

Izzy glanced up at Seth's handsome face. He looked unusually serious, and he'd been a bit quiet for a while now. She hoped he wasn't regretting asking her along. But he held her hand firmly enough and pulled her in front of him as they went through the gate.

'Good evening, Ms Grant, Mr Roberts.' The elegantly glossy woman smiled as she checked their passports and boarding passes. 'Good luck with the tour.'

'Thanks.' Seth flashed her his cheeky grin which made her blush. *How did he do that?* He slipped his arm around Izzy's waist and leaned in to whisper, 'Too late to back out now, Ms Grant.'

Izzy laughed. 'Who says I want to?'

'No one, I hope.'

They followed a couple Izzy felt sure were famous but couldn't remember what for. Two stewards were standing at either side of the entrance to the plane and greeted them courteously.

'Up the stairs on the left, Mr Roberts,' said the woman. 'You know the way.'

'Should do by now,' said Seth. He led Izzy up the stairs to the first class section and, once again, she felt in awe of her surroundings. They walked through the lounge area with actual sofas and cushions, to the seating area with individual seats as big as single beds and real pillows instead of the tiny ones supplied in economy class. There was even a huge display of flowers in the lounge; Izzy didn't think they'd survive take-off somehow. Perhaps one of the cabin crew would sit and hold them.

'And you travel like this all the time?'

Seth ushered her into her seat and sat opposite. 'Yep – no point in earning shedloads and not enjoying it.' He shrugged. 'Plus, I'll be working soon, and this is a long-haul flight, so I needs me beauty sleep.' He wiggled his eyebrows.

Izzy raised her own back. 'Any more beauty sleep and I might have to prod you awake.'

'First with the poking and now with the prodding.' Blue eyes sparkled with amusement, as he accepted two glasses of champagne from a clearly star-struck member of the cabin crew. Handing one of the glasses to Izzy, he clinked his own glass against hers and said in a passable Fagin impression, 'Help you to sleep, my dear.'

For the first time since leaving that morning, Izzy felt herself relax, and she laughed. 'Thanks Mister, you're a real gent,' she said, attempting to channel her inner Nancy.

'You're not going to burst into "Feed the Birds", are you?'

'Definitely not.'

'Shame.'

'I told you, I will never sing in your presence.'

'Again, I say, shame.'

It was an interminably long flight. Izzy had known exactly how long of course, because she'd Googled the times, the changes, the flight to Adelaide and even checked all the time zones. But she'd watched four movies, eaten a fairly decent meal and drunk more wine than was wise, yet still didn't feel particularly sleepy.

Seth, however, was fast asleep. And didn't he look gorgeous when sleeping?

Izzy noticed a lot of longing glances from cabin crew – women *and* men – and, in fact, every female who passed by him cast a lustful look at him. Who could blame them? He looked like a fallen angel with finely sculpted features, his long brown eyelashes tinged with gold making little shadows on his cheeks, and the thick mane of chestnut curls almost reaching his broad shoulders. The term "rock god" could have been created just for him.

Leaning forward, Izzy tucked the blanket round him. He didn't move, and Izzy felt a wave of tenderness run through her. She could only guess at the stress and hard work involved in a massive tour such as the Scarlet Gryphon one. Plus, he'd gone against every rule in the book and taken a week out. For her. Heaven knew how unpopular it had made him – and, by default, her too. Although knowing Seth, he'd charm everyone with the greatest of ease once he was back in the fold. Sitting back, she pulled her blanket round herself and closed her eyes. Surely she'd fall asleep soon; if only she could just turn off her busy brain for a few minutes …

Seth opened his eyes the moment coffee arrived; it was an uncanny knack he had. Izzy was still asleep burrowed down inside the blanket, her fiery hair spread over the pillow. *Adorable*, thought Seth, and he didn't think that about anyone often – if at all. Not even Sheryl. He'd been besotted with his beautiful first wife at first for sure, but "adorable" wasn't a word that ever sprung to mind when describing her. He glanced over at Izzy again – adorable *definitely* described her perfectly. *Oh man, you've got it bad.* He watched her for a moment longer, wondering whether or not to wake her for breakfast, but decided instead to let her sleep.

He ordered the smoked salmon and scrambled eggs with toast and more coffee, telling the steward he'd ring when his girlfriend woke up so she could order for herself. She looked so peaceful asleep, and she'd been wide awake for most of the flight to his knowledge. At least until he'd managed some down time himself.

His breakfast arrived, and he'd almost finished when Izzy finally stirred. She blinked around owlishly, and then grinned at Seth.

'Hello.'

He pointed at her with his fork. 'And good morning to you.'

'What time is it?'

'Well, it depends where you are in the world.'

'Funny. Where are we?'

'No idea.' He pressed the buzzer, which immediately brought one of the cabin crew.

'Yes, Mr Roberts?'

'Izzy – what do you want for breakfast?' He passed the menu card across to her.

She stared at the card for a moment. 'Breakfast?'

'Yeah, you know, the meal you eat when you wake up?'

'Didn't we just have dinner?' She looked confused. 'Have I been asleep?'

Seth laughed. 'Yep, sound-o … so what do you fancy?'

Izzy looked at the card again. 'Maybe the continental breakfast, please? With orange juice … and coffee … lots of coffee.'

'Would you like more coffee, Mr Roberts?'

'Love some, thanks.' When the cabin crew member hurried away to fetch their order, Seth checked his online journey map. 'Just over halfway,' he commented.

Izzy's breakfast arrived and looked pretty good too. Seth eyed the croissants and fruit with interest.

'Can I get you some pastries, Mr Roberts?' The eagle-eyed stewardess had noticed.

‘You certainly can, thanks.’ He gave her his killer grin, and she hurried off again to get them, a faint flush colouring her cheeks.

Izzy giggled. ‘You’ll be the size of a house if she feeds you all the way to Sydney.’

Seth raised his eyebrows. ‘The food will be worked off in no time, I’ll have you know.’

‘Maybe you’d better give me a job then.’ Izzy took a bite out of a *pain au chocolat* with obvious enjoyment, and followed it with a large strawberry.

‘How are you at setting up a drum kit?’ Seth accepted the newly-arrived plate of pastries and tucked in with relish. He pointed a partially demolished Danish at her. ‘Any good?’

‘Sorry, no. I wouldn’t have a clue where to start.’

‘Ah well, Micky’s a tad possessive over his gear anyway. He doesn’t even let Caz near it – in fact, he probably loves his kit more than her.’

‘Scary – and a bit sad.’

‘She is, however, holder of the spare drum key, which is a very important and trusted position.’

‘Perhaps I could be holder of the plectrum for you?’

Seth laughed. ‘Sounds a bit risqué, but hey, I’m all for it.’ He gave her a cheeky grin and picked a strawberry off her plate. ‘You going to eat that?’

‘Help yourself.’

One of the cabin staff came to clear away their empty plates a while later, and Seth had very efficiently polished off anything remaining on both plates.

‘If you want to grab a shower, I think we’re the first one along. There’ll be towels and stuff in there.’

Izzy was staring at him in amazement. ‘There are showers?’

'Sure.'

'Wow.' Izzy blew out a breath. 'This is one incredible plane.'

'Yep – beats the English flights hands down.'

'But now comes the tricky part of actually having to take a shower in mid-air.'

'Do you need any help?'

Izzy gave him a stern look. 'You stay right where you are, Seth Roberts,' she said, making him laugh again.

'Spoilsport.'

He watched her grab her flight bag and walk off towards the shower rooms. Just before going into the cubicle she'd been shown to by a member of the crew, she turned and blew him a kiss. He winked at her and then settled back in his seat to listen to Jonno's bloody annoying track again through his earphones. No way were they playing *that* on this tour – actually, no way they would ever play that track on any tour. Not without a lot more work and time spent on it. He really hoped, once again, that Jonno's exceptionally annoying girlfriend, Sophie, hadn't flown out yet either. He *still* couldn't remember her full name. He'd met a few like her over the years. What did they call women like that again? Oh yeah … *The Yoko Factor*. Could even split the band if he wasn't careful. He hoped the others were keeping an eye on things. Micky, he knew, wouldn't take any crap from anyone, and the girls could take care of themselves without any problem at all, but Joe was more pliable. An all-round good guy, cheeky and fun, but maybe too nice … although Gina, his wife, would fight tooth and nail for him.

He sighed. Jonno's track certainly didn't improve with more listening – no matter how many times you heard it.

'Ladies and Gentlemen, we will be landing at Sydney Kingsford Smith Airport in twenty minutes. We hope you've enjoyed the flight, and we look forward to seeing you again soon.'

Izzy peered out of the window. 'Just clouds,' she reported. She hadn't felt this excited since her first proper date with Seth last year … well, maybe at her graduation … but *this*! She was in *Australia*. Very nearly anyway. In Australia with Seth. She turned back to look at him; he'd showered too, and changed his T-shirt for a long-sleeved sweatshirt, explaining that it was winter there, although still nowhere near as cold as English winters, of course. She thought it must be amazing to travel as much as he did, knowing the various time zones and seasons.

One of the cabin crew stopped by them. 'Your luggage will be taken directly on to the Adelaide flight, Mr Roberts,' she said. 'Yours and Ms Grant's.'

'Thanks,' he said. 'You don't happen to know which gate we need, do you?'

'I'll find out right now.'

She hurried away. Izzy found herself staring at Seth again. The man was a revelation. Of course she'd only seen him in work mode a couple of times, but he'd switched so quickly, and was now flipping efficiently through messages on his phone, his brow furrowed with concentration. It reminded her of the first time she'd seen him.

'Gate seven, Mr Roberts,' said the stewardess on her way by.

Seth looked up and smiled. 'Thanks,' he said.

The seat belt sign came on and Izzy felt butterflies pinging away in her stomach. She was on the opposite side of the world from home. With an internationally famous rock star and his band. Was she completely insane?

Supposing the tales of bands' overseas tours and their behaviour were all true?

'What if I get thrown off the tour bus?' she suddenly said aloud.

She met Seth's amused eyes, as he leant across and took hold of her hands. 'Iz, nobody is going to throw you off the tour bus – actually, I don't travel on a tour bus and neither will you.'

'Why not?'

'Because usually I'm either writing or sleeping on the way to gigs, and both are impossible on a bus with that lot. We have the noisiest bunch of roadies and crew in the business. Out here I tend to fly to gigs.'

'What about the rest of the band?'

'They travel by plane too. The gear has to go by road and quite often takes at least a few days to get from place to place.'

The plane was losing height now, and Izzy gazed out of her window at the approaching landscape. How different it looked from England …

'The current temperature in Sydney is a pleasant sixteen degrees centigrade,' said the captain's voice over the cabin's speakers. 'We hope you enjoyed your flight with us, and we wish those of you travelling onwards a safe trip.'

Seth kept a firm hold of Izzy's hand on the way to gate seven. He had a long stride and Izzy found herself almost running to keep up.

'Are we in danger of missing the flight?' she asked breathlessly.

'Nah, shouldn't think so,' he replied.

'Then any chance of slowing down a bit?' He looked down at her and grinned. 'You know – shorter than you – trying to keep up …'

'And you, a qualified Zumba instructor,' he responded lightly.

She narrowed her eyes at him, which only made him laugh again.

But he slowed his pace slightly, only relaxing his grip on Izzy's hand when they were safely aboard the Qantas flight for Adelaide, proving even he felt nervous sometimes. This time they were the only people in the small first class section of the plane, and Seth appeared to be getting everyone's undivided attention – certainly as far as the female crew were concerned. They were given champagne within seconds of sitting down, as well as little dishes of pretzels.

The plane took off within twenty minutes, and it felt hardly any time had passed at all when they began the descent to Adelaide airport.

'Zach's meeting us,' said Seth, and Izzy breathed a sigh of relief that they wouldn't have to queue for a taxi or hire car. She felt really tired now and a bit light-headed. Seth gave her a concerned look as they were whisked through immigration and security. 'Are you okay?'

'Tired,' admitted Izzy. 'And a bit woozy.'

'Too much champagne, young lady,' came the amused reply.

He appeared to know exactly where he was going, and a man pushing a trolley with their luggage joined them within a few minutes. Seth cast a cursory look over their cases and nodded.

'All there,' he said.

One less thing to worry about. Their luggage had arrived safely with them in Adelaide and not careered off to Bangkok.

Zach was indeed waiting with Anna in Arrivals, standing with a bunch of other drivers all holding up notices. Zach's said: *Mr Rock God and his lovely lady.* Seth laughed aloud when he saw it, and Izzy, in spite of the weird feeling that she'd somehow landed on a different planet, joined in.

'Hey man, how's it going?' He shook hands with Zach and dropped a kiss on Anna's cheek. 'How's my second favourite girl?'

'Good to have you back,' said Zach. 'Really.'

'Sounds ominous.' Seth shot him a look.

'Nothing you can't sort,' said Zach quickly. 'The odious Sophie arrived a couple of days ago.'

Seth rolled his eyes. 'Now I know it's ominous.'

'Sophie?' Izzy looked at Anna, fearing Sophie might be another Gracie, and, to be honest, one of those was enough for any one lifetime. Gracie was one of Seth's ex-girlfriends – demanding, jealous and verging on stalker-like.

'The love of Jonno's life – apparently,' said Anna. 'Interfering and *really* annoying – just like the woman in *Spinal Tap*.'

'I'm betting Iz has never seen *Spinal Tap*,' said Seth with a grin. He raised his eyebrows at Izzy in question.

'Sounds like an affliction,' muttered Izzy.

'In all the years I've worked for the band, I've never *ever* known Gina and Caz to argue. They're like twin sisters, but the moment *she* arrived, they've been arguing,' said Anna with a sigh.

Seth frowned. 'Over what?'

‘Sophie *“borrowed”* Caz’s personal mic, so she could sing Jonno’s track yesterday. Without asking I might add, and her voice is bloody awful. When challenged, she told Caz that Gina said she could use it, so it was Gina who got yelled at.’

Izzy didn’t know much about band politics, but even she knew personal equipment was just that – *personal*.

‘What fun she’s having,’ said Seth grimly.

‘Anyway, we need to get back to the car quickly,’ said Anna. ‘We left Micky doing a few laps.’ She pressed a button on her phone. ‘Hey Micky, we’ve got them. Yep, coming out now. Great.’ She turned to Seth. ‘He’s just driving round now.’

‘Not supposed to leave your car when picking anyone up,’ explained Zach to Izzy. ‘Cars get towed pretty damn quick here. And we’ve got a people carrier, so it’s a bit big to hide.’

They encountered a bank of photographers outside; all the cameras flashed at once the moment Seth stepped out. He waved good-naturedly and grinned around at the reporters as Zach wheeled their luggage towards a large black Audi Q7.

‘How’s the family, Seth?’

‘All good now, thanks guys.’

Keeping a protective arm around Izzy, he hustled her to the car as quickly as possible, shielding her from the cameras as much as he could.

‘You didn’t go and get married on us did ya, Seth?’ a woman’s voice called.

He merely grinned back at them, tapping his nose lightly with his free hand.

‘Who’s the red-head?’ another voice shouted.

Seth opened the rear door and Izzy dived in, followed by Seth. Anna and Zach got in the front and Micky drove quickly away.

'Hey Micky, how's your luck?' Seth clapped a friendly hand on his shoulder.

'Fair to middling,' he answered. 'Hey, Izzy.'

'Hey,' she said. 'I hear you had to keep driving round in circles.'

'Yeah, weird rules over here. Someone has to stay with the car when you do a pickup or it gets towed. So we all drive round and round.'

'Makes you dizzy, huh?' Seth grinned. His eyes shone and he looked pleased to be back with his bandmates, Izzy thought. Excited and raring to get back on stage, no doubt. He suddenly leaned in and plonked a kiss on her lips. 'Welcome to the madness of my life for a few weeks.'

'Thanks – I think,' she said.

He cupped her face in his hands and kissed her again. 'It's me who should be thanking *you* for coming all this way.'

'No accounting for taste,' muttered Micky, earning him a cuff round the head from Seth.

Izzy smiled. *Oh yes, he's definitely pleased to be back on the road.*

Chapter Six

The band and their immediate entourage had taken over the top two floors of a huge hotel just outside the city. It had been built roughly in the style of a Baroque castle, and was set rather pompously in its own secluded grounds. At first glance, it looked like something from a raving mad fairy-tale. Although, to Izzy's tired eyes, it also simply looked like heaven. She'd completely lost track of whatever time it was wherever she was, and felt more than a little light-headed, with a sinking feeling in her stomach that could have been hunger, nausea or just plain excitement. Or possibly a mixture of all three.

'Anyone hungry?' Zach twisted around in his seat to ask.

'I'd honestly just like to sleep somewhere that isn't moving and doesn't have in-cabin speakers,' Izzy said. 'For a couple of days.'

'Ah-ha,' said Seth with a grin. 'Now she understands the jet lag.'

'Fair cop.' Izzy nodded. 'Can I *please* sleep now?'

'You can.' He turned to Zach. 'What time are we needed?'

Zach glanced at his watch, 'You'll be needed after lunch, I'm afraid. But it's only ten now, so you can get four hours if you like, although we need to get over to rehearsals by two.'

Seth kissed the top of Izzy's head, 'Don't freak,' he said kindly. 'You can stay sleeping and we'll catch up for dinner.'

'No gig tonight either,' reminded Zach. 'You should be raring to rock by tomorrow.'

Izzy's head was buzzing now. *So this was how Seth's touring life panned out?* Her admiration for his professionalism continued to grow the more she learnt about his crazy lifestyle. Like he'd said to her once, he worked damned hard for his money.

Micky pulled up outside the front doors, which immediately opened to reveal two uniformed porters with a trolley. They had the luggage stowed on the trolley in seconds.

'Mr Roberts, if you'd like to follow me to the lift,' said one.

Izzy scrambled out of the car, followed by Seth. She stumbled and he grabbed her arm to prevent her falling.

'We need to get you some sleep, Ms Grant,' he said with a grin. 'Or less champagne.'

She rubbed at her eyes. 'Or both.' She wondered how he managed to look so awake and gorgeous after twenty-three hours travel. She didn't even want to hazard a guess at what she looked like.

'Who chose this place?' Seth looked singularly unimpressed as they went through reception. 'It looks like Sleeping Beauty's bloody castle.'

Anna and Zach laughed, and he pointed at her with his thumb. 'This one thought it looked romantic for you guys.'

'And for us,' she corrected, thumping him on the arm.

'Well, this sleeping beauty is going to fall flat on her face if I don't get her to the room soon.'

'See you later then.' Zach did a fist bump with Seth, and steered Anna off towards the nearest restaurant.

Seth and Izzy got into the lift with the porter and their luggage, and were whisked up to the top floor. The porter wheeled the trolley along a thickly carpeted corridor, and then opened the only door along there with a key card.

Izzy gave an audible gasp at the suite inside. 'It looks like a castle in here too.'

'That it does,' Seth said a little drily. 'If I didn't know better, I'd think someone somewhere is having a bloody good laugh at my expense.'

Izzy walked into the suite and turned back to grin at him, 'Aw, come on, Seth. You have to admit it's kind of fun. Why don't you like it?'

He muttered a few expletives under his breath. 'I hate hotels at the best of times,' he said, pushing a hand through his hair. 'The only way I can relax after a gig, or a long flight, is in a plain, but very comfortable room – tasteful duvet covers, white walls and preferably no bloody over-the-top paintings on those white walls.' He eyed the garish landscape opposite the bed with undisguised distaste.

'Anything you need, Mr Roberts?' The porter gave an apologetic cough to interrupt his rant.

Seth shook his head. 'Nah, mate. We're all good, cheers.' He thrust some notes at him with a grin.

'Thank you.' The younger man looked up at him shyly. 'We're all coming to the concert tomorrow.'

'Good man,' said Seth. 'I hope you enjoy it.'

'We will.' He scuttled out with his trolley and closed the door quietly behind him.

Izzy could feel a hysterical bubble of laughter building up. It must be the lack of sleep. The enormous four-poster bed, in spite of looking like something from *Beauty and the Beast*'s worst nightmare, still appeared comfortable and inviting, and she really wanted to snuggle down in it.

She looked around the suite instead: heavy red curtains framed the Australian version of mullion windows, and fake tapestries adorned some of the walls. She walked over to the bathroom, and that's when the bubbling laughter finally escaped. Seth came in to see what she was laughing at, and his raised eyebrows made her laugh all the more.

'Oh, for f—' He stopped short and she laughed even harder.

She moved closer to him and wound her arms around his waist. 'It's just a place to sleep, Seth,' she said. 'And I for one would like to do just that.'

'You'll drown in that bath,' he said sardonically. 'I've seen smaller swimming pools.'

He put his arms around her nevertheless, and she looked up at him. 'It's only a hotel stay for … how many nights?'

'Four.' He looked grumpy. 'I still think this is someone's idea of a laugh because I went AWOL for a week.'

'It's a bit over the top, I agree.' Izzy bit her lip to stop herself from laughing again.

'A bit?' Seth looked over at the huge sunken bath and its gold, dragon-shaped taps. 'I mean, *dragon taps*?'

'Dragons for a gryphon.' Izzy hugged him.

'God, I really hate hotels. Why couldn't we have rented a house somewhere? What was Anna thinking?'

'The grounds are lovely.'

'Maybe I'll sleep out there then.'

Izzy pushed playfully at his chest. 'You're being spoilt.'

He laughed suddenly. 'You're right, of course. Thank god for you, Isabelle Grant.' He picked her up suddenly under one arm, and striding into the bedroom, dropped her laughing onto the enormous bed, then flung himself down next to her.

'So …' He reached out and stroked her hair. 'Exactly how tired are you, Ms Grant?'

Seth showered, changed and went back in to the bedroom to find Izzy fast asleep, curled up in the middle of the huge bed like a contented cat. He covered her with the duvet she'd managed to throw off, and then pulled the heavy curtains across the windows. What was it about her that made him feel so protective? Was this what love felt like? He wasn't the best judge of real love, that was for sure; his track record certainly wasn't great. But he knew if anyone or anything threatened Izzy, he'd sort them out without compunction. Just like he intended to sort out whoever had booked this damn hotel. What the hell were they thinking? He couldn't believe it had been Anna – not his uber-efficient, ultra-trustworthy Anna. Unless being in love had made her go all Disney Princess on him, which he found hard to believe.

The car was waiting to take them to rehearsals, and Seth felt relieved to see only Micky, Caz, Zach and Anna were in it. He didn't feel in the mood to tolerate Jonno and Sophie at the moment. *That damn track*. He slid into the back seat of the car, immediately putting an arm around Zach's neck in a mock strangle hold.

'Right,' he said. 'Who the hell chose this Disneyland monstrosity and why?'

Zach pretended to splutter and gag. 'Mate, we really thought you'd like it. Romantic – you know?'

'*Like* it?' Seth tightened his hold. 'I think it needs demolishing.'

Zach laughed. 'Well, I think it might cost you a packet if you did.'

'Shame.' Seth released his friend. 'Couldn't you have found somewhere less offensive to the eye?'

Anna turned around with an apologetic look on her face. 'Seriously Seth, there's some kind of convention on at the moment and thousands of people are in Adelaide for it. This was the only place with decent security and outside space that had enough room for all of us. Probably because nobody else could afford its crazy prices.'

'It's hideous.' Seth sat back in his seat. 'Really, truly hideous.'

'The grounds are fabulous.' Caz joined in the conversation. 'And our bath has taps shaped like mermaids.'

Seth frowned. 'We have bloody dragons.'

'And we have dolphins,' Zach chipped in. 'It's all a bit Disney meets Gaudi, isn't it?'

'I keep expecting to bump into Mickey and Minnie,' Seth grumbled. 'Or those bloody chipmunks.'

'And there was us thinking you'd be all sweetness and light with Izzy here,' commented Zach.

'Hey – if she wasn't here, you wouldn't want to be anywhere near me, trust me.' Seth shoved at Zach's shoulder playfully.

Anna looked worried, and Seth grinned at her. 'Just joshing,' he clarified. 'I get the reasoning behind the hideousness.'

Micky turned into a car park behind a building proclaiming it was Sunbury Studios. The band's other cars were already there.

Seth instantly perked up. 'Okay – let's do some work.'

The raised voices could be heard all the way down the corridor to the front doors, and Seth looked at Zach with raised eyebrows. The loudest voice they could hear was definitely a woman's.

'If that's who I think it is, she's on the next flight home,' he promised.

He flung open the doors to the studio and stood, hands on hips, without saying anything at first. The shouting stopped as if a switch had been thrown. Jonno looked embarrassed, but his girlfriend merely shot a defiantly angry look at Seth, who raised an eyebrow without commenting.

'We could hear your dulcet tones out in the car park,' Seth exaggerated slightly. 'Have you no pride?'

'You've been away for nearly a week,' Sophie said accusingly.

Seth walked slowly towards the gaggle of people in the middle of the room until he was directly opposite her. 'And that's your business because …?'

'Anything that affects Jonno *is* my business.'

'Ah, well, that's where I beg to differ.' Seth's voice was purposefully calm and quiet. 'You see, Scarlet Gryphon is *my* band. I am the founding member. I started the band and I recruited everyone here. I'm also the main songwriter and lyricist. But, strangely, I don't recall ever giving *you* a job.'

'Jonno wants—' she began, but Seth cut her dead merely by raising his hand.

'I haven't finished,' he said firmly. 'You're therefore here by default, and as far as I'm concerned, under *sufferance* – you play no useful part in the band, and I hear you've done nothing but cause trouble ever since you arrived on the scene.'

Jonno looked even more uncomfortable. 'Seth, mate—'

Seth turned to face him, his blue eyes steely. 'Don't "Seth, mate" me, Jon. I'm well aware your … *lady* here has been using a band member's personal equipment without asking, and deliberately causing trouble between the girls while I've been away, and it's unacceptable.'

He turned back to Sophie, who was looking less sulky and a bit apprehensive now. 'I don't know what your agenda is, but you will not cause ructions with anyone in my band and that includes Jonno. Any more nonsense and I will personally put you on the next flight home. Understand?'

'*Your* girlfriend's allowed to be here though.' Sophie's tone turned spiteful.

Seth could feel his temper rising, yet he managed to speak quietly enough, 'Do you see her here at this rehearsal? No.' He turned back to Jonno. 'Get her in a car back to the hotel. Now. Before I really lose my temper – then get your arse back here and do some work.'

They both hesitated. 'Now,' Seth reiterated coldly. 'Or I make a call to Qantas and send you *both* the hell back to Blighty. In economy class.'

Jonno handed Sophie's jacket and bag to her and, taking hold of her hand, led the way out. Everyone watched the doors swing shut without a word.

Nobody said anything until they heard the front doors slam, then Joe let out a whoop and started applauding. Everyone else soon joined in with the applause and, for the first time since they'd arrived, Seth laughed.

Zach slapped him on the shoulder. 'Wow, remind me never to piss you off.'

Seth gave him a sardonic look. 'You do it all the time.'

'You know what I mean. That was spectacular, man. So good!'

'What the hell's been going on?' Seth stopped laughing and looked around at everyone. 'I was only gone six days. Someone *speak*, for heaven's sake.'

‘Jonno brought up the track thing every practice session we had,’ Joe volunteered. ‘And ever since that bloody woman arrived, she’s been sticking her oar in, pushing for the track, and now the latest thing is – she wants to be the one who sings it on stage!’

‘Is that so?’ Seth pushed a hand through his hair. ‘Have any of you heard her sing?’

‘She’s in tune – just.’ Gina grinned. ‘But only just, and she can’t hit any high notes to save her life.’

‘She sings like a rusty hinge,’ said Caz. ‘And Seth – she is *so* not singing with us.’

Seth draped a brotherly arm around her shoulders and dropped a chaste kiss on the top of her head. ‘Too right she isn’t, my little nightingale.’ He looked around at everyone again. ‘Who wants to play something while we wait for Jonno?’

There was a collective cheer from everyone, and Seth felt an overwhelming sense of relief. *Nothing like really loud rock music to banish the blues, so to speak.*

Whilst Seth was busy rehearsing, Izzy decided to wander around the beautiful, lush hotel gardens. Brightly-coloured birds swooped about overhead; some tiny, and others the size of parrots. She watched them, fascinated; they certainly made a lot of the native British birds look a bit *brown* by comparison.

‘Taken to birdwatching?’ An acerbic female voice interrupted the peace and quiet.

Izzy turned towards the voice. ‘I’m sorry, I don’t think I know you,’ she said lightly, hoping she wasn’t a reporter of some kind, although her accent was clearly very British. The newcomer was blonde and beautiful, immaculately dressed as though for the cat walk in Paris or Milan. She wasn't exactly wearing the right kind of shoes for a stroll around the gardens either. Izzy glanced down at her own faded jeans and dust-covered trainers, and decided they were much more sensible. She refused to feel intimidated.

'I'm Jonno's girlfriend, Sophie.' The reply came in cold, clipped tones. 'And I already know who *you* are.'

'I'm sure I don't know how,' replied Izzy, still keeping her voice light and non-committal. 'We haven't ever met, have we?'

'We weren't introduced in London, no, but you were pointed out to me as Seth's latest.'

Nice, thought Izzy. Aloud she said, 'Good to know I'm referred to as the latest.'

'I'm sure you won't be for long.' Sophie allowed her gaze to travel the length of Izzy's slight body, lingering on her gleaming red hair. 'He usually favours blondes.'

'Did you miss out then?' *Oops.* It came out before Izzy could check her fiery temper.

Sophie gave her an unpleasant look. 'Jonno and I were *ejected* from the rehearsal.'

'For?' Izzy crossed her arms and regarded the taller woman with interest. *So* this *was Sophie*. 'There must have been a reason.'

'Someone, somewhere has been causing trouble ... I think it's you.'

Izzy grinned. The woman was being ridiculous. 'I thought that was your job.'

Sophie clearly wasn't amused. 'Jonno listens to *me.*' She turned and strutted away like a super model, which, *to be fair*, thought Izzy, *is no mean feat in those shoes!*

Chapter Seven

Arriving back at the hotel later, Seth admitted to Zach he was "kind of getting used to the place". But then said it was probably only because he was shattered and starving as usual. He arranged to meet Zach and Anna in the bar later, and Anna said she'd book a big table for dinner.

When he went into the suite, he felt surprised to see Izzy wasn't there. He thought she might have still been asleep, but the bed looked pristine and very empty. He checked the lounge area, no Izzy, and then peered into the bathroom which was also devoid of Izzy. He was about to call her when she came through the front door.

'Hey, Music Man,' she said, her lovely face lighting up at the sight of him. 'How's your luck?'

'Getting better by the second.' He pulled her into his arms and kissed her. 'Where've you been?'

'Just walking round the grounds. Good rehearsal?'

He grimaced before telling her what had gone on, and then Izzy joined in with a story of her own.

'Actually … I just met the famous Sophie.'

'You did? Where?' Seth was gobsmacked. The woman clearly hadn't wasted any time seeking out Izzy when she returned to the hotel.

'Out in the gardens. She told me you preferred blondes and that Jonno listens to *her*,' Izzy said blithely. She didn't appear too bothered by the encounter.

'I did get the impression she wouldn't play that nicely with other women,' Seth said grimly, but then he grinned. 'I will always protect you, of course.'

Izzy gave him a look that said she could look after herself.

'Hungry?'

'Starving.'

'I'll grab a shower, then we'll hit the bar, shall we?'

'Will there be pretzels?'

'Who knows in this land of Disney?' Seth sauntered off towards the bathroom. 'Do you need a shower too?'

She made a shooing gesture. 'I know all your tricks, Seth Roberts, and if I ever meet your mother—'

'You can't tell her anything she doesn't know or guess,' Seth said. 'My mum is all-knowing and scarily wise.'

'She'd get on well with mine then.'

'Let's hope they don't meet any time soon ...' *Actually, that really* is *a scary thought.* Seth could only imagine the kind of notes they'd have to compare. And heaven help them both if the sisters joined in.

Once in the bathroom, he stood under the large shower head, letting the jets blast the stresses of rehearsal away. He shook the tangled mane of hair out of his eyes as he turned around, humming softly to himself. No alcohol tonight; he needed to protect his voice for the gig tomorrow. He couldn't wait to get back on stage. And no *way* was that bloody woman joining in.

Izzy was on the phone when Seth came out of the bathroom with just a towel draped around his lean hips. She almost drooled at the sight. He looked totally scrumptious.

'Izzy, are you still there?' Izzy's mum said in her ear. 'Did something happen?'

'No – no – sorry Mum, I'm still a bit jet-laggy.' What else could she say? *Sorry but Seth just came out of the bathroom wearing only a towel and I really wanted to yank it off him.*

Seth caught her glance at that point and his mischievous grin said he knew exactly what was going through her mind. She felt her cheeks flush – even now, after almost a year. She still felt quite shy with him sometimes, and he always appeared so confident and sexy. She realised her mum had still been talking while she stared at the Adonis in a towel. What was she saying? Ah yes, the concerts …

'There's a concert tomorrow and the next two days, then a day off to get everything packed up for Brisbane.'

'Will you get to see anything of Australia?'

'I hope so.'

'Me too. It's a long way to go just to see hotel rooms.'

'I think Seth feels like that sometimes.'

'I'm sure he does. But he's seen it all before and you haven't.'

'Don't worry, I'll have my tourist hat on in the morning.'

'Does it have corks round it?'

'Definitely not.'

'All right, my darling. Have a good evening and I hope the concert goes well.'

'Thank you. Love to Dad and Ben – and to you too, of course.' Izzy put her phone back on the bedside table, and breathed a sigh of relief when she noticed Seth now had his jeans on. No shirt still – and he was definitely rocking that look – but the jeans were on.

He was rooting around in one of the cases that had been forwarded for him, and turned to Izzy with two shirts in his hand.

'How smart should we be for dinner in this Disney hell place?' he asked.

She laughed. 'Well, when I went for a nosey round while you were at rehearsals everyone seems pretty casual during the day, but no clue about the evenings. Shall we ask Anna?'

'Good idea.' He reached for his phone, which was on the bed, and dialled. 'Hey Anna, is there any kind of dress code here for dinner? No Mickey Mouse ears?' He laughed at her reply. 'Cheers, doll. See you guys in half an hour then.'

'Cheap shot with the Mickey Mouse ears,' commented Izzy.

'Yeah, good though, huh?'

He grabbed a dark green sweatshirt from the case and pulled it on. 'Folks okay?' he asked as his head popped out through the neck.

'Yes, good thanks.' Izzy studied her hair in the wardrobe door's mirror and looked around for her brush. For some reason completely unknown to her, it was happily sitting on the nearest window sill. She picked it up and started brushing her hair, suddenly aware Seth was watching her. He sauntered towards her, and taking the brush out of her hand, continued brushing for her.

'You remember last year I told you never to change?'

'Yes. Do you think I have?'

'Nah, not a bit, thank goodness.' He tucked her hair behind her ears and leaned down to kiss her. 'I love you just the way you are, Izzy Grant, and don't you forget it.'

Wow ... he actually said he loves me. Izzy's senses whirled.

Seth brushed her flushed cheek with the back of his fingers. 'Just the way you are,' he said again. 'Now – let's get to dinner. I'm absolutely starving.'

The place was buzzing with people when Seth and Izzy arrived. Zach and Anna were already at the bar drinking huge cocktails. Izzy watched as Zach tucked a bright orange umbrella from his cocktail glass behind Anna's ear.

'Ah … young love,' said Seth in her ear.

'Poor old man,' muttered Izzy. He merely plonked a kiss on her cheek with a laugh.

'What are you drinking?' he asked as they drew nearer to Zach and Anna.

'Cosmos,' said Zach. 'And they're really strong. Want one?'

'Yes please,' said Izzy at once.

Seth shook his head, 'Alcohol free for me tonight so fruit juice and soda, I think.'

'Professional as always,' commented Zach.

'I try.'

There was no sign of Jonno and Sophie in the restaurant, but the other band members were already at the table reserved for Seth's party.

Seth looked around and raised his eyebrows at Micky.

Micky shrugged. 'No sign, mate,' he said. I phoned him but he's not picking up.

'Do we need to get ourselves another bassist stroke keyboard player?' Seth sat down and Izzy sat next to him. She was no expert but this didn't look good.

'Here he is,' said Caz waving in the direction of the door. 'On his own – thank god!'

Jonno made his way over to the table before sitting down next to Joe. He looked uncomfortable and didn't offer a greeting to anyone.

'Everything okay?' Seth asked him directly.

'Sophie isn't feeling very hungry,' was all he said. He signalled a waiter and ordered a double scotch on the rocks.

'I think we should have a band chat,' said Seth quietly.

Izzy stood up and so did Anna. 'And I think we'll go back to the bar for a bit.'

Anna picked up her drink and linked arms with Izzy. 'Grab your drink,' she instructed.

They walked over to the bar, and once they were out of earshot, Izzy turned to Anna. 'Will Jonno leave the band?'

Anna blew out a breath. 'I honestly don't know,' she said. 'But he's totally infatuated with that bloody awful woman, that's for sure. I've never seen him like this before.'

'Unfortunately for me, I ran into her out in the gardens while you were at rehearsals. I can certainly see she has an attitude problem. But why does she behave so badly towards the band?'

Anna perched on a barstool and pulled a dish of pretzels towards her. 'How unlucky for you! I don't know the answer to that question, but any conversation including Sophie needs pretzels and more cosmopolitans.' She waggled her nearly empty glass at the barman who nodded and started mixing the drinks. 'I'm not sure where she met Jonno, but Caz said it was Annabel's club in Berkeley Square one Sunday night. Sunday is the "anything goes" night, as in you don't have to be a member.'

'I get why she was there on a Sunday, but surely you guys are all members?'

'Seth is, so I'm guessing Zach is too, but the other guys – apart from Jonno – are happily married, so maybe not. Seth and Zach are the only ones who hang out on a regular basis.'

'Perhaps he was lonely?' Izzy suddenly felt sympathy for the enigmatic Jonno.

'Perhaps.' Anna smiled and helped herself to another handful of pretzels. 'Hey check these out, they're so good.'

The new cocktails arrived and they both picked up the glasses at the same time. Izzy clinked hers against Anna's.

'Well, here's hoping Seth can get things back on track – pun intended.'

'If anyone can, he can.'

'We need you to talk to us,' said Seth without preamble. 'Clearly things have been said – on all sides – so we need to clear the air here.'

Jonno gave him an unfriendly look. 'Sophie was devastated by what you said.'

'I'm not even considering any kind of apology,' said Seth firmly. 'She's apparently been mixing things up since she first arrived on the scene, and I get that you love her; that's not my concern, and I'm happy for you. But when she starts undermining me and other band members, then I'm not happy.'

'She just wants my track played on the tour.'

'And wants to sing it too, so I hear.'

Jonno looked embarrassed. 'That's just her dream … but even I don't think she's got the voice.'

'The track needs a lot of work, man.' Seth made his voice softer. 'A hell of a lot of work. And I'm being straight here; it has potential, it does.' He put his hand on the other man's arm. 'But the hook needs cleaning up, it's ragged, maybe a few new phrases added. So I don't think it's ready for this tour, plus the set list is really cast in concrete because of the album. The encores will be the old favourites and so on.'

Jonno nodded his head. 'So?'

‘So when we’re back home, after the tour, you come to my Sussex place in – say – early September sometime, and we’ll work on it together. Zach can come along and mix for us.’

For the first time that day, Jonno smiled a proper smile. ‘Really?’

‘Of course, really – but you come alone. Deal?’ He stuck his hand across the table. Jonno took it and the two men shook hands.

Seth looked around at the others. ‘Anybody else want to say anything? Because now I’m even more bloody starving – and I think my woman’s getting drunk with your woman.’ He looked at Zach.

Zach rolled his eyes and got to his feet. ‘I’ll go get ‘em,’ he said. ‘Let’s hope to god they don’t start singing as well.’

Chapter Eight

When Izzy forced her eyes open the next morning, she couldn't remember where she was, why she was there or what time of day it was. For one weird moment she thought she was back in halls after a night out on the town with Jo.

Cocktails … always her downfall … why did she ever think they were a good idea?

And those cosmopolitans had one hell of a kick. She'd be joining Seth on the wagon today, so to speak.

The man in question wandered into the bedroom at that moment with two cappuccinos and a very cheeky grin. He passed her a cup and regarded her over the brim of his with shining blue eyes. She waited for a rude comment but none came. He sat on her side of the bed and continued drinking his coffee. She took a grateful swig from her own cup and sighed.

'Are you going to send me back to Blighty?' she asked when she couldn't stand the suspense any longer.

He laughed. 'What – for swigging down one too many cosmos? Nah, you're safe, Iz.'

'We thought we were being tactful, leaving only band members in the discussion.'

'And you were very tactful, so thank you.'

'Is everything okay?'

'It will be. At least the tour's safe. I'm still not sure what to do about the Sophie woman though.'

'Obviously I don't know her that well, but she does seem to be trouble from what I've seen so far.'

'That she does.' He finished his coffee and put the cup on the bedside cabinet. 'I'm not needed until later this afternoon – the crew are setting up for tonight, and we'll go in for the sound checks about five. So let's go out somewhere.'

'Where?'

'There's the botanical gardens, the zoo, the Japanese Garden …' He ticked the sights off on his fingers.

'You sound like you've already seen them all.' Izzy laughed.

'*Or…*' His eyes gleamed. 'We could fly a helicopter over the spectacular Ayers Rock, now known as Uluru.' He grinned at her expression. 'I haven't done *that* yet.'

'Which is probably why you've arranged it? I hope you don't expect me to picnic there,' said Izzy. 'I've seen that movie, and it didn't end well.'

'Let's get breakfast.' He changed the subject and handed Izzy a menu.

'You're always giving me a menu wherever we are.'

'Probably because I'm always hungry. And Kathleen told me to look after you – I'm under pain of death if you don't go home tanned and healthy.'

Izzy took a quick look at the menu. 'Fruit, continental breakfast and coffee, please.'

Seth headed for the hotel phone and Izzy headed for the shower. A helicopter flight over Ayers Rock sounded the kind of trip only the very wealthy could afford. She wondered how far it was and how long the flight would be. If she showered quickly, she might just have time to Google it ...

Seth drove one of the band's cars out to the nearest heliport. He parked and jumped out of the car, looking like a kid on Christmas Day.

'C'mon Izzy, out you get.'

She scrambled out, smiling at his enthusiasm. 'Is this a bloke thing?'

'Course it is.' He grabbed her hand and strode out towards a shiny, red helicopter which was standing waiting for them. A tall, tanned man with sun-bleached hair came towards them.

'Mr Roberts?' He held a hand out. '*Strewth* – nobody told me it was *Seth* Roberts who'd booked my 'copter.'

Seth grinned and shook his hand. 'Good,' he said. 'We like keeping things a bit quiet sometimes.'

'Your secret's safe with me, mate.' He held a hand out to Izzy. 'Jacko.'

'Izzy,' she said.

'You got a gig later?' Jacko led the way back to the helicopter.

'Yep,' said Seth. 'Just taking a few hours out to see some sights.'

'Well, you're going in the right direction. We'll refuel in Alice Springs which is about halfway to Uluru, and then we'll fly directly over it before we fly around.'

'Sounds fantastic.'

They climbed up the steps into the cabin, where Jacko made sure they were strapped in and handed them headphones with mics so they could talk to each other.

'Home from home,' commented Seth. Izzy jumped, his voice sounded intimate and very close in her ears. He reached over and took hold of her hand. She felt a bit nervous now, never having flown in a helicopter before. 'Ready?'

'Erm … yes?'

'I'm guessing this is your first helicopter flight?'

'You'd guess right.'

'You'll love it.'

Izzy hoped that was true. He squeezed her hand as the engine revved and the rotor blades started turning. Izzy swallowed nervously and held on to him tightly. The helicopter rose gracefully in the air and moved off swiftly. It was a slightly weird experience – nothing like flying in a huge plane. To take her mind off the fact her stomach seemed to have been left on the ground, Izzy looked out at the scenery, watching as Adelaide thinned out.

'Okay?' Seth said in her ear.

She turned to look at him, seeing the concern in his eyes.

'All good,' she said. 'How long will it take us?'

He shrugged. 'How long's the journey, Jacko?'

'Couple of hours to Alice Springs, half an hour's refuelling stop and then an hour or so more,' Jacko replied. 'It'll be worth it, trust me.'

He was right – the moment the sand and rocks turned red, Izzy was completely captivated. The vast rust-coloured desert-scape below stretched for miles and miles, and she didn't think she'd ever seen anything more beautiful. The grassy scrub appeared almost fluorescent in colour against the vibrant red of the sand, and, at one point, they flew low enough to see the crowd of people hiking towards Uluru, which rose impressively up from the desert floor. By the time they flew over Uluru itself, Izzy had forgotten she was scared of helicopters.

The sheer exhilaration of skimming over the majestic Uluru had Seth whooping and Izzy shrieking. Jacko flew lower and around the sacred rock, before flying up again and over the top of it.

'Are all those people going to climb up the rock?' Izzy asked.

‘It’s not permitted these days.’ Jacko turned the helicopter around, homeward bound. ‘It’s been reclaimed as a sacred monument.’

‘I can see why – that was awesome,’ said Seth. ‘Totally, unbelievably awesome.’

‘What he said,’ said Izzy.

Seth had loved watching Izzy’s enraptured face when they flew over the top of Ayers Rock. Her eyes were wide and shining with pure joy, as she clung on to his hand for dear life – especially when Jacko banked the helicopter to give them a better view. The man’s piloting skills were off-the-scale brilliant, and Seth briefly wondered about getting himself some flying lessons, finally deciding that it would probably be a bit too time-consuming.

As they drove back to the hotel, he could already feel the adrenaline building at the thought of tonight’s concert. He literally couldn’t wait to be on stage again. He felt the familiar tingle in the knowledge he would be performing soon – he had the best job in the world. Even the hotel’s Disney-style turrets looming ahead couldn’t dampen his mood.

Just as they entered their suite, Seth’s phone rang. He answered with a ‘yep?’ without noticing who the caller was. He frowned when he heard an unfamiliar female voice. ‘Say that again?’ He watched Izzy tactfully head towards the bedroom to give him some privacy with the call.

‘I want to sing Jonno’s song tonight.’ No doubting who the caller was now.

‘Never going to happen.’

‘Then Jonno won’t play.’

‘That’s not your decision to make. Or his come to that.’

'He told me.'

'Look, Sophie ... I don't know what your problem is exactly, but Jonno and I had this all out last night – sorry, but you lost.' Seth hung up and immediately dialled Jonno.

'Get yourself here now,' he told him, and then hung up before Jonno had time to utter a word. Then he called Zach. 'We've got trouble,' he said. 'Need you here, please.'

Izzy came back into the room at that point, giving him a questioning look.

He chucked the phone on the bed and blew out a frustrated breath as he looked over at her. 'That bloody woman.'

'Do you need me to disappear when they get here? I can go downstairs with Anna or something.'

He shook his head. 'No need, unless you want to.'

A few minutes later there was a tap at the door.

'I'll get it,' said Izzy.

She opened the door to a worried-looking Zach, who gave her a quick smile before walking into the sitting room towards Seth.

'What's going on?'

Seth told him.

'I thought we sorted this out last night.'

'Me too. But she's had his ear all night and all day.'

'Sex is clearly a powerful weapon.'

Seth grinned. 'Ain't that the truth?' His eyes sparkled when he glanced over at Izzy. 'Know where we can get a good bassist and keyboard player at very short notice?'

Another tap at the door signalled the arrival of the current bassist and keyboard player, and he wasn't alone. He came into the sitting room followed, unsurprisingly, by Sophie, strutting in on her pink, spiky-heeled, completely inappropriate sandals. She was dressed in dusky pink from head to toe today, and looked striking but scarily defiant.

Seth regarded her with some considerable annoyance. 'You weren't invited.'

'It's about me.' She glared up at Seth who merely raised his eyebrows.

'It really isn't,' he said dismissively, gesturing to the door.

'My father will have something to say about this,' she said petulantly.

'Should I be worried?' Seth looked anything but. What he felt was anger, not just towards her, but towards the unfortunate bassist, who seemed incapable of standing up to his own girlfriend. He opened the door and motioned for her to go through.

'With all due respect, you aren't welcome at this meeting,' he said coldly. 'So I suggest you go back to your own room.'

'Jonny …?' Her voice took on an unattractive whine. Seth wondered if it was the same voice she used on her father to get her own way.

'I'll send him back when we're done.'

It was obvious Sophie wanted to say more, but the look on Seth's face changed her mind. She turned gracefully on the spiky heels and stalked towards the lift.

Seth closed the door with a determined slam before striding back towards Jonno. 'I thought we sorted this out last night?'

Jonno shrugged. 'We did. Well … *we* did, but Soph wasn't happy. She's desperate to sing the song tonight.'

Seth sighed. 'How long have you been with the band?'

Jonno appeared to think hard for a moment. 'Five years, give or take.'

'And how well do you know me?'

'Pretty well, I guess …'

'Right – so you know I'm dedicated to the band and its members.'

'Yeah …'

'And I hope you know me well enough to appreciate that I will not compromise a live tour for one bloody track – no matter who the hell wrote it?'

Jonno stuck his hands in his jacket pockets. He shrugged. 'I guess.'

'Do you want out of this tour?'

'No – man – really.'

'Because that's what your lady said to me on the phone. That if she can't sing, you won't play tonight.'

'I never said that, Seth – honest.'

'I hope you didn't, because I won't be blackmailed either.' Seth leaned back against the sofa and folded his arms, his face set and unsmiling.

'I want to play, of course I do. But it's difficult; her dad being who he is and all …'

'And that is?'

'Mega rich and titled.'

Seth turned to Zach and Izzy with a sudden unamused laugh. 'Sounds horribly familiar.' He turned back to Jonno. 'How serious are you about this relationship?'

'Very, but this conflict is doing my head in.'

Seth held his hands up. 'It's okay, I don't need to know the details. All I need to know is you're committed to the band and this tour.'

'Absolutely. I won't let you down, Seth.'

'And you'll play tonight.'

'Of course.'

'And if she tries to change your mind?'

'She won't.'

'Fair enough. See you later.'

Jonno nodded and left the room.

'What do you think?' Seth asked Zach.

'I think we can't afford to run the risk of him not turning up.'

'I agree. Okay, so who've we got among the stage crew who can play keyboards and bass well, *and* knows the songs?'

'Charlie and Dan always set up keyboards and bass for the sound check … which we need to get to in half an hour, by the way. Let's try 'em out.'

'Good call. Iz, do you want to come along to the sound check?'

'Will it be okay?' She looked a bit worried. 'I don't want to be seen as another Sophie.'

Seth raised his eyebrows. 'Hey, who's the boss here?'

'You.'

'Exactly right. So – let's move it.'

Chapter Nine

The first time Izzy visited a Scarlet Gryphon sound check had been at Wembley, and she'd been amazed then at the sheer number of personnel rushing around, but there appeared to be even more people hurtling about today.

Anna was already there, clipboard in hand, head mic and ear piece in place, directing who knew what where. Izzy felt huge admiration for the calm, confident way she handled things.

She was introduced to Lenny, Scarlet Gryphon's tour manager, whom she'd only seen in the distance at Wembley. A big, beefy man in his early forties, his huge hand dwarfed hers when they shook hands. Excusing himself after a few minutes, he strode towards the stage bellowing at the posse of men setting up the lighting rigs.

Zach also excused himself and went over to the mixing desks, where he was ensconced in seconds. He spoke into his own head mic and nodded a couple of times, then turned towards Seth and put his thumbs up.

'Which means?' asked Izzy.

'He's just spoken to the two guys in the crew who will be good stand-ins for Jonno should he go AWOL on us.'

'Do you think it's likely?'

Seth sighed and rubbed his eyes. 'For once, I've got no idea,' he said. 'That woman is playing with his head, and I almost feel sorry for the guy.'

'Spoilt little …' Izzy muttered, and stopped before she finished the sentence. 'What makes her think she can just swan in and demand this or that or whatever takes her fancy?'

Seth shrugged. 'Because she's always been spoilt by Daddy dearest, I expect. Who does that remind you of?'

'Gracie.'

'Yep. All I can say, in both mine and Jonno's favour, is life on the road is tough, tiring, very stressful, and can get bloody lonely. We do it because we love it, we love the buzz of performing – and the money ain't bad either.' He laughed. 'But it can lay us wide open to all sorts of things – not least certain types of women, and I should know: I married one of them!'

Izzy reached up and touched his cheek gently. 'I'm amazed you're still the adorable person you are,' she said softly. 'You have so much integrity, Seth Roberts. I will personally see off anyone who tries to take advantage of you, and that's a promise.'

Seth turned his head and kissed the palm of her hand. 'And that, Izzy Grant, is why I love you so much.'

Izzy flushed with surprise and gave a nervous laugh.

'Sorry, Seth ...' Zach appeared. 'We need you on stage for a few, please.'

'Sure.' He kissed Izzy softly on the lips and pointed towards the VIP seats. 'You know the drill.'

Izzy watched his tall, lean figure lope confidently towards the vast stage. How incredible must it feel to have that amount of self-assurance, and to know thousands of people would be cheering just for you later?

He greeted Caz and Gina with a kiss on the cheek, high-fived Micky who was already behind his beloved kit, and fist-bumped Joe, who was strapping on his guitar.

There was no sign of Jonno.

Seth adjusted the mic up to his height and spoke into it. 'Anyone seen Jonno?'

There was a general shaking of heads and shrugging of shoulders. Seth swore quietly, which was picked up by the mic. He spoke again – louder. 'Can we have Charlie on stage to stand in for Jonno on bass, please? Thanks,' he added as Charlie came running.

Micky counted them in on the cowbell, and they swung into 'Stepping Stones' –a fast, pulsing rock track. Seth looked fierce and primal in the centre of the stage, holding everyone in the auditorium spellbound as always. Izzy could scarcely breathe as she watched. She didn't think she would ever get tired of watching him perform.

She always found it difficult to believe *her* Seth was the same man as the one who appeared on stage – although she knew a lot of performers used a different persona when performing. The band ended on a triumphant blast of sound and Seth nodded his head.

'Yep. That's good, Charlie, thanks. Dan, can we have you on keyboards please?'

A young, slim man with long, dark hair pulled back in a ponytail ran on stage and stood behind Jonno's bank of keyboards.

'Let's go with "Heart Breaker", guys,' said Seth. Dan and Joe led the rest of the band into the ballad Izzy loved. Gina and Caz's backing harmonies melded so beautifully too, but once Seth started singing, time stood still for Izzy. She lost herself in the beauty of the music and his voice.

But there was still no sign of Jonno.

A couple of hours later, with Scarlet Gryphon's sound check over, everyone dispersed back to their various hotels to eat, change, and, in Seth's case, find Jonno. He'd tried his phone a few times during the ride back, but Jonno hadn't picked up. Seth tried to hide both his annoyance and his worry. The only thing that comforted him was the thought that he didn't really think Jonno would go off anywhere and leave his beloved bass behind, even if he had decided to abandon the tour.

Seth wanted nothing more than to help him see Sophie for what she appeared to be to everyone else: a manipulative and self-seeking woman. But he suspected it would only make things worse between the two of them if he tried – and possibly the rest of the band too. Love clearly was blind in this case. He'd tried everything to win him back onside: his offer of working on that damn track had been genuine, and he knew Zach would lend a hand too. But there was no way on this earth that bloody woman would ever be singing it. The only singer in Scarlet Gryphon was him, although he had allowed Gracie to sing with them a couple of times as a guest artist. A lot of bands did that. But in all fairness to his ex, she could really sing, and Sophie – according to Caz – sang like a "rusty hinge". A harsh critique maybe, but he trusted her judgment.

When they went through the hotel reception, the receptionist looked up and signalled to Seth.

'Note for you, Mr Roberts,' she said.

'No prizes for guessing who that's from,' muttered Seth. He went over to take the note and thanked the receptionist. Coming back to the others, he tore open the envelope, pulled out the note and read it aloud.

Seth, mate, I'm really sorry. I just can't handle the conflict between the band and Sophie. So we're going home. Got a flight out tonight. I didn't want things to end like this, honest I didn't. I know I promised not to let you down, but I don't think I'd be any good to you the way I feel at the moment. Take good care of my equipment, I know you will. Again – sorry. J.

'Bloody hell.' Zach looked furious. 'That damn woman.'

Seth nodded. 'All I can say is the writing was already on the wall weeks ago, if any of us had bothered to read it.'

Anna frowned. 'So do we need to advertise?'

Seth shook his head. 'Not just yet. Dan and Charlie can play tonight and even cover this leg of the tour if they have to, then we're all on a break anyway. We can't really interview when we're on tour, can we? People can't afford to fly out to Japan for auditions. But we should be able to think of someone we know in the business to recruit between us.'

'Good idea,' said Zach. 'We'll get thinking.'

Seth's frantic thoughts filled his head. Jonno was an important member of the band, the fans adored him and he had absolutely no idea how this would affect the tour. He didn't feel particularly worried about the record company bosses; he knew he could handle them. He just really wanted Jonno to come back of his own accord, but at this moment in time, he hadn't the faintest idea how to make it happen.

Izzy sat alone in the VIP seats, completely lost in the music, the problems with Jonno temporarily forgotten. The atmosphere pulsated with the audience's excitement; every seat in the huge arena was filled, whilst Seth held the crowd in the palm of his hand as usual. Ever since the very first time Izzy heard Seth perform, she'd been lost; hanging on to every golden note he sang, almost drowning in his hypnotic voice. She still couldn't believe the charismatic man up there on stage had told her earlier he loved her. *Twice.* How was it even possible that this beautiful, god-like creature even *noticed* her, let alone actually *loved* her?

Izzy felt the sudden need to speak to Jo – she hadn't spoken to her in ages, and she needed to hear her friend's reaction when she told her Seth *actually loved her. Unless he says that to all his girlfriends*. Izzy wondered about that too. Showbiz types told everyone they loved them, didn't they? All the time. But did it mean anything?

The band swung into 'Stepping Stones' and the whole place erupted. Izzy looked around at the members of the audience closest to her and smiled as a whole row of girls leapt up and started dancing. The security guys here were a lot more laidback than the Wembley ones. One of them even joined in the dancing.

When the song ended, Seth waited for the rapturous applause to die down before stepping back up to the mic.

'We're going to take a short break, folks,' he said. 'Back in a bit, so don't go home.' He grinned at the crowd.

Anna slid into the seat next to Izzy. 'Care to come backstage and mop his fevered brow?' she said mischievously. 'He'll appreciate that.'

Izzy chuckled. 'You mean he doesn't have a person to do that?'

'I'm sure he could get one easily enough, but it's you he wants,' she assured her.

'Fair cop then,' said Izzy. 'Lead the way.'

She followed Anna to the dressing rooms and tapped on the door Anna indicated before she hurtled off to find Zach.

'If you've got red hair and you're called Izzy, come on in. Otherwise, sod off,' Seth's voice responded.

'Nice.' Izzy pushed open the door.

Seth looked up from towelling his damp hair and beckoned her in. 'Fancy a sweaty hug?'

‘Always,’ said Izzy. ‘Sweaty rock god is my favourite.’ She walked into his arms and stood on tiptoe to kiss him.

‘Mmmmm,’ he murmured against her hair. ‘Do you need anything?’

‘Just you.’

‘And that you have.’

‘Can I get you a drink or anything?’

Seth peered at her in amusement. ‘We’re Scarlet Gryphon,’ he said. ‘And Anna tells them what to supply up front.’ He gestured to a large fridge in the corner with his thumb. ‘What can I get for you is more the question?’ Slinging the damp towel over his shoulder, he sauntered over to the fridge and opened the door. He looked inside. ‘Soft drinks, beer, wine, probably the makings of a cosmo in here if you know how to make it?’

‘Beer, please.’

Seth pulled out a bottle of lager, opened it with an attachment on the fridge door and then passed it across to Izzy. He picked up a stainless steel drink flask from the table and took a large swig.

‘What’s in there?’

‘Fresh lemon juice, room temperature mineral water and a spoonful of honey.’

‘For your voice.’

He raised the drink in a mock salute. ‘I always knew you’d be a quick study.’ He put his drink on the table and pulled down a dark blue shirt from a hanger on the door. ‘How’s it going out there?’

‘I’m sure you can tell better than I can,’ replied Izzy. ‘But to the uninitiated, I’d say the whole place is hopping and bopping.’

Seth picked up a plastic bottle of water from the table and thrust it under Izzy’s nose like a mic. ‘Can I quote you on that, Miss?' He grinned. 'Hopping and bopping. I like it.'

'Did you notice much difference out there without Jonno?'

Seth's grin faded. 'I'd like to say no,' he said. 'But the truth is ... yeah, I really miss him. He's a good bloke – or used to be, before – and he's a damn good keyboard and bass player – one of the best in the business, in fact. Maybe even *the* best. I really thought I could persuade him ... guess I'll just have to get over it.'

'And if he comes back?'

'Well, that would be a joint band and management decision, not just mine. And sadly, I think he might have shot himself in the foot.'

'Because ...?'

'Because he walked out on the band in the middle of a big world tour. And that, I'm sorry to say, is a heinous crime. Although management at home don't know anything yet.'

'But you came home for ...' Izzy stared up at him.

Seth put a finger across her lips. 'The crew don't know much about that,' he said. 'The general story given out was that I had a family emergency. No doubt this thing with Jonno is the bad karma I deserve.'

'It's all my fault ...'

'Nah, Izzy, not a chance, don't ever think that. I'm a grown man, making my own decisions. Rightly or wrongly.' He grinned. 'Now get over here and kiss me. I've got to be back on stage soon.'

Izzy moved closer and put her arms around his waist. He cradled her face in his hands and leaned down to kiss her, his lips soft at first, gradually growing more demanding.

A sharp rap on the door made Izzy jump violently and Seth laugh.

'Five minutes, Seth!' Lenny's voice shouted.

'On it,' he shouted back. He turned back to Izzy. 'C'mon you, walk me back.'

'As long as you don't expect me to get up on stage, we're good,' she replied.

'One day maybe ...' He dropped a kiss on her forehead.

'And I didn't even get to mop your brow.' Izzy pouted.

'You can mop anything you like back at the hotel.'

Izzy giggled.

Walking back towards the stage hand in hand with Seth felt surreal. With a whispered 'good luck', she watched him run nimbly up the stairs to the stage and nod over at Micky to start the intro. A roar from the crowd greeted his arrival, and Izzy went back to her seat to watch the rest of the show.

Seth felt so elated after the success of the show that the journey back to the hotel was punctuated with him and Zach cracking jokes and insulting each other in the way only good friends could. Izzy and Anna couldn't stop laughing at them, which made Seth even worse if that was possible. He really needed to let off steam because of the stress over Jonno, and the gig had helped a lot, but now he wanted to relax and unwind over a few beers before sleeping for hours.

'Izzy's on mopping duty when we get back,' Seth announced as the car turned into the open gateway at the hotel. 'Which is a very important job, isn't it, Iz?'

She turned to smile at him, and he caught his breath at the amused sparkle in her eyes. 'Very important,' she agreed.

Zach gave them a strange look. 'I think you two are as barking as each other.'

Anna laughed and patted his arm. 'I'll explain later,' she said.

'You might want to ask for a demo,' suggested Seth. 'Don't want you getting FOMO.'

Izzy raised her eyebrows.

'Aw come on Ms-I've-got-a-First,' he teased. 'Don't tell me you've never heard of FOMO?'

'We obviously move in very different circles,' she said.

'Not if I have anything to do with it,' he assured her. 'It's an acronym … *fear of missing out.*'

'Ah – with the very important mopping.'

'See?' He draped an arm around her. 'A quick study.'

The driver pulled up outside the main doors of the hotel and they all scrambled out.

'So no partying as you're – erm – mopping?' Zach asked politely with a straight face.

'Yep, that's us.' Seth's roguish grin made Izzy smile. 'Mopping and sleeping.' Keeping his arm around her shoulders, he led the way into the hotel. 'And a late breakfast.'

'See you tomorrow then.' Zach raised a hand before walking towards the bar with Anna.

'Go easy on those cosmos,' advised Izzy. 'They're lethal here, remember?'

'Yes, and I really hope they're lethal tonight too. I need them to be,' said Anna. 'Goodnight, sweet things.'

Seth hustled Izzy into a lift and pressed the number for the top floor. 'Sweet things?' He made a frown of mock disapproval. 'Girl's getting a mite cheeky, I think.'

'You must have known her a long time?'

'Eight years or so …'

'And did you—' Izzy stopped herself from asking a question she really didn't want the answer to.

Seth moved closer. 'Nope. She's like another sister, nags me like a sister too.'

'Sorry …'

He swooped down to kiss her and stopped her from saying any more just as the lift doors opened, then he grabbed her arm to pull her out.

'And that, my lovely, is a forfeit,' he said triumphantly. 'You might have forgotten there's a forfeit every time you say "sorry", but I haven't – and I do believe that's the first "sorry" of the trip.'

'What with all the mopping and forfeiting, when will we ever sleep?' Izzy widened her eyes at him.

'Who said anything about sleeping?'

'*You* did …' Izzy squeaked in surprise when Seth took off down the corridor at a rate of knots, hauling her behind him.

Seth opened the door and they both almost fell into the living room, laughing.

'I need a beer,' he said, heading for the fridge. 'How about you?'

'Please. But your voice?'

'No gig tomorrow, and I've really earned a few beers, I think.'

'Absolutely.' Izzy kicked her shoes off and collapsed on the sofa with a contented sigh. She watched Seth kick off his boots and socks, pad over to the fridge, and come back towards her with two bottles of beer. His hair looked even wilder now, and there was still a primal air of rock star about him; dangerous and feral. Izzy felt slightly shy with this Seth. He handed her a beer, sat in the armchair opposite her, his long legs stretched out in front of him, and flexed his bare feet.

'You have no idea how good that feels,' he said. 'And you have no idea how good it feels to have you here after a gig.'

'It gets lonely sometimes, you said …?'

'I'm not much for the after show party scene, you know that.' He took a large swig from his beer. 'But coming back to a soulless hotel room alone is sometimes worse.'

'I get that.'

He regarded her seriously with intense blue eyes. 'I think you do,' he said softly. 'Want to come and share my armchair?'

'There's more room here.' Izzy gestured at the sofa.

'Who needs more room?' The mischievous grin and dimples were suddenly back, and he crooked a finger at her. 'You have some mopping to do.'

Izzy stood up and walked over to share the armchair, and soon found it was indeed a perfect fit for two.

Chapter Ten

The two last shows went down a storm, and Izzy quickly became used to the way things were done. She knew when Seth would make his entrance, if and when he'd either announce a short interval, or saunter offstage for ten minutes leaving the girls singing. The set list got shuffled every other night in order to keep everything fresh for the musicians too, and Izzy found it all fascinating. It was on the last night that she thought of something she was surprised no one had brought up before – although she didn't feel too confident in suggesting it to everyone, and wasn't even sure if she should broach it with Seth. The last thing she wanted was to be thought of as another Sophie.

When they were at the hotel, packing to move on to Brisbane, she listened to Seth as he brought up the subject of Jonno again.

'Seth?'

He stopped talking and raised his eyebrows at her. 'That sounds serious?'

'If I suggest something … you won't mind, will you?'

He put his hands on his hips and looked at her quizzically. 'Well…spit it out, woman. I don't bite.' He wiggled his eyebrows. 'Unless you want me to.'

Izzy chose to ignore that. 'You play piano, don't you?'

'Sure. I write most of our songs on the piano. Why?'

'I read somewhere that a lot of frontmen sing a few songs at the piano … Freddie Mercury did, Chris Martin …'

Realisation dawned when he understood what she was getting at. 'You think I should sing at a piano?'

‘The slower tracks, one or two maybe …? It’s none of my business, of course. It’s just a thought.’

Seth moved closer and touched her cheek gently with his fingertips. ‘Iz, I love that your busy brain has been thinking things up for me, but it’s pretty funny you thought I’d get all cranky over it.’

‘*Are* you cranky?’

‘Hell no.’ He leaned down to kiss her. ‘It’s something Zach and I have talked about occasionally over the years, but naturally I didn’t want to step on Jonno’s toes – band politics.’

‘I thought it might help with his – erm – defection.’

He gave a low, bitter laugh. ‘Defection, yeah, good word.’

‘Take the audience’s minds off the fact he isn’t there.’

‘Now, *that’s* good reasoning.’ He fished his phone out of his pocket, stared at it for a moment, then put it back. ‘But it would need to be discussed face to face with everyone, I think, and not on the phone.’

Seth thought a lot about Izzy’s suggestion as they finished packing. He didn’t feel like offering it up for discussion just yet – too much like “dead man’s shoes” in his opinion, although he was possibly being a little oversensitive about it. After all, Jonno had left them all in the lurch.

One thing it had made him realise though, with startling clarity, was that he wanted his amazing Izzy with him all the time. Forever.

He felt relieved they were flying to Brisbane – it was a hell of a long drive otherwise. The crew had left with all the equipment at the crack of dawn the previous day – all two juggernauts of it. The lighting rigs and gear took up most of one. Rock bands didn’t exactly travel light. The flight took a mere two hours and twenty-five minutes, and that Seth could cope with. It meant they'd be at the hotel around lunch time. No gig until tomorrow would allow them all time to relax and recharge their batteries.

He packed his beloved acoustic guitar carefully in its case. No way would he trust that in with all the equipment. He wondered whether he should have taken Jonno's bass on the plane. Frowning, he pulled his phone out again and called Anna.

'Yes, Seth?' She answered on the second ring.

'Do you have Charlie's number?'

'Of course, I'll WhatsApp it to you.'

'Cheers. See you later.'

That girl was completely amazing. Heaven help them all if she left. He hoped she wouldn't go down the marriage and kids route just yet. She was a one-off and more difficult to replace than Jonno.

His phone pinged with the number and he keyed it in to call Charlie. Obviously, it took him longer to answer than it had Anna.

'Yeah?' The background noise told Seth they were still on the road.

'Charlie, it's Seth,'

'Oh hi, what's up?'

'I need to ask a favour.'

'Sure, anything.'

'I want you to take very good care of Jonno's bass. Don't let it travel with all the other gear. Nurture it, sleep with it and *never* leave it unattended.'

Charlie gave a good-humoured laugh. '*Sleep* with it, huh?'

'Yeah, do not lose it *or* break it.'

'No pressure then.'

'If you do, I might just have to kill you, and that would be a shame for the rest of the tour.'

'You have my word. I'll look after it.'

'Good man. Thanks.'

Seth hung up and added his guitar to the growing pile of cases.

'All done?' he asked Izzy, and she nodded.

'Yes, I'm good to go. *Who* are you going to kill?'

'Only Charlie.'

He didn't elaborate, and she didn't ask. Musicians on the road had their own particular brand of humour, and he felt sure she got most things anyway.

Izzy bought a bright green T-shirt for Ben at the airport. It had a yellow map of Australia on the front and the word "Straya", which she thought was probably Australian for Australia. She had no idea whether he'd like it, but it looked fun to her. At least no one at his school would have one the same. She wondered back to the VIP lounge where the others were waiting. Seth was sitting in a comfortable armchair, staring intently at his phone, which once again reminded her of the day they met. His beloved guitar was between his feet and he looked every inch the famous musician on tour. Tendrils of curls flopped into his eyes, and he pushed them back impatiently, then suddenly looked up as if he sensed she was there. She caught her breath as he smiled slowly at her. She reflected again on how it was no wonder every woman in the world fell for him. She slid into the chair next to his and leaned across to kiss him.

'Hey, Mr Cool. How's your luck?'

'Getting better all the time.' He pulled her back for another kiss. 'Whatcha been buying?'

'T-shirt for Ben.'

'What a good sister you are.'

'Not what he says.'

'He should try mine. He'd soon want you back.' He grinned.

Their flight was called a few minutes later, and they all stood up to go through the gate. Izzy wondered how they could do this all the time. It must be hard on Seth now Zach and Anna were an item; he'd be on his own a lot more when she wasn't around. Then her busy brain wondered if he'd seek out female company once she'd flown home. It would be easy for him, after all. She really didn't want to go down that route with her thinking; it would lead to sleepless nights and potential misery. His voice in her ear startled her out of her morbid thoughts.

'You look very serious.'

'Sorry ...'

He laughed. 'Oh Izzy, Izzy, that's two forfeits now.'

She pulled a face at him.

He tapped her gently on the nose. 'And I'm saving 'em up for the holiday.'

'Evil.'

'Oh yeah ...' He treated her to his delicious, mischievous grin and took hold of her hand as they passed through the departure gate.

Chapter Eleven

Seth breathed a sigh of relief when he caught sight of the hotel they were staying in. There didn't appear to be a Disney theme in this one – not a turret in sight for a start. Perhaps the room would even be tasteful with a nice conventional bathroom. Hopefully there wouldn't be gold-plated dragon taps and a huge whirlpool bath … although a huge bath did have its advantages.

'Wow, this place looks almost normal, Anna,' he said. 'You're slipping.'

She laughed. 'Our rooms are normal,' she said. 'Yours, however …'

Izzy patted him on the arm, 'Don't panic. There won't be dragons.'

Seth narrowed his eyes at her. 'I shall hold you personally responsible if there are.'

The driver pulled up outside the hotel's main doors and out spilled several porters with trolleys. Seth levered himself out of the car and Izzy handed his precious guitar carefully out to him.

'Let's check it out then,' he said. 'And if there's anything looking remotely like a dragon, Anna, you're in big trouble.'

'What's the big hate for dragons all of a sudden?' asked Zach, joining them on the forecourt. 'I think they're pretty cool.'

Seth prodded him in the chest on his way past.

'Boy's gone mad,' said Zach conversationally.

'Working too hard,' commented Izzy.

'Too much loud music,' chipped in Anna.

‘I can still hear you,’ Seth called back as he walked into the hotel foyer.

Anna scurried in after him. ‘I have to sign us all in,’ she said to anyone who might be listening.

The “room” for Seth and Izzy actually turned out to be the penthouse suite at the top of the hotel. It was accessible only by the penthouse lift, which also needed a special key card. Luckily, it all met with Seth’s approval.

He went straight out on to the balcony and gazed down at the outside pool. It looked beautiful – and empty. Graceful palm trees bordered the pool and comfortable looking sun loungers were arranged around the edge. The view across the city was spectacular from this vantage point. Skyscrapers jostled for space with each other against a fresh blue sky. If this was the Australian winter, he’d take it over the UK’s attempt at summer any day.

He sensed Izzy next to him and turned to look at her. Casually dressed in faded jeans and an oversized black shirt, she looked delectable. Glancing up at him, her eyes glinting with fun, she linked her arm through his.

‘Have you checked the bathroom?’

‘Not yet. You?’

‘Oh yes.’

Seth eyed her suspiciously.’ And …?’

‘Dragon-free.’

He laughed. ‘Good news.’

‘Is it lunch time yet?’

Seth pulled his phone out of his pocket. ‘It’s gone midday, so it can be. Are you hungry?’

‘A bit.’

‘Me too. Let’s scope out the restaurant.’

‘There are three in this place.’

‘Good. So if we’re ever not speaking, we can still eat.’

Izzy thumped him on the arm. 'Nice to know you have your priorities straight.'

Seth shrugged. 'What can I say? I get hungry.'

They turned to go back inside just as Seth's phone rang. 'Yep. Malcolm, hi. How's it going?' He frowned. The voice on the other end sounded less than happy. Seth really hadn't been looking forward to this call, and he'd guessed it would be coming soon. All about Jonno, of course. *Why hadn't Seth tried harder to keep him, what had he been thinking?*

Seth let him carry on a while longer before he decided to actually join in the conversation.

'Right, so let's get this straight, you think I should have let Jonno's girlfriend loose on stage with her god-awful voice – which, I quote is "like a rusty hinge" – singing a god-awful song in the middle of a world tour?'

Malcolm stopped mid-rant. 'Well, no, not when you put it like that.'

'Surely you aren't scared of her old man as well?'

'No – no ... although he's influential in the City apparently, so we have to wonder what kind of trouble he could actually cause us.'

'Doesn't mean anything to me, mate. Load of claptrap.'

'Seth, be reasonable—'

'No – *you* be bloody reasonable! Scarlet Gryphon is *my* band, and what I say goes. I don't care if you're the biggest cheese in our label's management hierarchy – I own a big bundle of shares too – and you need me a hell of a lot more than I need you. I'm gutted Jonno left – truly – but I will not compromise our sound *or* the tour for one spoilt little girl.'

Malcolm sighed. 'I'm on my way out. I'll be there in a couple of days.'

'Waste of time, mate.'

'Yeah, I get that. But I have to keep the promotors happy by reassuring them the punters are happy, and I can only do that by seeing for myself and reporting back.'

'By that I imagine the tabloids have managed to get hold of some version of the story?'

'Jonno's girl, Sophie – is it? She told the press.'

'Of course she did.'

'What does he see in her?'

'Got me beat.'

'See you soon.'

'I'll get in the garlic and crucifixes.'

The line went dead.

Seth pushed a hand through his hair and blew out a frustrated breath. He could hear the shower running in the bathroom, which was either Izzy taking a shower, or running the shower in order not to intrude on his conversation. He called Zach and relayed Malcolm's phone call.

'Only a matter of time before he turned up,' was all he said. 'But like you told him, they need us more than we need them. We're the money-makers – at least you are.'

'Still, maybe I should have been friendlier?'

Zach snorted out a laugh. 'You think? And made him even more suspicious?'

'True enough.' Seth raised his eyebrows as Izzy re-emerged from the bathroom, amidst a cloud of fragrant steam and wrapped in a huge, fluffy towel. She gave him an impish grin as she went into the bedroom.

'You going down for lunch any time soon?' Zach's voice startled him back to the conversation.

'Give us half an hour or so,' muttered Seth.

Seth had gone out early to the venue with Zach for a "reccy" and to check on the equipment with the road crew. Izzy had opted to stay at the hotel for a change – she'd discovered a Zumba class being held in the hotel's dance studio, and found herself itching to do something energetic. It was always fun doing another instructor's class; it made a change from doing her own.

Making sure she had the room key card with her, Izzy took the lift down to the sports floor in the basement, feeling quite excited at the thought of an hour's dance. She pushed open the door to the dance studio to see quite a few people standing around. For a split second she nearly greeted everyone, like she usually did in her own class. Instead, she positioned herself near the back of the studio, careful not to be in anyone's way.

Seconds later, a tall, willowy blonde almost exploded into the room, dressed in a black Lycra crop top and leggings with a fluorescent green stripe down each side.

'Hi guys!' she shouted. 'Anyone here new to Zumba?' She cast a professional eye over Izzy, who shook her head.

'I do Zumba at home in the UK,' she said.

'Great stuff. I'm Roz – who are you?'

'Izzy.'

'Hey, you aren't here with that British rock band, are you?'

'Erm … yes.'

'Which one of 'em's yours?'

Izzy laughed. 'I would say they're all their own men.'

Roz smiled. 'That singer's a real tasty morsel though, isn't he?' She turned back to the rest of the class. 'Okay, let's dance.'

An hour later, a very hot and sweaty Izzy took herself back up to the penthouse. She really needed a shower now, but that class had been just what the doctor ordered *(what did that even mean?)*. Australians certainly had a lot of energy. Letting herself back into the suite, she made straight for the fridge and, opening the door, pulled out a welcome bottle of ice-cold water.

She was about to head off to the shower when there was a tap at the door. Puzzled, she peered through the security peephole, but could only make out the back view of a slim, dark-haired man who looked slightly familiar. She slipped the chain on and opened the door a little.

'Yes?'

The man turned around; he looked tired, paler than usual, and was definitely the last person Izzy expected to see. *Jonno.*

'Hey Izzy, is Seth there?' He ran his hands nervously through his hair. 'I really need to speak with him.'

'I'm sorry but he isn't at the moment. Come on in though.' She slipped the chain off and opened the door wide. 'He should be back any minute.'

'I don't want to be a nuisance …' Jonno really did look wretched.

'As if,' said Izzy. 'Get in here and I'll ring down for some coffee. Are you hungry? I can order food too.' She had a horrible feeling she might be babbling, but there was no way on earth she wanted to let him go before Seth got back. 'Come in.'

Jonno came in somewhat reluctantly, and Izzy waved him to the nearest sofa. She picked up the phone. 'What can I get you?'

'Lots of coffee would be cool, thanks.'

Izzy ordered two pots of coffee and a plate of pastries and fruit. She felt worried about Jonno, who appeared not to have slept, showered or eaten for some days, which he probably hadn't, with all the to-ing and fro-ing between London and Australia he'd been doing.

'Coffee's coming. I'll just get a sweatshirt.' She went into the bedroom but kept the door open so she could make sure he didn't suddenly make a run for it. Although why would he when he'd clearly just flown all the way across the world again to come back? Anyway, Izzy hadn't the faintest idea what on earth she'd do if he did take off. Rugby tackle him? Picking up her phone from the bedside table, she dashed off a quick text to Seth.

Jonno's here. Get back asap! Iz x

Izzy remembered the sweatshirt excuse just in time, and grabbing the nearest one, slung it around her shoulders before going back into the lounge area. A knock at the door heralded the arrival of the coffee and she dashed to open it. A waiter wheeled in a trolley laden with coffee pots, milk, sugar, several mugs and a large plate of tasty-looking pastries with various berries and melon slices. He loaded plates, coffee and food on the coffee table in front of Jonno, and had left before Izzy ever thought to give him a tip.

'Was I supposed to tip him?' she asked Jonno. 'I'm seriously rubbish at living the high life.'

He gave her a tired smile. 'You're all good, Izzy,' he said. 'We pay enough to stay in the best places, but I'm sure Seth will drop him a few notes when we leave.'

Izzy nodded and poured coffee into two mugs. She pushed one across to Jonno. 'Help me out with the pastries,' she said. 'I've just done an hour of Australian Zumba, and eating more than one of those will destroy all the good work.'

'How is Australian Zumba different?'

'The instructor here is stark staring mad,' said Izzy fervently. 'Good fun – but bonkers.'

Obligingly, Jonno took a large croissant from the plate and bit into it. 'This is good.'

'How are you, Jonno?'

He peered at her sadly, and then sighed. 'I've been a total prat,' he said. 'Sophie was hoping to use me as a shoehorn into our band … or any other band. I don't think she's too fussy. I don't even think she really loved me ... and that hurts ... the joke is she can't even sing. I guess the joke's on me now.'

'I'm no singer either,' said Izzy. 'But I'm more of a foghorn than a shoehorn.'

Jonno gave a hollow laugh and poured milk into his coffee. 'Turns out, after her little prank with the tabloids, Daddy Dearest has been trying to buy out our record label.'

'And did he manage it?' Izzy felt a cold shiver run down her spine. '*Will* he manage it?'

Jonno shook his head. 'No chance,' he said. 'In fact, I think he's already gone after one of the others. Kind of a "if you can't get a record deal, buy the bloody label deal".'

Izzy touched his arm gently. 'I'm sorry about Sophie.'

'Don't be. Blokes like us – me and Seth – we're kind of married to the band, to life on the road. Relationships don't often work out. Marriage certainly doesn't. Seth's living proof of that. We'll both probably die on the road back home when we're too old to travel far. Can't stick in one place for long and can't stay with one person too long either, see?'

Izzy concentrated on nibbling at her Danish in order to avoid looking at Jonno. She wondered whether what he said was true. She'd never really thought about rock stars getting old, but of course some did. They didn't all go out in a blaze of glory and alcohol before they were forty. But it was also true that very few of them stayed married for long. She wondered why Jonno would say things like that to her; it seemed tactless and inappropriate. Perhaps he was hurting so much, he just wanted to lash out. *Or maybe he's simply trying to cause trouble between me and Seth?*

'It's a tough life,' she said after a while. 'And I know absolutely nothing about it of course, but even I can see how tough it is. So you have to really love what you do, or it simply won't work.'

Jonno nodded. He was about to comment further, when the door opened and both Seth and Zach came in. Izzy could almost have cried with relief.

She stood up. 'There's loads of fresh coffee and pastries,' she said. 'I'm going for a shower.' She went into the bedroom and was about to shut the door when Seth came in after her and kicked the door shut. He held her arms and stared down at her, his vivid blue eyes searching her face intently.

'What's he said?'

'Go easy on him, Seth, he looks washed out.' Izzy touched his face gently. 'He's been flying back and forth between here and home for days after all.'

'You look upset.'

'I feel sorry for him.'

'And?'

There was no hiding anything from Seth. 'He ... said you and he are very much alike ... married to the band, relationships don't work, can't stay long with one person ... that kind of thing.'

Seth muttered something extremely uncomplimentary. 'So he's split up with the spoilt heiress then?'

'It looks like it, and he's devastated as far as I can tell. But you need to go talk with him. I have to shower.'

'Do you now? What have you been up to?'

Izzy smiled. 'I did an Australian Zumba class and it nearly killed me.'

Seth brushed her damp hair back from her face with his fingers. 'I doubt that, my little dancing queen. Is that my sweatshirt you're nearly wearing?'

Izzy stood on tiptoe to kiss him and his arms tightened around her. 'You're a very special person, Isabelle Grant.' He whispered against her ear. 'Now, me and Zach have to have a chat with the wayward waif and stray.'

Chapter Twelve

Anna and Izzy had opted to eat dinner together in the smallest of the three hotel restaurants whilst the band members were in the biggest one having dinner and a chat with Jonno.

'He looked so … broken,' said Izzy, sipping at her second cosmopolitan.

'Jonno's always been kind of vulnerable where women are concerned.' Anna took a healthy swig of her own drink. 'The wrong kind of woman can easily manipulate him – and usually does.'

'He said how he and Seth are the same, can't stay with one person for too long or make relationships work, that kind of stuff.'

'He said that to you?' Anna looked outraged. 'Bozo.'

'Well … he's hurting …'

Anna shook her head. 'No excuse. He and Seth are nothing alike. Seth's a good guy. You saw how he looked out for Gracie last year, and she can be a total pain in the …'

Izzy laughed. She felt better being in Anna's company – sometimes only a chat with another woman would do.

'Plus,' Anna continued, 'most band problems start with the bassist. After all, nobody wants to hear a bass solo, do they? How long can you keep an audience interested with a walking bass riff?'

'I don't know what that is,' said Izzy, laughing as Anna played an air guitar whilst humming her version of a walking bass.

'And the bassist rarely gets to be up front unless he's another Paul McCartney and writes half the songs.'

'Jealous?' Izzy finished her cosmo. 'You think he's jealous of Seth?'

'It's possible,' agreed Anna. 'Seth gets – or did get – all the women, like most front men do. The next in line is the lead guitarist, except ours is happily married.'

'Complicated stuff, band politics.'

'But as I said, Seth's a good guy – one of the best.'

'Well, I think Seth's a good guy too, but I'm biased.'

Anna leaned across the table and stared at Izzy with dark, serious eyes. 'And he loves you to bits, trust me.'

'Thank you for saying that.'

'More of these, I think.' Anna peered at her almost empty cocktail glass, and then looked around for a waiter.

'Did we order food?' Izzy was having difficulty remembering. 'What did I order?'

Anna laughed. 'We ordered the salt and pepper calamari … and here it comes … I'm starving.'

They ate in silence at first, enjoying the huge portions of Sri Lankan style calamari, which had been wok-fried with garlic, green onions and chillies. Izzy felt she'd been transported to a restaurant in heaven. The different tastes were certainly out of this world, and it almost took her mind off their current problem.

Almost …

'Will they let Jonno back in the band?' Izzy couldn't help remembering Seth's words. *He's shot himself in the foot this time.*

'I expect they will, and just in time if manky Malcolm is coming out here.'

'Manky who?'

Anna waved her fork in the air. 'Big shareholder and one of the top guys at the record company,' she said. 'But luckily Seth owns a bigger chunk of shares than he does, so he won't take any rubbish from him, which is good.'

'Is he that bad?'

'Arrogant, bullying and verging on sexist,' said Anna. 'You'll see. But he won't dare be awful to you. Seth would have his guts for garters, and I'm being polite here.'

'You're funny,' Izzy popped a piece of calamari into her mouth. 'I did a Zumba class here today.'

Anna raised her eyebrows. 'Seriously? How'd that work out for ya?' She adopted a passable American accent. Izzy laughed, thinking it must be all the travelling she did that enabled her to switch accents with such accuracy.

'The instructor said Seth is a tasty morsel.'

'Did she now? Well, wouldn't that just float his boat?' Anna grinned, switching accents to a less accurate Australian one. 'Was she scary? She sounds scary.'

'Tall, slim, beautiful, blonde with an even tan, pierced nose and perfect teeth.'

'Good job Seth prefers a pale, diminutive redhead then.'

'Let's hope.'

'Don't let Jonno's mood affect you.' Anna sat back in her chair with a contented sigh. 'I'm pretty full, but I still feel the need for a dessert. How about you?'

Seth sat alone in the apartment once the others had left. For once he didn't feel particularly hungry. Jonno's words to Izzy had rattled him more than the band situation if he was honest. What was the man thinking? Just because he was having relationship problems, did he really need to try and create some for Seth too?

His phone rang, interrupting his surly thoughts. A London number he didn't recognise ...

'Yep?'

'Jacob Reynolds here, Mr Roberts.'

He didn't think he recognised his name either. 'And you are?'

'CEO of your record company.'

Ah, he probably should have recognised *his* name. 'What can I do for you?'

'Mr Roberts, we've had an extremely substantial offer for the company – not that we were exactly in the market to sell, but as a major shareholder, obviously we have to let you know there's been an offer.'

'From?'

'Sir William Etherington-Smythe.'

'And apart from being knighted, who is he?'

'Well, I understand from Sir William that his daughter is engaged to your bass player.'

Seth's gut twisted at those words. *What the hell …?* 'News to me, Mr Reynolds,' he said, trying not to sound as taken aback as he felt. *Engaged?*

'He apparently wants to take more of an interest in his daughter's future.'

'Perhaps he should try getting his facts right then,' Seth replied.

'As the major shareholder, a refusal from you would stop the sale,' Reynolds continued.

'I'm refusing,' said Seth shortly.

'I hoped you would.'

Seth could hear the relief in the other man's voice.

They said their goodbyes, and Seth sat for a while longer, staring at the now silent phone. He really hoped his bass player hadn't suddenly become engaged to the ruthlessly ambitious Sophie, because that certainly *wasn't* what Jonno had told them earlier.

Chapter Thirteen

Seth idly watched two young women execute perfectly synchronised dives into the swimming pool below. They scarcely made a ripple in the water's surface, and one turned to float on her back and give him a cheeky wave. He was used to women waving at him – it went with the turf – but there were times and places to wave back, and he didn't think this was one of them. Especially with his own gorgeous woman still fast asleep in the room behind him. He grinned to himself. She really did have trouble with those cosmos. Or maybe it was Anna's fault, leading her astray. Although in all fairness to Izzy, she was definitely her own person; he knew that all too well. He also knew she loved cocktails, even if she couldn't drink too many of them. She'd certainly been a little worse for wear last night when he and Zach had retrieved them from their restaurant. He could recite what they'd eaten word for word because Izzy had told him more than once. And, she'd told him proudly, she'd eaten a dessert. Almost unheard of for Izzy to eat dessert. That had definitely been Anna's doing; he knew how much she loved her desserts.

A noise from the room caused him to peer in through the open French window. But it was just Izzy rolling over and muttering in her sleep. He looked back at the pool, to see what the swimmers were up to, and watched them do a few laps before he turned and went back into the room. He wouldn't have minded doing a few laps himself but didn't fancy having to avoid other swimmers. Izzy had once called him unsociable, and perhaps he was becoming more like the recluse people thought he was. What he did know was he tolerated less rubbish now than he had at the start of Scarlet Gryphon.

He should probably have a word with the others about the lovely Sophie's father making an offer for the label. He had to be mad if he thought it would further her singing career. She needed to be able to actually *sing* first. He wondered again whether she and Jonno really were engaged, although he should know by now how easily rumours started. No doubt he'd get home to discover he and Izzy were "married with twins" or something. He grinned to himself. Then he thought about *actually* having children with Izzy ... and *marrying* Izzy. The idea no longer seemed to terrify him. In fact, he had a whole heap of ideas on that score, *and* he knew just the person to help him. *But first he really needed to focus on the rest of the tour ...*

Wandering into the lounge, he scrolled down through his messages. *Oh deep joy!* There was one from Malcolm – he was here in the hotel. Seth wondered whether to call him or wait for him to make contact first. He was saved from making the decision when his phone buzzed.

'Malcolm,' he said. 'You know it's only seven in the morning, I take it?'

'Too early for breakfast?' Malcolm sounded grumpy, but that was nothing new.

'Nah, never too early for food.' Seth supposed he could be a little sociable, seeing as Jonno was back in the fold and Malcolm didn't actually have anything to moan about.

'I'm in the Bluebird Restaurant. Care to join me?'

'On my way.'

Seth hung up and looked over at Izzy again; she looked adorable and extremely tempting. He'd rather get back into bed with her for a few more hours, but needs must. He checked his appearance before leaving because … well …

that's what he had to do. Stepping into the lift, he pressed the button for the restaurant's floor, texting Izzy on the way down.

Moaning Malc is here and has demanded my presence in the Bluebird Restaurant. No idea how long, but come on down if I'm not back when you wake up. I might need rescuing. S xx

He strolled into the restaurant and spotted Malcolm at a window table working his way down a pot of coffee. He waved a hand at Seth but remained seated when Seth reached the table. *No excuse for bad manners*, thought Seth, but he still held out a hand to the older man. 'Good flight out?' he asked.

'Bloody awful,' said Malcolm, shaking Seth's hand with an air of reluctance. 'Any news?'

Seth signalled a waiter with the minimum of fuss and ordered another pot of coffee. 'I'll have the full breakfast works, please.' He turned to Malcolm and raised his eyebrows.

'Same for me.'

'Coming up,' said the waiter.

'So … as I said … any news?' Malcolm wasn't going to waste any time on niceties, that much was obvious.

Deliberately, Seth took his time pouring himself a coffee from the pot on the table and adding milk to it. After taking a few healthy gulps, he eyed Malcolm suspiciously. 'About?'

'Don't play games, Seth. News of Jonno, of course.'

'I'm not one of your minions, Malc, so don't treat me like one.'

Malcolm gaped like an out of water fish.

Luckily, the food arrived at that moment, which distracted Malcolm for a few minutes, and Seth managed a whole sausage before he asked the same question again.

Seth sighed and put down his knife and fork. 'Jonno is back in the fold, the annoying girlfriend appears to be history and the guys are working on forgiving him. Now can I eat my food?'

'He's *back*? She's gone?'

'Yep. And her dad's attempt at buying out the company has been thwarted.' Seth polished off another sausage with relish. 'By me. And these sausages are awesome.'

'Buy the …? *What?*'

'You didn't know?' Seth felt marginally happy about that. 'As a major shareholder, I got a call, and so would you, but I guess you'd have been on the plane. I turned down the very kind offer, which meant he failed. Going after someone else now I hear, so good luck with that.'

Malcolm sat back in his chair, staring at Seth as if he'd suddenly sprouted another head. 'The man sounds as mad as his daughter.'

'Is that sexist or people-ist?' Seth speared his final sausage and waved it at Malcolm. 'Either way, you're insulting somebody.'

Malcolm resumed eating, still watching Seth through narrowed eyes. 'You're not exactly sane either.'

'Oh, I'm deadly sane, trust me.' Seth flashed his wicked grin. 'And here is my most favourite person in the world.' He'd spotted Izzy coming into the restaurant and stood up to wave her over.

'Who's that?'

'The love of my life.' Seth loved watching her walk towards him. When she reached the table, he leaned down to kiss her before introducing her to Malcolm.

'Meet Malcolm Dodds, record company exec and shareholder.'

Izzy turned to Malcolm and held out a small hand. 'Good to meet you.'

Malcolm took her hand. 'And you … Miss …?'

'Izzy,' she said firmly. She sat in the vacant chair next to Seth. 'Any coffee left?'

'I'll get more.' Seth signalled to a waiter.

Malcolm stood up then. 'I'll catch you later, Seth.' He strode away without a backward glance. Seth frowned.

'Was it something I said?' Izzy didn't look too bothered.

'The man's an imbecile.' Seth didn't feel too bothered either.

'Anna did mention that about him.'

'But less politely, I imagine.'

'He can't fire Jonno, can he?' It was clear that Izzy was still having problems getting her head around who was more important than who in this strange world of rock music.

'Strictly speaking, the only person who can legally fire Jonno is me.'

'Wow … no pressure then.'

Zach and Anna arrived at that moment and scooted into the vacant chairs opposite.

'I'm starving.' Anna reached for the menu. 'What did you two have?'

'Nothing yet,' said Izzy.

'I'm working up to a second breakfast,' said Seth.

'You're way too tall to be a hobbit,' commented Izzy.

'He's got hairy feet though,' offered Zach.

'I can fire other people too,' said Seth conversationally to Izzy. 'Especially ones who make personal remarks.'

'Is Malcolm here?' Anna chose to change the subject.

'Izzy scared him away.'

'Good job, Iz.' Anna looked around for a waiter. 'Where are all the waiters?'

Seth looked around, stuck his hand up anyway, and one materialised as if by magic at his side.

'Yes, Mr Roberts?'

Anna and Zach laughed.

'Every time,' said Zach.

'You've either got it or you ain't,' said Seth with a grin.

Chapter Fourteen

There was only one week left of this part of the tour before everyone disappeared off for a fortnight's break, which Izzy found hard to believe. She'd become acclimatised to the band's on-the-road way of life really quickly, although she couldn't escape the feeling she should somehow be earning her keep. It really went against her values, letting someone else pay for her all the time when she'd paid her own way for most of her adult life.

Soon she'd be on her way back to the normality of England, but without Seth, and she realised she ought to be thinking about finding work of some kind. Although exactly what kind, she had no idea. What she really wanted to do was enrol for an MA in journalism, and she knew several London universities offered the course. She felt sure she'd be accepted – her professor had told her it was pretty much a given with her grades. But when should she apply – this year or next?

She kept thinking about Seth's offer of staying at his farm in Sussex, and the thought of riding his horses was really tempting. But she also couldn't help thinking it would feel like taking advantage of his generosity. Again. She wasn't looking forward to life without him either. *How do other girlfriends of musicians cope?* she wondered. Perhaps that was the reason Jonno's Sophie had wanted to be part of the band so desperately?

Personally, Izzy couldn't think of anything more terrifying than standing on a stage in front of thousands of people. She felt sure the only sound she'd be able to make under those circumstances would be a petrified squeak. Hardly the stuff rock singers were made of.

Izzy braved the Zumba class a couple more times, and enjoyed the enthusiasm of both Roz and the students. They were a friendly bunch and happily included her in coffee after the class without question. She left Seth sleeping in if it was the morning after a show, knowing he probably wouldn't surface much before eleven. She attempted to persuade Anna to join her, but she'd looked horrified and said she'd leave Zumba to the experts.

On her way back up to the penthouse after one particularly energetic session, Izzy's phone rang. She didn't recognise the number but answered anyway.

'Is that Ms Isabelle Grant?' A youngish sounding female voice asked.

'Yes.'

'Hi, my name is Lucy Evans. I'm one of the researchers for *Today's Women*.'

'Erm … yes?'

'We'd like to invite you onto the show.'

A giggle escaped from Izzy – she couldn't help it. The lift doors opened and she stepped out into the corridor outside the suite.

'So who is this really?' She fiddled with the key card, juggling the phone at the same time, only to have the door opened from the other side by Seth, who raised his eyebrows at her in mock horror as she almost fell into the room.

'I really am Lucy Evans,' said the voice, sounding a bit peeved now.

'And why on earth would you want *me* on *Today's Women*?'

At that, Seth turned back and held his hand out for the phone. She passed it over with a shrug.

‘Who’s this?’ he asked, putting the phone on speaker so Izzy could hear too.

‘Lucy Evans from ITV. I’m a researcher on *Today’s Women*.’

‘And where did you get this number?’

‘We spoke with Mrs Grant the other day and she gave us the number.’

‘Well, Ms Evans, this is a private number, and Ms Grant doesn’t give interviews.’

Izzy suppressed a snort of laughter as Seth ended the call.

‘I think we may need to have a word with your mum about *not* handing out your number to every TV researcher who calls.’ He looked serious.

‘Does it matter?’ Izzy felt suddenly concerned. ‘It’s not a big deal, is it? I wouldn’t have done the show.’

‘I know that, Iz, but if your mum gives out your number willy-nilly, you’ll get bombarded with calls until eventually you’ll agree to an interview just to get them off your back. Then once you’ve done one …’ He trailed off, but gave her a shrewd look and raised his eyebrows.

‘That’s a bit scary.’

‘It can be.’

‘Sor—’ she stopped herself in time when she noticed amusement flicker across Seth’s face. ‘Ah no. You’re not getting me again.’

‘Go shower, Zumba Queen. I’m taking you to see cute, fluffy marsupials this morning.’

‘Really?’ Izzy didn’t think that sounded even vaguely like Seth.

‘Raising money for koalas, that’s the kind of interview I *will* do. Good cause, good press, and you get to come too and cuddle koalas.’

‘Do you think they just want to find out juicy stuff about you?’

‘Who? The koalas?’

Izzy laughed. ‘*Today’s Women*.’

‘Maybe.’

‘Every day’s a school day.’ Izzy headed for the shower. *And koalas?* Who knew?

The Koala Sanctuary was only a short drive away and Seth had arranged for a driver to take them there and then back to the hotel.

‘I’ve never seen a real koala,’ said Izzy. ‘Have you?’

‘Yeah, cute and surprisingly heavy.’ Seth grinned. ‘Which you might be one day, if you keep having cosmos and desserts with Anna.’

Izzy elbowed him swiftly and none too gently in the ribs, and fixed him with her scariest steely glare. ‘Which is still better than finishing this part of the tour with a broken leg, I’d have thought.’

Seth laughed. ‘You don’t scare me, Izzy Grant. I’ll set the sisters on you.’

‘From what I’ve heard about your sisters, they’re more likely to be on my side. And both my weight *and* my appetite are just fine, by the way.’

Seth held up his hands in mock surrender. ‘Scarily all true.’ He rubbed his ribs ruefully. ‘I think you’ve broken something.’

They drove into the Sanctuary, and Izzy could see lots of enclosures filled with dense trees … but there wasn’t a koala in sight.

‘Where are they all?’ she said as they got out of the car.

‘Asleep, I expect.’

‘Asleep?’

‘They’re nocturnal.’

‘So we’re here because …?’

‘I told you – good publicity and a photo op.’

Seth was already striding towards a bunch of people who were obviously waiting for him. He was shaking hands with everyone when she reached the group. He put an arm around her shoulders and introduced her. One young woman was holding a koala in her arms. She noticed Izzy staring.

‘Would you like to hold her?’

‘Yes please!’ Izzy held her arms out to take her. ‘She looks half asleep.’ Taking hold of the koala, she felt surprised to discover it was indeed heavy.

In a matter of minutes, Seth was holding a koala too, and cameras were clicking from all directions. The keeper, Sally, kept up a running commentary about the danger of habitat loss for koalas due to dying eucalyptus trees, owing to bush fires, land clearance and the different diseases which killed the trees.

Izzy had immediately fallen in love with the koala she was holding, who seemed to be happily snoozing with its fluffy arms wound around her neck.

Sally explained about the babies – or Joeys – who were born very immature and then developed in the mother’s pouch for a further six or seven months. ‘An adult koala will sleep up to eighteen or twenty hours a day,’ she went on.

‘Bit like you after a concert,’ said Izzy to Seth cheekily. He narrowed his eyes at her.

After a further fifteen minutes, Izzy reluctantly gave the sleepy koala back to Sally, Seth having already relinquished his koala earlier.

‘Time to get back,’ he said. ‘Duty calls.’

Amidst more hand shaking and thanks for Seth's donation and appearance, they returned to the car and headed back towards the hotel.

'Do you do stuff like that a lot?' Izzy felt amazed at the diverse amount of work involved in being famous.

'Nah, only if it's something I agree with.' He turned to look at her. 'And I happen to like koalas.'

Chapter Fifteen

It seemed like no time at all before it was the last night in Australia, and everyone was euphoric. A two-week break was in sight. The fans appeared to have forgiven and forgotten Jonno's temporary desertion, and Malcolm had flown home, having not found anything else to moan about. Everyone felt better after he'd left, especially poor Lenny, Scarlet Gryphon's long-suffering tour manager, who'd born the brunt of his interfering this time. Not that Len ever seemed to take Malcolm too seriously – he himself was an extremely valued member of the team and Seth made sure he knew it.

The final Australian concert was filmed both for Sky Arts and MTV Australia and New Zealand, and Seth enjoyed every second. Everything went without a hitch for a change, and when the band came back on stage for their encore, every member of the audience was on their feet. They finished with 'Take Me Back', Seth's favourite tumultuous rock track, and he sang his heart out. He felt they'd almost blown the roof off. Twirling the mic by its lead, he caught it deftly, and took a bow as the last notes died away and colourful indoor fireworks rocked the stage. Izzy was on her feet too, he noticed, as the lights travelled out over the audience, and that made him feel ten feet tall. *What a night.*

Everyone stayed around for the last night party, including Seth and Izzy. Even Jonno stayed, albeit drinking far more than he usually did, and spending a lot more time with the female hangers-on. *Strange behaviour from a newly-engaged man*, Seth mused. If indeed, that piece of information really was true. Seth certainly had no intention of asking him tonight, but stored the information away for after the holiday.

'Will he be okay?' Izzy frowned.

'Iz, he's thirty-three years old, it's up to him. We're officially on holiday for two weeks, so if he wants to take all those girls back to the hotel, it's his call.' Seth took hold of her arm and steered her away from the area with Jonno and his fans.

Izzy was still frowning. 'I expect this is when he misses Sophie the most?'

'No idea,' said Seth. 'We're all different, no matter what he said to you.'

'Which means?'

Seth stopped and turned her to face him. 'Which means I know you well enough by now to know the way that busy brain of yours works.' He stroked a hand down her glossy hair. 'And no, I won't be behaving like that in Japan, even though I will be missing you like crazy.'

'Can we get a drink now?' She changed the subject.

'Trying to get me drunk and incapable?'

'Definitely not. Where's the fun in that?'

'Where indeed?' He bent down and kissed her. 'We could just get the hell out of here instead?'

'Could we?' Her eyes sparkled. 'What about your stuff in the dressing room?'

'That will be taken care of, but I do need to get my guitar.'

'Let's go get it then.'

He grinned and took hold of her hand. 'Plenty to drink back at the hotel, after all.'

Izzy woke up early, in spite of the late night and copious glasses of champagne back at the hotel. She rolled over and peered at Seth. How could he still look so gorgeous when sleeping? She'd never even heard him snore. She hoped she didn't snore either, but knowing her, she probably did.

His unruly curls framed a face that could have been carved by gods – for female gods – or would that still be goddesses? Izzy was never sure these days.

Either way, he had an ethereal quality about him which made him appear not quite of this earth. And those eyelashes … most women would pay good money for eyelashes like that.

Idly she reached out a tentative finger to tease one of those curls and yelped in surprise when a strong hand grabbed her wrist. Drowning blue eyes stared up at her, glinting with fun.

'Never play with a sleeping rock singer,' he said quietly. 'Dangerous …'

'Well, you won't hear me apologising again. I've gained enough forfeits.'

'About those …'

The only thing Izzy knew about their departure from Australia was they had a plane to catch. Seth still remained tight-lipped over their destination, and no amount of pleading, cajoling or dire threats moved him in any way.

'You'll soon see,' was all he'd say, flashing his cheeky grin.

'You're not just taking me home, are you?' Izzy decided to try out her last idea.

'Oh please.' Seth gave her an exasperated look. 'Give me a little credit.'

At last they were headed out to the car to begin their journey to the airport. Izzy hugged Anna and Zach, promising to catch up in August.

‘WhatsApp me,’ instructed Anna. ‘Tell me where you are.’

‘She’ll be sworn to secrecy,’ said Seth.

‘I’ll be in touch,’ said Izzy with a grin.

‘She won’t,’ said Seth, shooing her into the car. ‘And neither will I.’

Then they were off. It felt strange being without the others, even to Izzy who’d only been around them for three weeks, so she realised it must feel totally weird to Seth who travelled with them all for most of the year.

‘Do you miss them?’ she asked him suddenly.

He turned to look at her. ‘Usually, yes,’ he said. ‘But not this time.’

‘Just the actual concerts.’

‘It’s what I was born to do,’ he said, taking hold of her hand. ‘It’s all I know.’

‘Total way of life then.’ She thought for a moment. ‘I wonder what you’d have been if you’d gone a different way?’

‘Probably a window cleaner or something.’ He grinned. ‘I like going up ladders.’

The driver took them to the airport’s first class entrance and helped load their cases onto a trolley. Seth shook his hand and gave him a hefty tip. Then they were checking in, and through to the VIP departure lounge.

‘You’ll have to tell me soon.’ Izzy felt the need to badger him a bit more. ‘Supposing I have to go to the loo, and the flight’s called? I wouldn’t know it was our flight because I don’t know where we’re going – then I might miss it.’

Seth laughed aloud at that. ‘I think you’ve watched *Home Alone Two* far too many times.’

Izzy shrugged. ‘Worth a try.’

Seth glanced at the departure board. 'Flight's up there.'

'There's a lot of flights up there.'

Seth sat down in a comfy armchair, his guitar case between his feet as usual. 'Sit down, Iz. You're making me nervous.'

She sat down reluctantly, feeling too wired to keep still. She had no idea why Seth continued to keep their holiday destination secret when they were now on their way. Unless he didn't want any reporters, who might be lurking, to overhear? Although she felt pretty sure reporters weren't allowed in the departure lounge …

'Coffee?'

Izzy turned to see a waiter standing at Seth's elbow. Zach and Anna were right; she hadn't seen him signal to anyone, yet here the waiter was.

'Cappuccino, please.'

'Espresso for me, thanks.'

Seth went back to scrolling through his phone and suddenly made a disgruntled noise, causing Izzy to look at him in surprise.

'What's up?'

'Zach and Anna were trying to keep an eye on Jonno, but he's already skedaddled apparently, taking his bass with him this time.'

'You don't think he'll let you down again?'

'Let's find out.' Seth scrolled through his contacts until he found Jonno's number and pressed the call button. 'Hey Jon, how's it going?' He listened for a few minutes. 'Yep, that's cool. Sounds great. Have fun. See you in Tokyo.'

Izzy gave him a questioning look.

'Apparently, one of the girls from last night has a place on the beach, so he's staying there for a week or so and then flying out to Japan.'

'Let's hope she's not an aspiring singer then.'

The waiter arrived with their coffees, and Seth picked up his and swigged most of it down in two gulps. 'Let's hope,' he agreed. He suddenly remembered one of the girls surrounding Jonno had been blonde, very slim, and had worn ridiculously high heels ...

Izzy drank some of her coffee, watching the departure board surreptitiously.

'We're good to board,' Seth said with a grin. 'Let's go on holiday.'

Seth tried to cover Izzy's ears when the captain welcomed everyone aboard their flight to Honolulu.

'I thought you wanted to go somewhere quiet,' she said, laughing.

'Where we're going will be quiet enough,' he said, tapping the side of his nose.

'Will there be crocodiles?'

'Alligators, I think,' said Seth calmly. 'Loads of teeth ... ever seen one close up?'

She narrowed her eyes at him. 'We're not going on some alligator safari, are we?'

'No, but it's a good idea.' He handed her a glass of champagne and took one for himself from the cabin steward's tray. 'Cheers.'

'I would have thought you'd want to be nearer Japan. Make the return-to-work journey easier for you.'

'Ah well, that just proves how much I was thinking of you.'

'Why?'

'Because the flight to Honolulu is about ten hours from here, which means you'll have a sixteen-hour flight home rather than a solo twenty-eight-hour flight.'

'And you'll have ...?'

'Around ten to Tokyo, but I do have to go straight to a sound check.'

'You're amazing.'

He grinned and finished off his champagne. 'I'm hungry,' he corrected.

The steward reappeared at his side. 'Can I tempt you with anything to eat, Mr Roberts?'

Izzy smothered a giggle. Seth ordered pastries and coffee then raised his eyebrows at her. 'How about you, Iz? Can you be tempted?'

'Just coffee, please.'

'You'll waste away,' said Seth, shaking his head.

'Not if I'm anywhere near you, I won't,' said Izzy. 'Although I might bite a corner off one of your pastries.'

'Highly unlikely,' said Seth. 'People have died for less.'

A large plate of Danish pastries and fruit arrived with two coffees. Izzy plucked a few berries from the plate, earning her a reproving look from Seth, which only made her laugh again.

He picked up a pastry and waggled it at her. 'Touch one of these and you'll gain at least two more forfeits.'

'That's fighting talk where I come from.'

He took a huge bite out of his pastry. 'And I always win.'

Izzy decided trying to steal food from a hungry Seth would be like taking food from a hungry bear. Better to let him eat the lot and save her own appetite for lunch or whatever meal came next.

She glanced out of the small window nearest to her at the huge fluffy clouds and the glimpses of pale blue sky here and there, daydreaming about exotic Hawaiian islands, and promptly fell asleep.

When she opened her eyes some time later, Seth was happily brandishing a menu card at her.

'Thought you were going to miss lunch,' he said, looking at her as though it would be a heinous crime to do so.

'I wouldn't dare,' she said sleepily. 'Anyway, I *am* hungry now.'

Izzy loved being alone with Seth – no phones, nobody wanting him for anything and, so far, no stress. Lunch was ordered, duly came, and was eaten quickly, after which Seth stretched his long legs out with a contented sigh.

'This is definitely the bonus we all work so hard for,' he said. 'This and the thought of a fortnight's holiday with just the two of us.'

'You love what you do,' said Izzy with a smile.

'Sure I do.' He nodded. 'But I love the bonuses too.'

Whenever he looked at her with those fathomless blue eyes, Izzy always lost her train of thought. Except she could still imagine two whole weeks stretching away in front of them ... so inviting and exciting in this fabulous part of the world.

Once the plane landed at Honolulu airport, Seth and Izzy were fast-tracked through immigration rather than towards a connecting flight to Hawaii itself.

'Honolulu is the airport on Oahu island,' Seth explained as they followed a porter with their luggage. 'Hawaii's about a thirty-five-minute flight from here. We'll have a day or so there at the end of the holiday.'

Two pretty, dark-haired girls ran up to them and put colourful leis of flowers around their necks. 'Aloha, Mr

Seth!' the girl putting the lei around his neck said shyly. He kissed her cheek and she squealed with delight.

'Even here …?' Izzy grinned at him.

'Even here,' he agreed.

The cameras were out in force too. How had they known Seth would be here when even Izzy hadn't known? Perhaps they met all long-haul flights just in case someone famous did turn up. Seth grinned and waved with his usual charm, holding Izzy's arm protectively as he guided her towards a waiting car.

'Are you tired?' he asked as they drove away.

'Hungry – again,' she said. 'Travel makes me hungry.'

'Welcome to my world.' He laughed.

The car drove smoothly away and Izzy stared out at a place she'd only ever seen in films before; the sunset over the ocean was spectacular, its vivid colours lighting the darkening sky and reflecting in the inky waters below. Feathery palms stood silhouetted proudly along the roadside, and she could just make out the silvery sands as the daylight faded.

'So beautiful,' she breathed.

'We're staying in an oceanfront house,' he said. 'A couple of miles from Waikiki Beach. I'm assured it's quiet at this time of year, and I am craving some quiet.'

'It sounds wonderful.' Personally, Izzy thought anywhere with Seth would be wonderful, especially if there was no one else around. 'Thank you for bringing me here.'

He draped an arm around her shoulders. 'Thank you for coming out here, and making this the best tour ever.'

'I think you did the tour bit all on your own,' she said.

The car drove up a sandy drive and came to a halt outside a large one-storey house surrounded by palm trees. Izzy scrambled out and rushed to get a closer look. She ran around the house, sliding to a halt in front of a huge glinting pool. The water looked really inviting too. Tropical plants with vividly coloured flowers graced the lush gardens surrounding the house. Izzy thought it looked like paradise.

She ran back to where she'd left Seth, who was leaning against the car with an amused smile on his face.

'There's a pool!' she shouted. 'A big, gorgeous pool. Is it just for us?'

'I hope so,' said Seth dryly. 'I didn't pay for seclusion only to share the pool.'

The driver carried their cases to the front door, while Seth retrieved the keys from the key safe.

'Good job you knew the number then,' said Izzy, rejoining him.

'It's in my phone,' he said, holding it up so she could see.

He paid the driver and then unlocked the door to let them both in.

'I wouldn't have thought you'd be allowed to stay somewhere without security,' commented Izzy, remembering the strict security they'd encountered back home in a London club.

'We have security,' he assured her. 'You might not see them, but they're here.'

'In the house?'

He did laugh at that. 'Of course not. But there are additional houses nearby, and we have gates that are usually closed.' He pointed his thumb behind him. 'Take a look.'

Izzy turned to look behind him, where, sure enough, the gates were closing electronically behind the departing car.

'You did your research well,' she said.

‘Fancy a swim?’

‘It’s getting dark.’

‘Floodlights! We have electricity too.’

Chapter Sixteen

Seth awoke to the welcome smell of food cooking and the distant clatter of crockery from somewhere on the other side of the house. Instinctively, he followed the aroma and found himself in a spacious kitchen, where a young Hawaiian woman was busy cooking a vast mountain of food.

'Would you be Makani?' he asked.

'Yes.' She turned and nodded, beaming a bright smile. 'I am honoured to meet you.'

'Likewise.' He sauntered over to inspect the pans. 'Whatcha cooking?'

'French toast, pancakes, scrambled eggs, sausage, hash browns, avocado salad, rice and fruit.'

'Did you invite the whole island?'

Makani giggled. 'They say you like to eat, Mr Seth.'

'They say right, Makani, and it all looks fantastic.'

Seth spotted the state-of-the-art coffee machine in the corner and started towards it, but she waved him away.

'Sit outside and I'll bring you coffee,' she insisted. 'How do you take it?'

'Espresso – large, please.' He walked over to the open sliding doors and out onto the huge veranda. The view was perfect, even better than the retouched photos he'd been sent. The villa's pool sparkled invitingly in the early morning sunshine, tall, graceful palm trees swayed in a light breeze, and he could see the ocean stretching for miles towards the horizon. Seth could feel himself already unwinding as he sat in the warm sunshine, enjoying the solitude and peace. Then he started thinking about the collection of rings Anna had been helping with. *Was it all too soon? Too optimistic? Was now the right time?* Especially if the Jonno/Sophie thing was true. It might look like he was deliberately stealing their thunder, so to speak ...

Makani set a large mug of coffee on the table in front of him without saying a word. He glanced up and gave her an appreciative grin. Now wasn't the time for serious thoughts.

Coffee, sunshine, a pool and, at some point, a pretty redhead – whenever she decided to grace him with her presence. She'd been a real trooper in Australia. Taking the whole mad circus of the tour in her stride, and getting along with everyone too. It had made all the difference to him having her around.

He laced his fingers behind his head and stretched out his long legs. It felt really good. A swim would be better, but he didn't want to go in and change, because it would probably disturb Izzy. She'd been really tired last night. And he didn't want to just strip off like he usually would and possibly frighten the hell out of Makani. Ah well, his jeans could probably do with a wash anyway. He pulled his T shirt off and then, kicking off his trainers, dived cleanly into the pool.

After a few lengths, Seth stopped to float on his back and gazed up at the brilliant blue sky. He'd been on the road since mid-January; he really needed this break.

There was plenty to do on the island, although he wasn't sure he wanted to particularly *do* everything, or even anything very much. He'd found out where to eat in the best ocean view restaurants, and he really fancied a few candle-lit meals with just the two of them, the ocean – and hopefully no damn reporters.

A slight splash made him turn his head, and there was Izzy, swimming out to reach him.

'Hello, floating man,' she said. 'How long have you been in here?'

'Hours,' he replied. 'Waiting for you.'

'Liar.' She prodded him in the chest, only to squeal as he grabbed her and rolled them both over and under the water.

They resurfaced, spluttering and laughing.

'What did I tell you about prodding?' he said, still holding on to her. 'You're a compulsive prodder.'

'You deserved prodding.' She squealed again as he took them both under water for a second time.

This time when they resurfaced, she held her hands up in surrender while she trod water. 'Enough,' she said. 'Look – here comes food.'

'Race you back,' he said and took off like lightning.

Izzy had no chance of keeping up with him; he was by far the stronger swimmer. But the main advantage was he'd found towels by the time she joined him on the veranda. He wound one of the towels around her and plonked a kiss on her lips.

'Food,' he said. 'Looks sensational.'

'Every day should start like this,' said Izzy, picking up a slice of French toast in her fingers and biting off a chunk.

Seth raised his eyebrows. 'Manners, Ms Grant,' he said. 'What would your mother say?'

'Quite a lot probably,' she said. 'What would yours say?'

'She'd wonder where on earth I got you from.' He laughed and ducked as she chucked a handy cushion vaguely in his direction. 'You really are a lousy shot.'

'I always have been,' agreed Izzy. 'Wow, this food is amazing.'

Makani came out from the kitchen with a newspaper. 'You made the front page, Mr Seth.' She handed it to him and turned to go back inside.

'What have I done now?' He thanked her, grinning ruefully as he took the paper. 'Ah, it's all because I arrived here with a gorgeous redhead.' He looked over at Izzy. 'I guess the English press didn't make it to Oahu. But they all want to know about you now.'

'I can't think why.' Izzy looked a bit worried. 'Which reminds me, I must phone Mum.'

'Breakfast first,' said Seth, pointing to a chair. 'No reporters here.'

Izzy started spooning scrambled eggs and hash browns onto their plates and pushed the dish of sausages towards Seth. He picked one out and bit the end off.

'Your manners are no better, I see,' observed Izzy, helping herself to more toast.

Seth chose to ignore that and carried on eating. 'I'm opting for a lazy day by the pool today, perhaps a walk on one of the beaches, and then a traditional slap-up dinner in this nice little place I found.'

Izzy looked up in admiration. 'Whenever did you find the time to plan anything at all?'

He grinned. 'Iz, I've had months away and plenty of alone down time.'

Makani reappeared with yet another plate. The tempting smells wafting from it were definitely *doughnutty*. Seth raised his eyebrows.

She set the plate on the table. 'These are called *malasadas*, and are best eaten like this – with cinnamon and sugar.'

Izzy's eyes widened. 'They look positively wicked.'

'Wicked for the waistline,' agreed Makani. 'But you have no worries.'

'Not yet …' Izzy took one anyway and bit into it. 'You won't like these, Seth. Best leave them for me.'

Makani laughed. 'I've put cold plates for your lunch in the fridge. See you tomorrow.'

'Makani, you're an angel,' said Seth. 'Have a nice day.'

'Both of you too.' With a wave, she went back into the house, and a few minutes later they heard the front doors close.

'Did you find her too?'

'Nah, she comes with the house.' Seth tasted a *malasada* and made an approving sound. 'I'd better put in a daily forty-lap regime if I eat too many of these.'

'I hear you.' Izzy nodded, pushing her chair away from the table. 'Don't swim straight after those *malasadas* – you'll sink like a stone. I'm going in to phone Mum.'

Walking along the white sands of Makua Beach later, Izzy thought she'd never been anywhere so beautiful. They had most of the beach to themselves; the only people she could see were far away in the distance, and there was nobody in the sea.

'No-one's swimming,' she observed.

'It's dangerous to swim here, apparently,' said Seth, clearly keen to show off his research. 'Strong currents here, and it's not protected by a reef like lots of the other beaches.'

Izzy felt impressed. Had he really spent all his spare time researching for this holiday?

'Plus,' he waved a finger in the air, 'the ocean bottom drops suddenly here ... so all swimmers should stick close to the shore where it's safer from the current.'

'Forget the window cleaning,' said Izzy. 'You could have been a lecturer.'

He gave her a sardonic look. 'What? You don't like my singing?'

'I love your singing,' she said quickly. 'As well you know.' She took a sideways glance at him; he'd taken his sneakers off, rolled up his jeans and looked totally at home. He obviously had the ability to relax wherever he might be. And he still managed to look totally gorgeous and fanciable at the same time.

'We missed the rainy season by a few weeks,' he said. 'And we'll miss the tourist season too.'

'It's so quiet here,' commented Izzy. She looked out at the turquoise sea fringed with frothy white waves. 'Are there really alligators?'

He laughed. 'Nah, I was teasing. You get those down in Florida.'

'Thank goodness.' Izzy felt she could now stop looking furtively over her shoulder in case an alligator was following.

'Get turtles here though.'

'Well, turtles won't eat me,' said Izzy. 'Or will they?'

'There's a bunch over there. Let's find out.'

Having not been eaten by turtles, Izzy and Seth sat at an ocean view table some hours later and enjoyed Mai Tai cocktails. They'd been assured the Mai Tai was the most famous cocktail in the world, and had even enjoyed an appearance in Elvis Presley's film, *Blue Hawaii*. Even Izzy had heard of him. She'd never liked his music much, but she'd heard of him.

'He died nearly ten years before I was even born,' said Seth. 'But I've still heard most of his music and seen a couple of his films.'

'It's your job to know about music,' said Izzy. 'Wow, what's in here exactly?' She held her glass up to the light. 'Pretty colours.'

'I should know better than to buy you cocktails by now,' said Seth with a slight grimace. 'Two different rums, curacao and various fresh fruit juices, I think.'

Izzy grinned. 'It's really good.'

Seth changed the subject. 'The fish tacos are good here,' he said. 'Apparently.'

'My kind of place.'

After sampling the fish tacos and a few glasses of wine, they strolled back to the house along the beach, hands clasped – Australia felt a long time ago already.

Seth felt less tense and wound up, and Jonno's problems seemed more trivial. So what if he did do another bunk? The band would continue; no one was bigger than the band. Possibly not even himself, although he did wonder about that. Seth knew bands split up all the time; it was inevitable, and often the cause was a girlfriend or wife. Life on the road was tough, as he'd explained to Izzy. Relationships were hard to maintain, and he hadn't exactly talked that through with her yet, but the hard fact remained that long-distance relationships *were* difficult to sustain. There had to be complete trust on both sides, otherwise it simply wouldn't work. He wondered whether their relationship was still a bit too new to insist on total trust. Although if he went ahead with his intentions, there would have to be trust between them. *Was this something else to worry about*? They'd met a year ago, but he'd been on the road for a lot of it. Most of this year, in fact. And when she went home in a couple of weeks, he wouldn't see her again for at least two months. Where would she live when she went back? He'd offered the use of both of his places, but she was an independent sort of person, and he wasn't sure she'd accept either offer.

'What will you do when you get back?' he asked suddenly.

'I'm still thinking about doing an MA,' she said. 'In journalism – I told you.'

He stopped walking and turned to face her. 'You're still thinking about *journalism*?' He still wasn't sure how he felt about that. 'Really?'

'Not the type of journalist you hate, so no throwing me out of planes or off buses,' she reassured him with a smile. 'But if I want to train as a TV presenter, I'd need an MA in journalism to even get a foot in the door as a runner.'

'Are you sure it's really what you want to do?'

'To be honest – I don't know until I try. I thought doing an MA would give me another year's grace. I can do the course pretty much online, so no living in halls, and I can start researching TV production companies and channels at the same time.'

'You *have* been thinking about it …' Seth continued walking again. 'So where can you do an MA? Please tell me you're thinking of London?'

'Goldsmiths is the best, I'm told,' she said. 'But Kings College and LSE are pretty good too. And yes, all in London.'

'Pretty tough gig, journalism in TV,' he said thoughtfully. 'And I hate to say it, but it can still be tough in some areas for women.'

‘I think there are laws in place these days,’ said Izzy with a frown.

‘And not before time, as far as I’m concerned …’ He pushed his free hand through his hair. ‘Although I’m pretty sure *you’ll* be a force to be reckoned with.’ He paused, lost in thought for a moment. ‘But I do know a lot of people in media ... I could certainly help you out with some contacts if you want?’

Izzy pulled a face. ‘Not sure about that. It sort of feels like cheating?’

Seth flashed her his mischievous grin. ‘Everyone does it, Izzy. You’re far too honest.’

‘I’ll think about it,’ she promised. ‘Thanks.’

‘But there’ll be hell to pay if anyone gives you a hard time!’

Chapter Seventeen

The days seemed to accelerate and fly past in a haze of island-hopping, sun, sea and surf, except Izzy's surfing lesson left a lot to be desired. She preferred watching Seth, to be honest, who seemed to take to the surf like a duck to water – so to speak. Was there anything the man couldn't do? He was definitely worth watching too – long, lean and tanned, his hair bleached lighter by the sun, his eyes almost the same colour as the sea – practically every woman on the beach stopped to stare as he rode the surf back to shore. He looked as if he'd been surfing for years, and Izzy had taken so many pictures she felt sure her phone would explode if she took any more.

Izzy's favourite island had been Kauai, the aptly nicknamed "Garden Isle". A perfectly preserved place of pristine beauty, with lush vegetation and over sixty beaches, it could have simply been called "Eden" in her view. Although Seth's charismatic company had a lot to do with how she felt too.

She'd now acquired the necessary tan to keep both Kathleen and her mum happy, having lost her university "bookworm" pallor in the bargain. But the holiday was drawing to a close now, Seth was back in regular contact with Zach and Anna. He'd touched base with Micky, Joe and even Jonno, and checked various tour stuff with Lenny. The difference in him felt tangible; he was rested and ready to – well … rock!

Izzy almost wanted to cancel her flight home and fly with Seth to Tokyo like he'd offered, but she also felt she didn't want to outstay her welcome. Something inside her told her he needed to be the usual "on tour Seth" with nobody to worry about other than the band and the set list. Plus, she realised she needed to follow up her own plans for the MA … although she already knew that being without Seth after weeks of being with him would feel as if she was being torn in half.

They spent two glorious days in West Hawaii, but the last day came around far too quickly as far as Izzy was concerned, and the hired car arrived to take them to Ellison Onizuka Kona airport at Keahole.

Izzy was steeling herself not to get upset when she had to part ways with Seth – it was only for a few weeks, after all. He'd be home by the end of August, although she wasn't sure which home he'd come back to. Come to that, she wasn't sure where she'd be either. Definitely London for a few nights; she needed to see the fam as well, and maybe she could visit Seth's horses at the same time …

Having gone through security to departure, Seth and Izzy sat in a quiet corner of the VIP lounge whilst Izzy struggled to keep the tears at bay. She mentally told herself to get a grip and not be so stupid, and that he'd be embarrassed if she cried. And someone, somewhere, would take a picture for sure. Then *she'd* be embarrassed. In fact, everyone she knew would be embarrassed. It would be an embarrassment-fest. Worldwide. *Breathe, Izzy.*

Seth turned to her and cradled her face in his hands. 'Where will you be when I come back?' he asked, his blue eyes searching her face. 'London or Sussex?'

'I haven't decided,' she said, feeling the tears trying to escape. *Hold on, Izzy.*

'Let me know, and I'll come straight there.'

She nodded.

'Just make sure it's one of my places, okay?'

She nodded again, not daring to speak past the lump in her throat.

He pulled her closer and kissed her gently. 'Be sure to miss me.'

And that did it. Tears trickled down her cheek, which he wiped away with his thumbs. He wrapped his arms around her. 'Iz, don't cry. It's only for a few weeks … then I'll be back for ages. Plus, everyone's gonna take pictures of you crying.'

Izzy hiccupped and giggled at the same time. 'Sorry…'

Seth laughed and tipped her face up to his. 'And there's the first forfeit for when I'm back.' He kissed her again. 'Your flight's been called.'

They stood up together, Seth grabbing his guitar case in one hand and Izzy's hand in the other. He walked to the departure gate with her, and then stepped in front of her so she had to stop.

'Safe trip, Isabelle Grant,' he said softly. 'I love you.'

'You too,' she said. 'On both counts.'

He grinned. 'I should hope so too. I booked you in to first class, after all. See you soon. Now go, or I'll be forced to drag you off to Tokyo.'

One last kiss and then she was through the gate, leaving Hawaii – and Seth – behind.

Izzy slept for a lot of the flight; several weeks of late nights, followed by a whirlwind tour of Hawaiian islands and beauty spots had taken its toll. She ate a meal at some point and watched a film, but didn't remember either what she ate or what she saw. She started watching a second film which had Tom Hanks in it but fell asleep when he was riding across the desert. By the time she woke up, Tom was reading a story to an appreciative audience and there was no desert or horse in sight. *Weird.*

And then, after a quick stopover, almost eighteen hours of travelling and a lot of hanging around in between, they were at last landing at Heathrow. *Home.* Well, not the airport itself, but dear old drizzly England in late July. Izzy shivered and pulled her trusty leather jacket out of the locker, along with her flight bag. It felt strange already without Seth's confident presence by her side. Izzy wasn't at all sure how she felt about that; she'd always been sure of herself in most situations, but this trip was the first time she'd travelled first class on her own, and it had felt a bit daunting at times.

Her phone pinged and she pulled it out of her pocket. It was Dave saying he was waiting outside and he'd see her at the pickup point as discussed.

'Discussed with who?' muttered Izzy. 'Not with me.'

Then she saw the message from Seth telling her where Dave would be.

Stay at the flat, Iz. Missing you already. S xx

You're amazing, thank you! Just landed. I miss you too. Look after my rock god.

I xx

It felt odd going out of the airport via a different exit and seeing Dave's familiar figure waiting for her. How the rich lived. She'd almost become used to it in the weeks she'd been away with Seth. No wonder he didn't appear fazed at all by the press and photographers everywhere he went.

Dave came forward to take her luggage and stow it in the boot of the car.

'Well, you look healthier than when you left,' he said with a quick grin. 'How's our boy?'

‘Taking the world by storm,’ said Izzy.

‘Course he is.’

Izzy must have dozed off in the car, because the trip back to Finchley seemed amazingly fast, and before she realised it Dave was pulling up outside the mansion block. There were a few fans lurking who recognised the car, but quickly lost interest when they saw their hero wasn’t in it. Izzy breathed a sigh of relief when she and her luggage were both in the lift and on the way up to Seth’s flat.

She wondered whether Kathleen would be there, but kind of hoped she wouldn’t be so she could just veg in front of the TV.

Letting herself into the flat, the unmistakable smell of furniture polish and fresh flowers greeted her. She left the cases in the hall and made for the kitchen. A huge bouquet of twenty-four red roses were beautifully arranged in a massive crystal vase with a card propped up against it. She opened the card, which had the simple message:

Best holiday ever – thanks to you. Love you loads, S xxx

He always thinks of everything. Izzy wondered whether he’d got tips or advice from Anna, but did it matter if he had? He’d bothered to ask her – if that’s what he’d done. She already knew she’d keep the card forever. And yes, she knew it had been written by a florist over here, but he’d dictated it, so the words were his, and that was all that mattered.

Next to the vase was a note in Kathleen’s small, neat writing.

Isabelle, I hope you had a lovely time and got some colour back in your cheeks. I’ll be there in the morning to make your breakfast, so I will, otherwise you’ll eat nothing. Ring your mother. K.

Izzy smiled. Seth was right – it really was like having two mothers. She looked at her phone to check the time, decided it was a bit late to call home now, so texted her mum instead.

Just got in and off to bed now. I'll call in the morning. Love I xx

The answer pinged back almost instantly. *Okay darling, sleep tight. Good to have you back in the same country again. Love M.*

Izzy trailed upstairs to the bedroom, leaving the cases downstairs, undressed and crawled into the very big, very empty bed.

Chapter Eighteen

Tokyo Airport, known as Haneda, was situated quite close to Tokyo itself if Seth remembered rightly, and he felt relieved he'd plumped for there instead of the larger airport of Narita, which was further out. The need to chill out had crept up on him, just as he'd known it would. He needed a shower, food and sleep in that order. He believed the others were mostly all in Tokyo already, and Zach would be waiting for him at the pickup point. It would be good to catch up with the guys again, and even better to get back on stage. Although he already missed having Izzy around more than he was prepared to admit, even to himself. This last leg of the tour was going to be full on, with very little time off, which was probably just as well. No time to dwell on the absence of a certain little redhead. He'd definitely never felt like this about anyone before. So why the hell hadn't he proposed on holiday? *Scared of being turned down, Seth, mate?*

He'd been so impressed by how Izzy had completely embraced life on the road, especially the cosmopolitans, and laughed when he remembered how she'd teased him about that god-awful hotel with the dragon taps and faux Tudor décor. No other woman had ever treated him both as a friend and a lover. It was a new experience for him, and he loved it.

Once ensconced in the comfortable hotel suite that took up a whole corridor, he brought out the ring boxes from his flight bag and opened them one by one. They should probably go in the hotel safe. He felt almost disgusted with himself that even now he felt so sure of his feelings towards Izzy, he simply hadn't plucked up the courage to ask the big question. *How pathetic*. How many more rings did he have to buy until he felt confident enough to ask her? It now felt totally insane that he hadn't. He sang about romance all the bloody time after all – *and* he wrote the damn songs. *Hawaii*, supposedly one of the most romantic places in the world … so Izzy might actually have been *expecting* a proposal. He didn't think so, but what the hell did he know? Hardly his area of expertise, even if he had been married before. *Look how well that turned out.*

Come to think of it, it had been Sheryl who'd instigated the whole getting married gig the first time, and he'd gone along with it. More fool him. The next proposal would be on his terms for sure. But supposing he'd blown it already? What if Izzy *had* been hoping he'd propose? What if, even as he was sitting here, she was being chatted up by a Mr Joe Normal, who was wooing her with compliments and plying her with cocktails? He felt a sudden surge of jealousy at the thought. What about all these damn rings he'd bought – with Anna's help – from various places they'd played in? Was it simply a seriously stupid idea? It had felt brilliant when he'd first thought of it. Yet somehow, he *still* hadn't managed to muster up a romantic proposal. *Pathetic Seth.* Totally and utterly *pathetic.*

Giving himself a hard mental shake, he put the ring boxes on the bedside table and picked up the hotel phone to speak to reception. The receptionist informed him he had his own safe installed in the wardrobe and he could programme it with whichever six-digit number he wanted to use for security. Now that was efficient. He felt a lot more relaxed when he'd stored the rings safely away, and stretching out on the huge bed, he scanned his own phone for messages.

Lenny had messaged earlier, checking Seth had arrived safely and reminding him about the sound check that afternoon.

'No peace for the wicked,' muttered Seth.

There wasn't a message from Jonno, so he decided to message him first.

Hey Jon, how was the holiday? All set for the sound check?

Jonno's answer pinged back almost immediately.

Great holiday thanks. How was yours? Yep, I'll see you downstairs in a few hours.

Seth breathed a sigh of relief. Jonno was here ... but he really hoped his girlfriend – *or was it fiancée now?* – wasn't.

Having woken up at some ungodly hour thinking it was time for dinner, Izzy gave up trying to get back to sleep after two hours of lying awake and went for a shower. By the time she'd dressed and dried her hair, Kathleen had arrived, and, after calling out a greeting, started cooking breakfast. Izzy wandered downstairs to the kitchen and hugged the housekeeper.

'Whatever you're cooking smells heavenly,' she commented.

'Sure, and bacon smells good at any time of the day or night.' Kathleen smiled as she dished up a plateful of food for Izzy. 'Sit yourself down and eat.'

Obediently, Izzy hauled herself up on to one of the tall stools at the breakfast bar. 'I'm really hungry,' she said, looking at the huge amount of food on her plate. 'But I'm not sure I'll finish all of this.'

'Give it a good go now,' said Kathleen. 'It's nice to see you looking healthy, so it is.'

In spite of thinking she'd never finish all the food, Izzy made short work of it, which earned Kathleen's approval when she placed a mug of coffee in front of her.

'You made the papers with your koalas.' She pushed a newspaper cutting towards Izzy.

Izzy smiled as she remembered the day of the visit. 'They're really heavy too,' she said. 'Cute though.'

Kathleen took Izzy's empty plate to the dishwasher, brushing aside her insistence that she could clear up after herself.

'You'll be ringing your mother, I expect,' she said firmly.

'Fair cop,' muttered Izzy with a laugh, and excusing herself, went back upstairs to do just that.

'So did he propose?' Jo squealed down the phone the moment Izzy answered.

'Propose? *What?*' Izzy felt bemused by the question. 'Of course not. Why would he?'

'Well … because he took you off on a romantic holiday for two?' Jo sounded disappointed.

Izzy laughed. 'We may have met just over a year ago, but in that time we've barely been together more than a few months.'

'He's clearly smitten.'

'Not that clearly.'

Jo sighed. 'I was looking forward to attending a proper show biz wedding.'

'And maybe you will, but not yet, and it probably won't be mine.' Izzy laughed. 'You just want to marry everyone off because you're so happy.'

'Is he romantic at all?'

Izzy thought of the roses. 'There was a huge bouquet of red roses waiting for me when I got back.'

'Well, there you go,' Jo said. 'Red roses are for lovers.'

'Lovers don't always want to get married.'

'He will ask you,' Jo insisted. 'And what will you say? No – I'm busy?'

'Depends whether I am busy or not.' Izzy giggled. It was good to chat with Jo again. 'Will your new husband allow you to come out for a drink and a pizza with your chief bridesmaid, I wonder?'

'Absolutely – tomorrow?'

'Don't you need to ask him?'

'No.'

'Sure?'

'Course not. He's out with his own mates tomorrow, so it's perfect.'

Jo looked tanned, happy and healthy, and hugged Izzy when they met outside their favourite pizza restaurant.

'Wow – Iz, you look amazing,' she said. 'Hob-nobbing with a rock god clearly agrees with you.'

'Thanks – I think.' Izzy led the way into the restaurant. She checked in at the desk, and a waiter soon showed them the way to their table.

'You booked a table?' Jo looked impressed. 'You've never done that before.'

'I wanted to make sure we could get in.'

They sat down at the table and started looking at the menu.

'I don't know why I bother to read this,' said Izzy. 'I always have the garlic bread to start and the margherita pizza.'

'One day you might not,' said Jo. 'You'll scare everyone – including the chef – by ordering the pepperoni meat fest.'

Izzy grinned. 'It's so good to see you. How's life as a married lady?'

'Pretty much the same,' said Jo, stretching out her left hand. 'Except I have this spiffy new ring.'

'Shiny,' agreed Izzy. 'Even after two months.'

The waiter brought over a bottle of wine and two glasses.

'So … he really hasn't proposed yet then?'

Izzy had wondered how long it would be before Jo brought that up again.

'He's said he loves me,' Izzy offered. 'Several times.'

'Talk's cheap,' said Jo with a sardonic look. She picked up her glass of wine and raised it to Izzy in a toast. 'He needs to know there is only one Isabelle Grant in the world, and he doesn't want to miss out.'

Izzy laughed. 'Well yes, because there are so many other men vying for my attention.'

'It wouldn't do him any harm to think there might be.'

Izzy thought back to Jo's wedding and the best man, shaking her head. 'Trust me, it would be a very bad idea.'

An impish look crossed Jo's face. 'Oooh, is he the jealous type? Do tell.'

Izzy told her about the best man and how Seth brought him up again at every possible moment.

'And you told him because …?'

'Well, he asked who'd been chatting me up at the reception.'

'I'll say it again: you told him because …?' Jo laughed.

'Actually, I don't know – and I wish I hadn't.'

'Lesson learned then,' said Jo, clinking her glass against Izzy's. She leaned forward. 'He's away a lot, Iz, but he still probably gets a lot of down time to think when he's alone. Don't give him anything to fester on – it could be really bad.'

'Wise words, married lady,' agreed Izzy. 'Oh good, here comes the garlic bread.'

On the other side of the world, Seth lay awake. He glanced at the clock on the bedside cabinet. *Four in the morning.* He had no idea what had woken him; the hotel was as quiet as the grave – not that he had any experience in that direction, thankfully. His brain was buzzing with the conversations over dinner. Everyone mostly seemed okay, although Jonno was still a bit quiet and that worried him. He wondered whether the odious Sophie had re-surfaced and started causing trouble. Then he wondered whether he should ask Jonno outright if they really were engaged. But was it his business? He thought probably yes, if it affected the tour. Although the band hadn't exactly been impacted in any way yet – not to his knowledge anyway.

He sighed and reached for his phone. Scrolling through various messages of no consequence, he spotted one from Izzy. *Hey – how's my rock god? Thank you for the simply amazing roses. I miss you. I xx*

That made him smile. He calculated it would be around eight or nine in the evening for her and decided to call. She answered immediately.

'Hi, how's Tokyo?'

'Lonely without you.'

'Same here.'

'What are you up to?'

'Having dinner in my favourite pizza place.'

'Not with the best man, I hope.' *Good one, Seth. What the hell did you say that for?*

'No – actually with the bride. Isn't it the middle of the night where you are?'

'Kinda … it's four-thirty in the morning.'

'Ouch! Why are you awake?'

'Busy Izzy brain must be catching.' He laughed. 'Going through the day, the gig … you know …'

'You need sleep so you can make music.'

'Just needed to hear your voice.'

Her voice sounded so close; it felt strange to realise she was thousands of miles away in some pizza place in Finchley.

'When are you back again?'

'Around the middle of August. I'll give you the specific dates tomorrow.'

'Get some sleep.'

'I'll give it a whirl.' He laughed again. 'Talk tomorrow then.'

They said goodnight, and Seth leaned back on his pillows with a sigh.

What had he expected? Declarations of undying love? With Jo sitting there? He should know by now that Izzy was a little shy of saying her feelings out loud. He wondered again whether she'd expected or hoped for a proposal on holiday. And there was him sitting here with a whole bunch of potential engagement rings in his hotel room's safe, waiting for him to get a grip and just *ask* her.

Why were relationships so damn difficult?

Chapter Nineteen

Two weeks later, Izzy impulsively packed a bag, and retrieving her car from one of Seth's parking bays, took off for Sussex. She felt in need of some family time and sea air. Although she had decided to stay at Seth's Tudor farmhouse rather than at the family home. She didn't feel as though she wanted *that* much company just at the moment. She'd had quite a few evenings with Jo which had brought a lot of her own questions to the surface … ones she'd been trying to ignore. Such as, how serious was Seth? Or was he, in fact, serious at all? The biggest thing in his life was the band. Where did she factor in to all of that? She didn't feel ready to field her mother's questions either, especially when she had no idea of the answers herself.

Beth had been less than happy to hear Izzy wasn't staying with them, and she'd tried to explain about the work she needed to do in order to apply for the MA; her application needed to be in pronto if she wanted to be accepted for October. And that meant a lot of work with no younger brother with his XBox games disturbing her thought process.

Reluctantly, Beth had agreed it would be more peaceful at Seth's place and was content enough to go along with seeing Izzy at weekends and for the odd evening.

The drive down was uneventful apart from the usual convoy of caravans and cars with boats on trailers making their way to the south coast. The holiday season was definitely in full swing, although Izzy lost a fair amount of the traffic at the turn off for Brighton.

The country lanes winding their way to Seth's secluded farm were busy with tractors, horse riders and, at one point, a herd of cows.

'So much for the quiet country life,' muttered Izzy, as she sat watching the big placid animals lumber past. One of them squished her wing mirror flat, but Izzy decided she'd leave it that way until they'd all gone by. Another stopped to peer in at her with huge, soulful eyes, which made her laugh.

The herdsman touched the peak of his flat cap in thanks as he wobbled slowly past on a rusty old boneshaker of a bike, and she waved an acknowledgment. His bike was probably better than walking, but only just. *Never a dull moment in the countryside.*

When she turned up the private track to Seth's place, she breathed a sigh of relief. In spite of her fears that she'd rattle around there feeling lonely, she felt happy and instantly calm when the huge wrought iron gates came into view. She wondered whether this was how he felt coming home here after a long tour.

Izzy fished in her bag for her phone and the entrance code he'd texted her for opening the electronic gates. When they swung quietly open, she felt like an intruder, even more so when the CCTV camera swung around to follow her.

'No pressure then, Seth,' she muttered.

The gates clanged shut behind her, and she drove up towards the property. The beautiful red-brick Tudor house came into view after the first bend in the drive. She remembered the first time he'd brought her here, and it did feel strange to just turn up without him. Almost voyeuristic. *He must trust me implicitly to allow me to come here*, she thought. The London flat was one thing, but this was his special place: his retreat from the mad world of rock and roll. And yet he'd allowed her in without any doubts at all, it appeared.

Unsure where she should park, Izzy followed the sweeping drive round to the back of the house, to the big wooden door she knew opened on to his very impressive kitchen – the kitchen nobody ever cooked in. A gunmetal coloured VW Golf was parked under the trees opposite the back door, so Izzy parked next to it, wondering who it belonged to. She got out of her car and stretched, feeling the need to walk off the hours spent driving.

The back door opened, and a sturdy-looking woman with grey-streaked brown hair pulled back in a severe bun stepped out.

'You Isabelle?' she called.

'That's me,' said Izzy.

'I'm Sarah, Seth's housekeeper.'

Another housekeeper. Izzy really hoped she didn't live in.

'Hello, Sarah,' she said, hauling her case out of the boot. 'How's everything?'

'Quiet with Seth away,' Sarah replied with a quick survey of Izzy's belongings. 'How long are you here for?'

'I'm not sure yet.' Suddenly Izzy didn't feel very welcome.

'I don't cook,' Sarah continued. 'You'll have to fend for yourself. And I don't clean either. I'm only here now to see you in.'

'Fair enough,' said Izzy, wondering what, in fact, she did do. 'I've brought supplies, and I'll be visiting my family a fair bit too.'

'Couldn't stay with them then?'

Izzy hid an inward sigh. This woman would take some winning over, it seemed.

'I could have, yes,' was all she said. She continued pulling bags of supermarket shopping out of the boot, and her laptop bag, but decided to leave her wellies where they were. Something told her she shouldn't appear to be moving in to this territorial woman. Slamming the boot shut, she locked the car and began taking her stuff into the kitchen. Sarah made no attempt to help, just continued standing in the wide doorway with her arms folded, so Izzy had to say 'excuse me' every time she wanted to get by.

'There's no milk either,' she said, seemingly as a last ditch attempt to rattle Izzy.

'I brought some,' said Izzy abruptly, wishing the woman would just go home.

'Or tea,' she continued.

'Don't drink it,' said Izzy, almost beginning to enjoy the exchange now.

'Or coffee.'

Izzy burst out laughing. She couldn't help it. What *was* her problem?

Sarah narrowed her eyes at Izzy as she carried the last of her bags into the kitchen. Still laughing, Izzy started unpacking the food and stowing it away in the vast fridge.

'Don't you go taking up all the fridge space either,' said Sarah, her mouth now a thin, disapproving line.

'It's a pretty huge fridge,' said Izzy lightly. 'And as you don't cook, and nobody but me is staying here, I think we'll be okay, don't you?'

'And don't you go bothering Ted neither.'

Aha. Now they were getting somewhere.

'Ted?' Izzy turned to face the older woman, leaned against the fridge doors and folded her own arms.

'My husband, Ted.'

Bingo.

'Ted, who looks after Seth's horses – that Ted?'

'He's too busy to be bothered with the likes of you.'

'Sarah, the only man I will ever be interested in is Seth.' Izzy smiled. 'And the only reason I need to speak with Ted is to find out which horse I might be able to ride without killing myself.'

Sarah eyed her suspiciously. 'So you say.'

'Promise,' said Izzy, opening the fridge door and grabbing a bottle of beer. She waved it at Sarah. 'Want one?'

'Driving,' said Sarah. 'House keys are on the hook over there. Lock up when you go out and reset the alarms – instructions are in that drawer.'

'Will do, thanks.' Izzy felt determined not to be intimidated.

'And don't make a mess.'

Izzy giggled again. 'I'll do my best not to.'

'And if you do go out to the stables, treat my man with respect.'

'The same respect you showed me?' Izzy's cool tone brought a quick flush to the woman's face, and picking up her own keys from the work surface, she turned and left, slamming the kitchen door behind her.

'Well, that was bracing,' muttered Izzy. 'Welcome to Seth's farm, Iz.'

That same evening, Izzy had the whole family hooting with laughter when she described her arrival at Seth's place.

'Not a fan of yours then, Iz?' Her dad laughed. 'Whatever must Seth have said to cause that reaction?'

'I'll have to ask him,' said Izzy, helping herself to more apple pie. 'He's usually quite tactful, but he's on tour and mad busy, so who knows?'

'Are you going to marry him?' asked Ben suddenly. 'I think it would be super cool to have him as a brother-in-law.'

Her mum and dad exchanged glances.

'Who knows?' said Izzy. 'I've only known him about a year, and for half that time he's been on tour. I think it's too soon to say.'

'So he hasn't asked then?' Ben persevered.

'No,' Izzy said firmly.

'I bet he'd buy you a really expensive ring.'

'Only if I said yes,' said Izzy with a mischievous grin. 'Otherwise, it would be a waste of money.'

'Would you say no then?' Ben really wasn't going to give up any time soon.

'Ben, that's enough.' Her mum stepped in to halt the conversation. 'Stop pestering your sister. She'll tell you when she has something to tell you.'

'When's he back?' Her dad changed the subject to something much safer.

'In a couple of weeks or so – middle of August, I think. I don't know the exact date.' Izzy gave her dad a grateful smile. 'He's coming straight to Sussex though, so I'll be around here longer.'

'That's lovely.' Her mum smiled. 'We should probably have a family party or something.'

'Then everyone really will think we're getting married.' Izzy rolled her eyes.

'Maybe just a slap-up Sunday roast then,' amended her mother.

'That sounds brilliant,' agreed Izzy.

After a shower the next morning, Izzy felt a lot more human. Although everything in Seth's state-of-the-art kitchen looked completely untouched – like it had never been used at all, which was more than a little daunting. Most of the equipment looked as if it had been installed from a very expensive show room specifically for a glossy magazine photo shoot – except for the hugely expensive-looking coffee machine that was standing proudly in the centre of the gleaming work surface. There was no doubting that had been used; Seth loved his espressos. Izzy had no clue how it worked and came to the conclusion she might need a degree in engineering just to turn it on. But needs must, and Izzy needed coffee in the morning.

'But there *is* no coffee, according to Sarah.' She laughed to herself. 'Although I bet there are *beans* ...'

She opened the cupboard door nearest to the coffee machine and, sure enough, there was a giant bag of coffee beans, together with the instruction booklet for the machine. Seth might not cook, but he wouldn't ever forgo his coffee.

Izzy soon had the beans in the grinder and everything set up for a large, much-needed cappuccino.

Seth had also laughed at Izzy's description of Sarah's "welcome" and felt he may well be at fault for inadvertently causing it. He thought she should perhaps forget the journalism idea and go straight to writing comedy; she had a certain deft turn of phrase which he loved.

He felt pleased she was staying at the farm. Although she hadn't mentioned the horses yet. He hoped she wasn't worried about Sarah. He'd never had a problem with her himself, but then she was a woman and he didn't often have a problem with women. Apart from his mother sometimes, and the sisters. He suspected Beth wouldn't be taken in very easily either.

Funny that he'd never noticed anything unfriendly about Sarah thought; she'd always been perfectly fine towards him. Probably because he paid her wages. He thought of her husband, Ted. Typical brawny farming stock; sturdily built and tanned all year round. Almost old enough to be Izzy's father too. Why would Sarah go all *Fatal Attraction* on Izzy? Perhaps because she was young enough and gorgeous enough to bring out the worst in his housekeeper.

'Good job I don't keep rabbits,' he muttered to himself.

The stables appeared to be almost the same age as the house, built with similar small red bricks, with a clay-tiled roof. In the early morning sun, the building almost glowed. Izzy wondered how anyone would ever want to leave this magical place for Finchley – let alone for the rest of the world.

A beautiful chestnut looked over the top of his stable door, snickering a welcome to Izzy. She stopped to stroke his glossy neck.

'Hello, you beauty,' she said softly. 'What's your name I wonder?'

'He's called Martinique, that one,' said a gruff voice behind her and she jumped.

'You must be Ted,' she said, holding out her hand. 'I'm Izzy.'

'Good to know,' he said. 'Otherwise, you'd be a horse thief.' He took her hand and shook it. 'He's mostly called Marty,' he added.

Izzy thought Ted looked a lot friendlier than his missus, although that wouldn't be difficult. Maybe that was the problem. There was a definite twinkle in his shrewd grey eyes when he looked at her. She went back to stroking Marty's neck.

'How many horses do you have here?' she asked instead.

'Four at the minute,' he replied. 'Marty here, the grey next door is Duchess; she's the lady of the stables.' Ted walked along the line, and Izzy followed him. 'This wicked one here is Marvel, Seth's favourite, and the bay is Jupiter. Not very big but takes off like a rocket.'

Izzy laughed. 'Well, I haven't ridden for a few years, so who would you recommend?'

Ted tilted his head to one side. 'Well, you're not that big yourself, are you?'

Izzy raised her eyebrows.

'If you're after going out on your own, take Duchess, she's good as gold and pretty bombproof. When you're back in the swing of it, I reckon Marty will suit you just fine.'

'Duchess it is for now then,' said Izzy. 'Thanks.'

'When the Boss gets back, you could try Jupiter.'

'Need backup for Jupiter, do I?'

Ted rasped out a laugh. 'Everyone does.'

'Might leave him for a bit then.' Izzy grinned.

'I'll show you where the tack's kept.'

Ted strode off again and Izzy followed.

The tack room was spotless and so was the tack. The leather looked like it was lovingly cleaned every day, and the silver of the bits and stirrup irons shone in the sunlight that filtered through the high windows.

'I've never seen such clean tack that wasn't actually brand new,' commented Izzy.

Ted looked pleased, and Izzy wondered whether that would count as being respectful in Sarah's book.

The name plates on the wall above the tack made it clear what belonged to who.

'Duchess has a rubber bit,' explained Ted. 'She's a soft mouth, so a light rein with her, please.'

Izzy nodded. 'I used to ride a pony called Bijou who had a rubber bit.'

'Lovely temperament has Duchess.'

'She sounds like your favourite.'

'Mebbe.'

Izzy looked around the tack room when she heard faint mews coming from the far corner. Unable to resist, she went over to look and found a tabby cat and four tiny kittens snuggled up together on a red blanket in a large cardboard box.

'How adorable.' Izzy crouched down for a better look. 'How old are they?'

'Couple of weeks, give or take.'

'Does Seth know?'

'Can't say he does.' Ted thought for a minute. 'You can tell him.'

Izzy fished her phone out of her pocket. 'I'll send him a picture or two.'

She took a lot more pictures than two, and the mother preened at the attention.

'What's mum's name?'

'Willow.'

Izzy stroked Willow's ears softly. 'Hello, Willow,' she said. 'Such a lovely, proud mum.'

'Yup, she's a good mouser too, that one.'

Izzy couldn't wait to send the pictures to Seth.

'Got a hat?' Ted asked suddenly. 'Can't go out without one.'

'Yes, I brought mine back from my parents' last night.'

'Close by, are they?'

'About forty minutes.'

Ted nodded. Izzy could almost see the cogs turning and felt sure she'd been the subject of discussion in his house last night.

'Let me know when you want to ride,' he said.

'I was thinking tomorrow morning if that's okay.' Izzy took the plunge. 'About nine?'

'Works for me. See you in the morning then. Must crack on.'

He turned and walked out of the tack room, leaving Izzy still stroking Willow's ears.

Chapter Twenty

One thing about mornings in rural areas is that they tended to start a whole lot earlier than mornings in cities. Izzy woke up when magpies tapped on the roof and the drainpipe with their sharp beaks whilst cackling morning greetings, sheep bleated somewhere, cows mooed and Seth's horses whinnied. She felt sure the kittens were probably mewing too, but in a much quieter way. The clock on the bedside table said it was six-fifteen, and she didn't think there ever was a time that early in Finchley.

What time would it be in Tokyo? Would he be on stage? She did a quick Google search and discovered they were eight hours ahead … two in the afternoon. Sound check time maybe? Perhaps a text would be better.

Hey Rock God, how's it going in the land of Fuji and Sushi? I xx

His answer pinged back almost immediately. *Hey Gorgeous. Have you and Sarah come to blows over Ted yet? S xx*

Oho funny man. Whatever did you tell Sarah about me?

Not much, just how young and fanciable you are.

That would have done it then.

Calling now, hang on.

Izzy's phone rang a few seconds later, and Seth's voice, sounding so close, whispered a very personal greeting which made her blush.

'Where are you and what time is it with you?' he continued with laughter in his voice.

'You'll be asking me what I'm wearing next.'

'I'd rather imagine that …'

'I'm in your bed and it's six-twenty.'

'Early.'

'Magpies woke me up.'

'You're in bed with magpies?'

Izzy laughed. 'Idiot. They're pecking the roof and cackling, and every animal in this part of Sussex is shouting for its breakfast.'

'Yep, that's the country for you. If it makes you feel better, Tokyo is a twenty-four-hour kind of city, and really bloody noisy too.'

'How are the concerts going?'

'Good, thanks. We still have Jonno and, at the moment, no Sophie.'

'How is he?'

'Suffering from a broken heart, I think – but playing like a demon.'

'That's something, I suppose.'

'Been riding yet?'

'I'm going out this morning.'

'Who's Ted recommended for you?'

'Duchess.'

There was a slight pause as Seth digested that information. 'Might be a bit slow for you, I'd have thought.'

'Seth, I haven't ridden for years and have no clue where I'm going either.'

'I suggest you ride round the two top fields then, to get the feel of riding again.'

'On your property?'

'Yep.'

'Okay.'

'And text me when you're back on your own two feet.'

'Will do.'

'Not long now, Iz. I'll be in Sussex on the sixteenth, then we can ride together.'

'I can't wait.'

'Gotta go and get the sound check done. Take care.'

'You too.'

And he was gone.

Izzy lay back on the pillows when she remembered she hadn't told him about Willow's kittens. The sound of his voice always made her forget everything, including her own name sometimes. She quickly sent him three pictures. His answer pinged back.

Does that make me a grandpa?

Kind of.

Shall we keep them all?

Definitely.

Pick one for the house then. That'll keep Sarah busy when I'm not there.

Wicked.

Uh-oh – being called – gotta go, sorry.

Good luck.

Cheers.

Izzy wandered down to the stables at eight-thirty, thinking she might be able to lend a hand rather than just turn up at nine like Lady Muck, but Ted was already in grooming Duchess.

'I could have done that,' she said over the top of the stable door.

Ted barely paused in his work. 'No need,' he said brusquely. 'You can fetch the tack if you like.'

'Sure.' Izzy walked towards the tack room. Did he think she was after his job or something? She checked on Willow and the kittens. There was one black kitten with a naughty glint in its green eyes who kept treading across the others to get to his mum.

'You're a cheeky one,' Izzy said softly. 'Do you want to live in the big house?'

The kitten opened its tiny mouth in a silent 'miaow' and batted one of the others who had the temerity to chew his tail. Izzy laughed. She'd chosen the one she liked the best already.

Standing up, she hauled Duchess's saddle down from its stand and hooked the bridle over her shoulder. It was a long time since she'd done this, let alone the riding bit. Reaching the stable, she put the saddle carefully over the half door but kept hold of the bridle.

Duchess looked a treat already, and this time Ted did turn around to face Izzy.

'She's a cracker, this one,' he said.

'She looks fit for the Queen,' commented Izzy.

'According to the Boss, that would be you.' A rare smile crossed Ted's face.

Izzy laughed. 'I'm sure his opinion will change when we have our first big row.'

'You've not had one yet?' Ted took off his flat cap and scratched his head. 'Why not?' He replaced his cap and gave Izzy an appraising look. 'You've got red hair, there has to be a temper.'

'Bad press for redheads,' said Izzy firmly. 'Although we had a few words when we first met.'

Ted took the bridle from Izzy with a short laugh. 'What did he do?'

'Sent his mate over to invite me for a drink,' said Izzy. 'I wasn't too impressed.'

'I can see why.' Ted nodded. 'Gave him what for, did you?'

'Something like that.'

'Fame does funny things to folk sometimes,' observed Ted. 'He's all right though is the Boss.'

'Yes, he is.'

Ted put the bridle on Duchess and buckled the throat lash. He stroked her glossy neck. 'Look after this one, milady,' he said. 'She's important to the Boss.'

He took the sheepskin numnah from underneath the saddle and put it carefully on the horse's back. He finished tacking up and patted Duchess's neck. 'You'll do, lady,' he said.

'She looks fabulous,' said Izzy. 'I hope I don't let her down.'

'Where are you riding?'

'Seth suggested the top two fields for the first time out.'

'Man's got a good head on his shoulders.' Ted nodded his own. 'Sounds about right.'

'And if Duchess comes back without me, you'll know where to look.' Izzy laughed.

'You'll be fine with this one,' said Ted. 'If it had been Jupiter, now, I might be worried.'

'Me too, now I've heard his reputation.'

'He's had the Boss off a few times.'

'He never mentioned that one.' Izzy gave Ted an impish grin. 'You'll have to tell me about it.'

Ted didn't reply, merely opened the stable door and led Duchess out into the yard.

Duchess walked out happily, ears pricked forward, her stride confident and steady. Izzy stroked her neck as she aimed for the first field Ted had pointed to.

The gate was already open, and Duchess quickened her pace as she spied the open field.

‘Not going to do a Jupiter on me, I hope?’ Izzy chuckled, feeling the mare’s muscles tense as she eyed the open gate when they passed by. ‘Gate going to get you, huh?’

Izzy gave her a long rein as they walked around the edge of the field, and then shortened them a little as she urged her into a smart trot. Duchess was more than happy to oblige, and before long they were cantering. Izzy had almost forgotten the thrill she always felt when riding, but it all came flooding back as she sat on top of this lovely horse.

She looked around at the fields and the rolling downs in the distance. A rabbit startled by the horse scampered away, its bright white tail shining like a warning beacon for any other rabbits who might be nearby. Duchess snickered softly after it, as if it was beneath her to notice something as small as a rabbit.

They slowed to a walk and Duchess tossed her head, eager to carry on cantering. Izzy patted her neck. ‘I can’t take you back all sweaty,’ she said. ‘I’ll get into trouble.’

The sun felt warm on her back now; it really was a perfect summer’s day. The slight drone of bees would have made Izzy sleepy had she not been concentrating on her riding. She looked behind to see how far they’d come, and the stable buildings looked a long way away already. She knew Seth worked long and hard, and as far as she was concerned, deserved everything he had, but how privileged was he, to own this fabulous place? Although Izzy felt anywhere with Seth would be blissful. He was just that kind of person. It sometimes felt as if she was holding her breath, waiting for something to go wrong, and she couldn’t get rid of the feeling. Hopefully it was only her lurid imagination.

The second field stretched temptingly ahead and Duchess quickened her pace again.

'Okay girl, let's see what you're made of then.' Izzy gave Duchess her head and urged her into a gallop. The warm summer air rushed by them as they raced up a small hill. On reaching the top, Izzy slowed Duchess to a halt and rode her into the shade of a huge oak tree.

'You enjoyed that, didn't you?' Izzy leaned on the pommel and stroked the mare's damp neck. 'But I do think a more sedate pace back will keep us both in Ted's good books.'

After a few more minutes, Izzy turned Duchess back towards home. She appeared more than eager to go too. When they clattered into the yard, Ted emerged from Jupiter's stable wheeling a barrow of soiled straw.

'How was that?' he asked, closing the door behind him.

'Brilliant!' Izzy jumped down and ran the stirrup irons up the leathers. 'She's a really lovely ride.' She gave Duchess a peppermint surreptitiously, although she felt sure Ted had noticed. He didn't say anything, so she undid the girth and slid the saddle from the horse's back. Ted came over and took it from her.

'She'll need a bit of a rub down,' he said.

'Of course,' said Izzy, leading her into the stable.

After rubbing Duchess down and filling up her water bucket, Izzy bolted the stable door and took the bridle back to the tack room. Just time to check on the kittens and then she should really get going on her application for the MA course.

The kittens were all fast asleep and looking too cute for words. Willow looked up at Izzy and mewed a soft greeting.

She crouched down and fondled her ears. 'Hey Mama, how's it going?' she said. 'Having a rest while the babies sleep, huh?'

'What's the Man think of the kittens then?' Ted spoke behind her.

Izzy stood up. 'Wants to keep them all.' She grinned. 'And told me to choose one for the house.'

'Is that right?' Ted scratched his ear thoughtfully. 'That'll annoy the missus.'

'Why?'

'She'll be the one looking after it when he's away.'

'Do you want me to take him back to London instead?'

'I'm teasing,' he said gruffly. 'Missus will be chuffed to bits; she loves cats.'

Phew, thought Izzy. She definitely didn't want another run in with Scratchy Sarah.

'I chose the black kitty,' said Izzy. 'He's the naughtiest one, I think. Will the others live out here?'

Ted nodded. 'Stables have plenty of mice and rats as I'm sure you know. The more cats the better.'

'Thank you for letting me ride Duchess today,' said Izzy. 'She's amazing.'

'Any time.'

Saying goodbye, Izzy left the tack room and walked back towards the house.

She felt relieved to see Sarah's Golf wasn't parked next to her own car and let herself in the kitchen door.

Another triumphant gig, and Seth had loved every second. There were not many nights left now, and then he'd be on his way home. *The end of a world tour* – it was hard to believe. All the months of preparation and rehearsing, sound checks, gigs, photo calls, interviews and marketing stuff. Now what he needed most of all was home and privacy, peace and quiet … and, of course, Izzy. Definitely *lots* of Izzy.

Midnight with him must mean it was around four in the afternoon for her. He wondered whether she'd be at the farm or with her parents. Did it matter? That's what mobiles were for, after all. He pressed her number in his contacts and she answered straight away.

'Hey, Music Man. How was it?'

'Spectacular, thanks. How was your ride?'

'Also spectacular.'

'No problems?'

'None at all. Duchess is lovely.'

'Yep, she's a real classy lady that one.'

'I've chosen a kitty for the house.'

'Have you now? What colour?'

'Black with green eyes, very naughty.'

Seth laughed. 'Sounds about right. Got a name?'

'Not yet.'

'Let's name him when I'm back then.'

'Deal.'

After another ten minutes, Seth reluctantly admitted to Izzy he was shattered and they said goodnight. Too wiped even to shower, he crawled into bed and closed his eyes. Whoever said the life of a rock star was all glamour had obviously never tried it.

Chapter Twenty-One

The wait for Seth almost over, Izzy found herself on tenterhooks and unable to settle to anything. She spent a lot of time at her parents' place, and even more time down at the stables. She helped Ted with the mucking out, cleaned tack – even cleaned the windows in the tack room – anything to keep busy.

And then, suddenly, he was there.

One evening Izzy took herself downstairs to Seth's "cinema room" in the basement, and was watching possibly the worst-written police drama *ever* on the gigantic, pretending-to-be-a-cinema-screen television, when she thought she heard someone moving around upstairs in the kitchen. Her heart leapt. *Seth!* Or possibly a burglar? She turned the sound to mute on the TV in order to listen out for more noises when the man himself dived over the back of the sofa, pinning her in place so he could kiss her.

Laughing, she wrapped her arms around his neck. *'You!'* she said.

He pulled back, and those mesmerising blue eyes looked down at her, a mischievous smile playing over his lips. 'Who were you expecting?' he asked. 'The best man?'

'You *are* the best man,' she said softly.

'Is there any food in the house? I'm starving.'

'I knew you would be.'

'That means there is.' He swung himself up to standing and pulled Izzy to her feet. 'Let's go find it.'

Izzy had brought in some food shopping the day before, knowing he'd be more interested in food than anything else for the first few hours or so.

'I bet you've been eating all the way back on the plane too.'

'Do you now?' He grabbed her hand and hauled her up the stairs to the kitchen. 'I slept too.'

'In between meals.'

'So what is there?'

'Salad.' Izzy laughed at the look of disgust on his face. 'Don't panic, it's for me.'

'You bet it is.'

She opened the fridge door. 'You choose it, I'll cook it.'

'Cook? Nah. I'll order something in.'

'You'll have to wait longer.'

But he'd already grabbed a beer and was on the phone to his favourite restaurant, ordering the things he liked best. He suddenly turned to her. 'What do you want, Iz?'

'I've eaten, thanks.'

He frowned and turned back to the phone. 'And one of your chargrilled tuna steaks for the lady.' He listened to the order being read back, and then confirmed it. 'Yep, just in. Thanks, I appreciate it.'

He grinned at Izzy. Food was on its way, so she knew he was now a happy man. 'Do you want to finish watching whatever the hell you were watching?'

She pulled a face. 'Definitely not. It was dire.'

'Why were you watching it then?'

'Because the waiting was getting to me.'

'Waiting …?'

'For you.'

He put his beer down on the counter and moved closer, wrapping his arms around her. 'I forget sometimes ... it's always worse being the one doing the waiting.' He kissed the top of her head, and she looked up into those startling eyes.

'It's so good to have you back,' she said, enjoying the fact he was home – at last.

'It's pretty good to be here,' he said. 'Now … what can we do for half an hour?'

There was no early start the next morning. It had been a very late night, and Izzy slept through the usual magpie alarm, the horses' breakfast alarm and any other alarm that might have inadvertently gone off. Seth still slept soundly on, even when she did wake up. Not wanting to disturb him, she slid carefully and quietly out of the bed and padded into the bathroom.

When she emerged, twenty minutes later, he was still fast asleep, looking cherubic and almost edible. Remembering the "never touch a sleeping rock star" mantra, Izzy dressed quickly and tip-toed out of the room to go and make coffee.

As usual, at the precise moment the coffee was ready, Seth wandered in, his glorious mane of hair sleep-tousled, shirt still unbuttoned and hanging loose over an old pair of faded jeans, and his feet bare. He looked gorgeous.

'Morning,' he said. 'Is that coffee?'

Izzy chuckled. 'Of course it is.'

'You're an angel of mercy.' He loped over to kiss her. 'What time is it?'

Izzy looked pointedly at the clock behind his shoulder. 'Eleven-thirty.'

He pulled her into his arms and waltzed her round the big kitchen. 'So do we have brunch or go out for lunch? Or …' He raised his eyebrows at her as they twirled. 'Shall we order something in and go out for a ride first?'

Izzy opened her mouth to say she didn't mind and he could choose, but before she could, he continued. 'And don't you dare say I can decide, because it will count as at least four forfeits.'

'I'd love to go riding with you,' she said instead.

'That's what we'll do then.'

The stables appeared quiet and there was no obvious sign of Ted. The tiny black kitten suddenly shot out of the tack room and disappeared into a bush by the path.

'Was that him?' Seth watched the bush with interest. 'Gonna be a mouser, I reckon.'

'Already is,' Ted's voice said from inside the tack room. He came to the door, his weathered face breaking into a friendly grin at the sight of Seth. He strode forward to shake Seth's hand. 'Welcome home, it's good to see you.'

'You too,' said Seth. 'How's everything been?'

'Your lady here's been a great help,' said Ted with a cheeky wink at Izzy. 'Couldn't keep away from the horses, she couldn't.'

'Poor old Duchess will need a rest today then,' said Seth. 'Let's get you on Marty.'

'Good idea,' said Ted. 'Come on, young Izzy, let's get your horse some tack.' He turned back to Seth. 'I take it you'll be riding Marvel.'

Seth nodded his head. 'Yep, thanks.'

As they rode out of the stable yard, Seth reflected on how good Izzy looked on a horse. She rode effortlessly for someone who said she hadn't ridden in years, her hands were light on the reins and she sat well in the saddle. No wonder Ted thought she was so wonderful. He watched as Izzy urged Marty into a collected trot out into the first field, changing smoothly to a canter, and he followed suit with Marvel.

It felt good to be home at the farm, and it felt wonderful to be out riding with Izzy.

Nearly two hours later, Izzy and Seth wandered back to the house hotter and stickier and, in Seth's case, very much hungrier. The breakfast brunch he'd ordered was due any moment, and he said in no uncertain terms that he had no intention of taking a shower until he was fed.

'What would your mother say?' Izzy wrinkled her nose at him.

'She'd probably hold the food to ransom until I showered.'

Izzy grinned. 'How's Jonno by the way?'

Seth rubbed the side of his nose, 'Hard to say. Played like a demon as I told you before, but it felt like all the heart's gone out of him.'

Izzy frowned. 'Sounds like he still misses Sophie.'

'There's more to all this … he's really quiet ... but I don't have a clue what it is.'

'Will he come here to work on the track?'

Seth turned to look at her. 'I really hope so.'

'If this place can't work its magic on Jonno, then nothing will,' she said resolutely.

After they'd eaten, Seth shut himself away in the studio with apologies to Izzy for leaving her alone. She thought it rather sweet of him, seeing as she'd been here alone for weeks. But his absence encouraged her to break out her laptop and do some work herself. She'd set herself a few projects to keep her hand in and had bought several top-notch magazines to compare writing styles. She still hadn't decided which area of journalism interested her the most.

Although it would probably depend on what spaces – if any – were available. She intended to keep all her options open for the moment; cover all bases by looking at everything.

Flicking open the nearest glossy magazine, she read the names listed on the inside front cover of all the people who worked there. There was even a sassy-looking photograph of each person beside their name, advertising their importance in this very prestigious magazine.

One name suddenly leapt out at her. *Sheryl Roberts*. Wait … hadn't Jo said Sheryl was Seth's ex-wife's name? Her friend loved all the glossy mags with celebrity gossip and probably knew more about Seth than Izzy did, even now. Would Sheryl really have kept her married name after all these years though? Didn't women revert back to their maiden names? Izzy felt sure *she* would in the case of a divorce – especially if the marriage had ended badly. Why would you want to be reminded every time you wrote your name? But then perhaps the connection to the famous Seth *Roberts* was what had secured Sheryl the job in the first place, if this was indeed her.

Not a very charitable thought, Iz, she told herself. *Shame on you.*

Then she peered at the photograph by the name. *Heavens.* And she'd thought Gracie was beautiful … Seth certainly had a thing for stunning blondes. Or used to have; Izzy really hoped they were all in the past now. *Fashion Stylist* it said next to her name. Well, of course she would be, looking like that. It was difficult for Izzy to tear her eyes away from the glacial beauty who used to be married to Seth. Silvery, blonde hair hung to her shoulders like a glossy waterfall, and cool, grey eyes stared out from a perfect face with skin like porcelain.

Suddenly, Izzy didn't feel like writing any more. She decided to walk back down to the stables and chat to Duchess. Leaving everything on the kitchen breakfast bar, she let herself out the back door and set off for the stables.

'Had your first row, have you?' Ted challenged her the moment he saw her walk into the yard.

Izzy gestured with her thumb over her shoulder. 'He's working.'

'Ah, the joys of being famous and wanting to stay that way,' said Ted wisely.

'Can I help with anything?'

'You can groom Duchess if you like. I was about to, but if you're after a job I'll get off home early.'

'Will do,' said Izzy, heading for the tack room, grateful for something to do. Anything to take her mind off Sheryl bloody *Roberts*. She didn't even know why she felt so rattled. Seth never mentioned her, she'd never lived here with him, there didn't appear to be any photographs of her anywhere either, and he certainly didn't seem to be suffering from a lack of Sheryl in any way. She remembered Jo mentioning they'd never had kids either (those gossip mags again) … but there was *something* … Izzy felt it. And Seth had fallen into another relationship with a cool blonde beauty, hadn't he? She wondered whether men really did prefer blondes.

She loaded the grooming kit into one of the wooden tack trays, trying to shake off the feeling of impending doom and gloom, that, if she was honest, she knew she'd just inflicted on herself.

When she let herself into Duchess's stall, the horse snickered a greeting. Izzy stroked the velvety neck and spoke to her softly.

'You are such a lovely lady,' she told her. 'And although you already look beautiful, I'm going to make you look even more stunning.' Duchess turned to eye her through immensely long white eyelashes, making Izzy laugh. 'How did I know you'd make me feel better?'

She set to work, brushing the horse's coat until it gleamed, and then started on the mane and tail. Losing all track of time, she cleaned Duchess's hooves and had just started oiling them when Seth's voice made her look up.

'Thought I'd find you here.'

He was leaning on the stable door, the customary mischievous smile lighting up his eyes. 'Looks like you've done a really good job. No wonder Ted thinks you're the best thing since sliced bread.'

'He's gone off a bit early, so that should make Sarah happy.'

'Or not.' Seth grinned.

'Or not,' agreed Izzy, pulling a face. 'Did you finish what you wanted to finish?'

'Yep.' He nodded. 'Just needed to get something down before I forgot it.'

'Do you forget things often?'

He gave a rueful laugh. 'I forget the words all the time, and *I* wrote most of them.'

Izzy leaned against Duchess's warm flank and smiled up at him. She still couldn't believe this gorgeous man could actually be interested in her – ordinary old Isabelle Grant – especially after seeing the photo of Sheryl.

He continued to lean on the wooden half door, his strong, tanned arms folded, his hair curling almost to his broad shoulders, and those fathomless blue eyes studying her intently. 'Has anything happened?'

Izzy should have known he'd pick up on her current mood.

'Not exactly …'

'Well, say goodbye to Duchess and let's put the brushes away.' He took the tack tray from her. 'And then you can tell me.'

'I'll show you instead,' Izzy offered.

'Deal.'

Once they'd finished putting things away, Seth held a hand out to Izzy as they walked back towards the house, and she took hold of it. His grip felt warm, strong and safe somehow. She wondered whether she was being ridiculous, getting antsy over a picture of Seth's ex-wife – if it even was her. But Izzy didn't believe in coincidence. She definitely remembered Jo saying her name was Sheryl, and Seth had mentioned she worked in the media. *Have you had your first row?* Ted had asked, and she couldn't help but wonder if they were about to.

The moment they arrived at the kitchen, Seth turned Izzy to face him. He had no idea what had spooked her but something had. She'd been fine when he'd gone out to the studio, so he didn't think she'd been upset by him disappearing. She simply wasn't like that.

'Okay – spill,' he said firmly.

'Like I said, I'll show you.' She pulled him over to the breakfast bar. He noticed her laptop open with a blank page on the screen alongside a big pile of expensive-looking women's magazines. He didn't think Izzy had bought them to actually read, so she must have bought them for research purposes.

She pushed a magazine across the counter to him, open at the first page.

'Is this your Sheryl?' she asked.

Now Seth felt really confused. *His* Sheryl? He glanced down at the photograph of his ex-wife and felt … nothing. Zilch. Nada. *Too much make-up as usual*, he thought, and the photo appeared to have been retouched. Was this all that had upset Iz?

Relationships were *really* difficult. He might have to ask his older sister for advice soon. Although … then again … maybe not.

He sat on a stool at the breakfast bar and motioned for Izzy to do the same. She turned to look at him, and he was quiet for a moment, admiring the gleaming reds in her lovely hair. He reached out, twirling a thick strand around with his finger, and smiled.

'Did I ever tell you how much I love your hair this length?'

'No.' She grinned back at him. 'But I'm pleased you do.'

He released her hair and pulled the magazine towards him. 'Yep, that's her.'

'Still using your name.'

Seth raised his eyebrows. 'Cheeky of her. But not illegal, unfortunately.'

He looked back at the magazine and wondered what he'd ever seen in Sheryl. He'd been taken in by her, that's for sure … but they'd both been so young.

'If I was feeling vindictive, I'd say she kept the name to get herself a prestigious job.'

Izzy looked uncomfortable. 'That's what I thought, I'm ashamed to say.'

Seth laughed aloud. 'That's my Iz,' he said. 'Just say what you think.' He grabbed her hand and kissed it. 'And please never, ever change.'

'It's none of my business of course, but …'

Seth leaned over and kissed her soundly on the lips. 'Iz, you can ask me whatever you want. There are no secrets between us.'

'Do you ever miss her?'

'*Miss* her? Hell no. Why would I miss her when I've got you? And before you ask, I don't miss Gracie either.'

'But you married Sheryl.'

Uh-oh – the marriage thing. Seth gave her a shrewd look.

'We were young, very young, but both sets of parents were keen for us to get married and settle down. Except I was on the road a lot with the band and things were starting to happen for us. To be honest, the last thing I wanted was to get married to anyone.'

'So why did you?'

Seth sighed inwardly. He'd have to tell the truth, he realised; there was no way he could lie to Izzy. Actually, he was pretty rubbish at lying to anyone. He felt the truth was always better.

'She said she was pregnant.'

Izzy gaped at him. 'But you don't have kids …?'

He shook his head. 'We didn't. She told my parents and the sisters, and they believed her – hell, *I* believed her. I even thought I was in love, so we got married. Iz, I was barely nineteen.'

Seth searched her face for a reaction. She looked a bit shell-shocked. He brushed the backs of his fingers gently down her cheek. 'But I definitely know the real thing now I've found it and I'm all grown up.' He smiled. 'I was infatuated and easily manipulated back then.'

Suddenly, Izzy smiled back – her usual no-holds-barred, dazzling smile.

Seth was on a roll now. 'It soon became apparent she wasn't pregnant, and the world wasn't going to be inflicted with a "mini me".'

Izzy laughed quietly but soon composed herself as Seth continued.

'She said she'd lost the baby. We had a terrible row, I called her a liar – amongst other things … it got ugly. I'm not proud of some of the things I said.' Seth sighed. 'I was never sure there ever was a baby, but I do know now that she never stopped drinking her favourite tipple, and she never saw a doctor to my knowledge. She never asked me to go with her, at least – and, as far as I know, she didn't have any scans done at a hospital either.'

Izzy laid a hand on his arm. 'You really don't have to tell me everything,' she said. 'Especially if it's too painful for you to talk about.'

His eyes met hers unflinchingly. 'You're the only person I've ever talked to at length about it.'

Izzy took hold of his hand in both of hers. 'Thank you.'

'I didn't know what to do ... I was being pushed by the label to get out on tour and I had no say in those days. They ruled the roost so to speak. So I had no choice but to go on tour for nearly a year.' Seth looked down at their clasped hands and then back to Izzy's face. He took in a breath and continued. 'When I got back from touring, it was to a completely empty place. She'd moved out of the house we were renting, taking most of our furniture with her, and was suing me for desertion.'

Izzy gasped. 'That's awful ... and you had no idea ...?'

Seth looked down again and shook his head. 'The tabloids were full of it as you'd expect, and I didn't exactly come out of it smelling of roses. I refused to speak to any reporters, and I'm the same to this day. This is the first time

I've said as much as this to anyone – even Zach. Although he obviously knows most of the story.'

Izzy's eyes filled with tears. 'I can't believe—'

Seth continued as if she hadn't spoken, almost as if he couldn't stop now he'd started. 'The divorce papers were there in the house, waiting to be signed. My lawyers had tried to contact me, or so they said, but kept missing me – you know how tours go, always on the move. Patchy internet in a lot of places back then too, and no reliable mobile phones. Not like today.'

'But she trapped you in the first place …'

'Difficult to prove, and, to be honest, by then I just wanted her out of my life.'

'No wonder you don't want to repeat the experience.'

Realisation hit Seth like a sledgehammer. He cupped Izzy's face in both hands.

'When I'm ready to repeat the experience, it will be with you, Iz, and only you.' He kissed her again. 'And that's a promise.'

Chapter Twenty-Two

It felt strange being back in London after the space and freedom of Seth's farm. Izzy had always felt at home in the city, but now she felt a little claustrophobic. It took a while to get used to the noise and pace again too. Everyone was in such a hurry all the time, and Izzy wondered how she'd ever managed to keep up before. She'd applied to do an MA, even though she felt it was probably far too late to get accepted and enrolled on the course for this year. But, luckily, she *was* accepted on the strength of her grades, helped by a very glowing report from her professor at uni. Checking the timetables they sent, she found out the course would only involve going in a few times a term too, as long as her work was kept up to date. This meant she could be wherever Seth was most of the time, which made them both happy.

Over an early dinner in their favourite pizza place, Izzy told Jo about the magazine photo and the tail end of her conversation with Seth afterwards, omitting his very private revelations about Sheryl.

Jo held up her wine glass and smirked. 'Sounds like a proposal to me, Iz,' she said.

Izzy laughed. 'Well, it was a promise rather than a proposal, to be fair. If he ever feels like tying the knot, he said it will be with me. But, of course, he may never feel like tying the knot.'

'I think he'll surprise you.' Jo treated Izzy to her wise old married woman look. 'Sooner than you think.'

'I'm not sure I'm ready,' Izzy protested. 'It still feels like we're getting to know each other.'

Jo broke off a piece of garlic bread and took a bite out of it with obvious enjoyment. She waved the surviving piece in Izzy's direction. 'And that excuse is already sounding tired, young lady.'

Izzy laughed again. 'What is it with blissful marrieds always wanting to marry everyone else off?'

'Just looking after my BFF's interests.' Jo polished off her garlic bread and turned her attention to the pizza. 'Just make sure you're good and ready when he does ask.'

'Yes, ma'am.' Izzy saluted before snagging the last piece of garlic bread.

Somewhere in an exclusive club in Soho, Seth, Zach and Jonno were discussing the dates when they could all go down to the farm and work on Jonno's track.

'We're talking earlyish next month – right?' Seth took a healthy swig from his beer. He took out his phone and scrolled through the calendar. 'We're down at the farm from the seventh, back in London second week in October when Iz starts her course.'

The others were busy checking their own calendars.

Seth laughed. 'Look at us checking dates on our phones, like a bunch of hormonal teens arranging a night out.'

Zach grimaced. 'Sad, eh?'

'Anna's welcome to come too, of course,' said Seth. 'Although knowing Izzy, she'll be on a horse most of the time.'

'You'll never get Anna up on one of those,' said Zach. 'She's a townie through and through. She'd probably love to come for a weekend though.'

'Sure.' Seth nodded. 'Wouldn't want her to go all agoraphobic on us, would we?'

'She might break out in hives or something that far away from All Saints.' Zach grinned.

'Not sure I know what that is, mate.' Seth looked puzzled. 'Not a religious thing, is it?'

'She likes to shop there,' explained Zach.

'In a church?'

Zach cottoned on to the wind-up and swatted at Seth with a beer mat.

'There's this new-fangled thing we have now,' Seth continued. 'Online shopping.'

Both Zach and Jonno laughed at the thought of Seth shopping online – or anywhere at all for that matter.

They eventually settled on a date, and Jonno looked the happiest Seth had seen him look for weeks. He only hoped it would be possible to do something with the damn track. His phone buzzed and he saw a message from Izzy.

I'm heading back to the flat in a bit. I xx.

Where are you? I'll pick you up.

Gino's.

Hang on for me then. xx

Will do. xx

Seth sent a quick message to Dave saying he was good to go, quickly finished off his beer, said goodnight and then left to collect Izzy. It gave him a warm feeling, knowing they'd be going back to the flat together.

Soon Dave was drawing up outside Gino's and tooting his horn. Seconds later, Izzy came out and headed for the car. Seth opened the door and she slid in next to him.

Seth draped an arm around her shoulders and pulled her close. 'How was your pizza?'

'Good, thanks. How was your night?'

'Also good, and we have a week sorted for the guys to come to the farm and work on that bloody track.'

'I hope it helps Jonno.'

'Me too.'

'Is Anna coming?'

'For the weekend only – Zach thinks she'll spontaneously combust if she's out of London for too long.'

'Ah, an urban chick.' Izzy nodded her head. 'And probably not a horse fan.'

'Definitely not.' Seth laughed. 'To quote Zach, "you'll never get her up on one of those things".'

Over the coming weeks, Seth found himself thinking about his first marriage more than he would have liked, and probably more than was healthy – although at least it was all out in the open as far as Izzy was concerned. He knew he'd been right to confide in her. There should be no secrets between them. But Seth was beginning to feel a bit like a prisoner in town now; he wanted to be somewhere without the constant invasion of photographers and fans, and he wanted a lot of quality time with Izzy. In spite of his minor wobble in Hawaii, he now knew without question that he wanted to ask Izzy to marry him ... but the rings he'd bought in Australia were beginning to burn a theoretical hole in his flight bag now, and the thought of them lurking there in all their sparkling beauty began to play havoc with his everyday life. So much so, that the more he thought about them, the more ridiculous an idea it seemed to be – in the harsh light of Finchley anyway. *Get down to Sussex, Seth, and* propose *for heaven's sake ...*

When the first week of September arrived, hinting at a warm autumn, Seth couldn't concentrate on anything much at all and definitely felt the need to be back at the farmhouse. He wondered whether Izzy would mind leaving town a week earlier than they'd arranged, and felt hugely relieved when she agreed enthusiastically.

'I thought you might prefer to be in town a bit longer,' he said. 'But I could do with a week on our own before everyone comes down.'

'And I could do with having you to myself too.'

'Then we'll go tomorrow, shall we?'

'Let's do it.'

'I'll ring Sarah … unless you'd like to?' Seth raised his eyebrows at Izzy and laughed at the look of horror on her face. 'That's a no then.'

'That woman hates me.'

'I'm sure she doesn't.' Still grinning, Seth picked up his phone to call her. 'But she will hate the fact other people are coming down in a week's time.'

'Well, you can tell her that too. She won't shout at you.'

'Good to know you're looking out for me.'

'Always.'

The drive down to Sussex in Seth's car was almost idyllic until he hit the country lanes near his home and drove far too fast for Izzy's liking. She almost wished he'd called Dave and got him to drive them down, although she knew that would have been a bit unfair to him. When the farm gates loomed into view at last, she couldn't suppress a sigh of relief. At Seth's soft chuckle, she shot him a shrewd look.

'You sped up on purpose,' she said accusingly.

'I always drive the last couple of miles fast,' he said, still grinning. He reached under the dashboard for the remote and opened the gates. 'Sorry, Iz.'

'There could be people on horses,' she pointed out.

'Nobody lives down this lane but me,' he said reasonably, driving through the open gates at a deliberately sedate pace.

'If Sarah spots you driving this slowly, she'll think you've parked,' Izzy said with a hint of sarcasm. Although she couldn't help smiling when Seth laughed aloud and sped up the drive at a more normal pace.

'How boring the drive down used to be before I met you,' he said. He parked next to Izzy's car, which they'd left behind last time, and she spotted Sarah's Golf in its usual spot under the trees.

As they got out of the car, the kitchen door opened immediately, just like before, except this time Sarah's face was wreathed in smiles. *What a transformation.*

'Hey Sarah, how's tricks?' Seth gave her a friendly grin as he hauled their cases out of the boot.

Izzy grabbed her laptop and bag from the back seat and followed Seth to the kitchen door.

'Do you need a hand with anything?' Sarah offered, much to Izzy's surprise.

'No, I'm good, thanks,' she replied.

Seth turned back to wink at Izzy, and she wondered what he'd said on the phone to her to cause *such* a change. Threatened her with a plague of ants maybe. She followed Seth upstairs as he pretended to struggle with her bags, huffing and puffing for good measure.

'What *have* you got in here, Iz? Bricks?' He dumped the cases in the bedroom and turned to face her, blowing wayward tendrils of hair off his forehead.

'Yes, because I wear nothing but bricks in the countryside.'

He gave her an appraising look. 'Not sure it would catch on,' he said. 'But I'm happy to see the look. It would probably beat the blue taffeta.'

'One day I will put that dress on for you,' she promised. 'And you'll see how awful it is. No idea what Jo was thinking … barmy bride brain.'

He laughed. 'Is that what happens to brides?'

'That and trying to get all their friends married off …' Izzy stopped short, feeling suddenly embarrassed.

'I have friends who try that when they aren't even married.' Seth gallantly came to her rescue. 'And, by the way, I have a mother who is desperate to meet you.'

Izzy shrugged. 'Well, you've met most of my family,' she said. 'It seems only fair.'

'I'll arrange it sometime then.' He looked back at the cases. 'Do you want to unpack now or say to hell with that and get a beer?'

'Get a beer,' said Izzy quickly.

'That's my girl.'

The sight that met them in the kitchen was as unexpected as Sarah's greeting. Platters of cold meats and cheeses had been set out on the breakfast bar, accompanied by gorgeous-smelling, fresh, crusty bread and granary rolls. There was even a large bowl of salad, which Izzy knew Seth would ignore on principle. Various bowls of dips, chips and pickles finished the impressive spread.

'Are we having a party?' Seth grinned, grabbed a handful of crisps and ate them appreciatively. 'This looks great, Sarah. Thanks.'

'It does look amazing.' Izzy felt she should say something too. 'Thank you.'

Sarah looked pleased. 'Enjoy,' she said. 'I'm off home now.' She picked up her keys from the counter and, with a cheery wave, let herself out of the back door.

The only sound after her departure was the crunching of crisps from Seth until Izzy heard Sarah's car start up and drive away.

Then she turned to Seth. 'What the hell did you say to her?'

He went over to the fridge, pulled out two cold beers, and, after opening them both, passed one to Izzy.

'I told her roughly what time we'd be here and asked if she could leave the makings for sandwiches as we'd probably be hungry.'

'Is it normal for her to do that?'

Seth began piling food onto a plate and waved at Izzy to do the same. 'When I'm back from a tour, she often gets food in if I'm going to be late, and when I come down at Christmas, she gets in stuff like this for me. But she knows I get takeaways or go out mostly.'

'No wonder she told me not to take up too much room in the fridge with my stuff if she buys this much for you as a snack.' Izzy laughed and started putting food on her own plate.

'She said that?' Seth paused before stuffing a chunk of fresh bread in his mouth.

'I told you she hates me.'

'Has a problem with all younger women more likely.' Seth reached for the cheeses and cut chunks from each of them. 'But she left two plates out.' He pointed at each of their plates with the cheese knife. 'So she didn't want to starve you.'

‘Good to know,’ agreed Izzy. Although she felt she’d never starve as long as she was around Seth and his appetite.

Chapter Twenty-Three

The first few days back at the farm flew by in a blur of riding, long walks and lots of eating out. They were due to have Sunday lunch with Izzy's family, and then Jonno and Zach would arrive on Monday. True to form, Anna had decided to come just for the weekend, and Zach was due to pick her up at the nearest station on the following Friday afternoon.

Sarah had even got two guest rooms prepared, in spite of her having told Izzy she didn't clean, cook – or house keep at all, it seemed – and the place looked fabulous. Seth wondered about Sarah's initial reaction to Izzy. Perhaps there was some previous history with Ted and a redhead? Maybe he'd ask him sometime, but not when Izzy was around. Luckily, Sarah seemed to have moved on from whatever her problem had been, which was great news to Seth. It meant the fridge and the freezer were always well-stocked and that made for one very happy rock star.

The black kitten had been christened Sinbad because he was mischievous and the name seemed to suit him. He'd grown a lot in the last few weeks and had recently taken to delivering small, furry presents to the kitchen. Being country girls, neither Izzy or Sarah were in any way fazed, but Seth couldn't help wondering how Anna would cope if a dead rodent came her way.

Seth decided to drive the four by four to Izzy's parents' on Sunday. He loved driving it, and as it stayed on the farm, he could only drive it when he was there. The thought of trying to park it in Finchley made him wince. And, of course, Dave drove him everywhere in town anyway.

Just for once, Seth woke up before Izzy on Sunday, and was showered and dressed before she made an appearance. He wandered downstairs and greeted Sinbad, who'd been snoozing on one of the kitchen windowsills in the morning sunshine. The kitten stood up and arched his back, looking like a miniature Halloween cat.

'You're a very handsome chap,' commented Seth, tickling his tiny ears. 'I suppose you want food?'

Sinbad miaowed and yawned at the same time, making Seth laugh. 'I take that as a yes.'

He picked up the cat's bowls from the floor and washed them up while the kitten wound its way in and out of his legs. Then he realised he wasn't sure which cupboard the cat food lived in. Whatever had possessed him to get so many bloody cupboards? What on earth was in them all?

'Second cupboard on the left,' said Izzy from the doorway. 'I don't think I've ever seen you do anything even slightly domesticated before.'

'Has it made you go off me?' Seth grinned, looking appreciatively at her standing there in snug-fitting cut-off blue jeans and a black top. She'd tied a green bandana around her vivid hair again; he loved it when she did that. 'You look gorgeous.'

'Well, I can't go off you when you throw compliments like that at me,' she said, reaching across him to the cupboard where the cat food was kept.

Seth wrapped his arms around her waist. Her hair smelt wonderful as he pulled her close. A tiny miaow brought them both back to earth, and, laughing, Izzy got the food out of the cupboard. She sprinkled it in the bowl and filled the other bowl with water.

'Here you go, Sinbad,' she said.

The kitten almost leapt into the bowl, he was so eager for food.

'He's grown so much.' Izzy sounded almost unhappy about it.

'I think he's the reason Sarah's more cheerful,' said Seth. 'She likes looking after him.'

'Ted said she loves cats,' agreed Izzy. 'Good job because there's four others in the stables.'

'Ted looks after those,' said Seth. 'What time's lunch?' he asked, immediately changing the subject to more important matters.

'You haven't had breakfast yet!' Izzy laughed.

'Clever – I meant what time are we supposed to be there?'

'Mum didn't say, but they usually have Sunday lunch around one-thirty.'

Henry, the Grants' enthusiastic, very large and exceptionally hairy lurcher, shot round the house from somewhere in the back garden, barking furiously at the sound of Seth's car pulling in to the drive. Seconds later, Beth came out of the front door and waved.

'Go round to the garden,' she called. 'Drinks will meet you there.'

Seth leaned down to Izzy, 'So … who is this guy called "drinks"?'

'No idea, but I want one,' said Izzy with a grin. She led the way around the side of the house with Henry jumping up every now and again. 'I think he's forgiven me for all the beach W-A-L-K-S last year.'

'He can spell now?' Seth stopped short when two tiny red-haired girls flung themselves at Izzy.

'Izzy, Izzy, take us to the sea!' They chanted.

A red-haired man scooped up both girls who squealed with delight. 'Let Izzy say hello and have lunch first,' he said with an apologetic smile at his sister. 'How's it going, Iz?' He kissed her cheek.

'Good, thanks,' Izzy said. 'Erm … Seth, this is my big brother, Jack, and these two imps are his daughters, Katie and Lucy.'

Seth shook hands with Jack and winked at the twins.

'And I'm Jack's wife, Fiona.' A pretty brunette stuck her hand out towards Seth, who obligingly shook it.

Ben suddenly hurtled out of the back door. '*They* aren't married,' he said with the air of someone in the know.

'Benjamin Grant, what did I tell you earlier?' Beth emerged from the kitchen door carrying two jugs of what looked like Pimm's.

'To mind my own business.' Ben looked chastened. 'But I haven't got any worth minding.'

Everyone laughed.

'From the mouths of babes,' quipped Seth, draping an arm around Izzy's shoulders.

'I'm a teenager,' said Ben and pointed at the twins. 'They're babes.'

Katie pouted. 'We're nearly five,' she said, putting tiny fists on her hips. '*And* we started school last week.'

'Then you'll have to tell us all about it,' said Izzy quickly.

Izzy's mum had managed, somehow, to get everyone sitting around the large garden table with a drink, after a slight difference of opinion with Ben who'd wanted Pimm's. Seth assured him that he would be drinking water after just one Pimm's because he was driving, and Jack agreed, saying he was driving too, which appeased Ben a little.

Izzy had gone a bit quiet and Seth, feeling concerned, leaned in to talk quietly to her. 'Are you okay?'

She nodded. 'Just sorry you've been inflicted with the whole family in one go.'

'Don't worry. I'm used to my tribe, and believe me, they will all be there when you come with me next time.'

'Somehow that's not very reassuring.' Izzy grinned, looking a little happier.

Seth clinked his glass with hers, and then turned to watch Izzy's parents carrying out the first of the food. His very favourite time of day ... food time.

It had been a long time since he'd eaten a traditional Sunday roast, and he'd forgotten just how good it could be. Beth had cooked a Christmas-sized turkey with stuffing and cranberries, complemented by a mountain of roast potatoes and assorted summer vegetables. The huge plate that came his way was piled high with portions of everything, and would have daunted a lesser man for sure. But Seth was made of sterner stuff.

'Beth, this all looks amazing,' he told her. 'Your roast potatoes are the best I've ever seen.'

Jack raised a glass in a toast to his mother. 'She's always amazing.' He turned to Seth and started asking about the tour, and tours in general. 'Must be difficult,' he continued. 'Being on the road a lot of the year. Tough for those left behind.'

There was no mistaking the inference and Seth frowned. He didn't think this was the time or place for a discussion like that. But he decided honesty was the best policy.

'It's tough all round for everyone,' he said. 'Being on the road and away from the people closest to you is always hard. Soulless hotel rooms in cities you never actually see in daylight, in countries you don't have time to explore properly. It's hard work too, exacting physical work, with hundreds of people depending on me and the band for their livelihoods. And the tour itself is the end result of at least a couple of years in the studio, rehearsing, recording and so on.'

Jack looked taken aback and was about to speak when Seth carried on.

'Don't get me wrong, I'm a musician first and foremost – I love what I do, and I feel privileged to be able to earn money doing something I love, but I do get more than a little irritated when people assume it's an easy life with a massive payout. Trust me, it isn't. We really *earn* those big bucks.'

Izzy put her hand on Seth's arm. 'I only saw the workings of the tour for a few weeks,' she said. 'But even in that short time, I noticed just how hard everyone works. It's like a well-oiled machine and amazing to watch – and Seth is the lynch pin.'

Seth took hold of her hand in his. 'Finding the right person to share our kind of lifestyle is a tough gig, and some musicians never do,' he said. 'But to put all of your minds at rest, I think I have.'

Izzy turned to smile at him and he leaned down to kiss her.

Ben made a sound of disgust and everyone laughed again, breaking the tension.

'I'm sorry,' said Jack. 'I didn't mean to be the overbearing older brother.'

'Yes, you did,' said Izzy, punching him on the arm.

'But if you ever hurt Izzy, I *will* hunt you down.' He smiled to take the sting out of his terrible Liam Neeson impression.

'Good job I have big security guys then.' Seth grinned.

The farm seemed like a peaceful haven after lunch with her family, but Izzy felt awful about Jack's big brother attitude, even though Seth had assured her he'd taken it all with a pinch of salt.

'Rock stars have a terrible rep,' he said. 'Mostly thanks to the shenanigans of the guys a few decades ago. Riding around hotel corridors on Harleys, driving a Rolls into a swimming pool – stuff like that.'

'I'm surprised hotels ever allow any musicians to stay in that case,' commented Izzy.

'Me too.' Seth cupped her face in his hands. 'If your brother or your dad hadn't said something about the tour or me being out of the country for months at a time, I'd have been very surprised.'

'He was out of order.'

'Iz, seriously, Jack was just looking out for you – in a heavy-handed older brother kind of way, but nothing I wouldn't do for my little sister.' He tucked a strand of hair behind her ear and treated her to his mischievous grin. 'If she was hanging out with a lawyer.'

'But it was the first time you'd even met.' Izzy looked up into drowning blue eyes.

'Yeah, and he might not get the opportunity to say his bit again for some time.'

'He won't ever again if I have anything to do with it.'

'Fancy a walk to see the horses?' Seth was clearly keen to change the subject.

'More than anything.'

Seth took hold of her hand and led the way out of the garden gate and across the first field towards the stables. Izzy turned round to see Sinbad scampering after them.

'Sinbad's coming to see his fam.'

'Must be the day for it,' said Seth, laughing as he watched the kitten bounding through the long grass, and occasionally pouncing on a dandelion clock that was definitely too evil to live. 'Let's wish the horses goodnight, which I'm sure you always do anyway.'

Izzy flushed and smiled. She had actually spent quite a lot of time checking on the horses while Seth was away, but mainly because she didn't want anything bad to happen when she was there on her own. She wasn't sure what kind of bad she'd been dreading, but she'd checked on them anyway. And always went to say goodnight too.

Sinbad suddenly shot past them and disappeared into the tack room.

'There'll be squeals in a minute,' said Izzy.

Seconds later, all four kittens shot out of the tack room and disappeared in the long grass edging the path.

They went in to check on Willow, who was nonchalantly having a wash and obviously enjoying a bit of peace and quiet.

'Hey, Mama.' Izzy bent down to stroke her soft fur. 'So what time are the guys arriving tomorrow?'

'Just before lunch, I think. No need to get up early.'

'Good.'

Ted had shut the stable doors for the night, so Seth and Izzy went into each stable to say hello. Duchess was especially pleased to see Izzy and nuzzled her pockets hopefully.

'After a peppermint, are you?' Izzy fished one out of her pocket and gave it to her. 'No more.' Duchess pushed at her arm. 'All gone.' Patting the sleek neck, she said goodnight and shut the door behind her.

'You spoil that horse,' commented Seth.

‘She’s a special lady,’ said Izzy. ‘Helped me get my riding mojo back.’

‘Ah, but you were born to ride.’ Seth smiled. ‘Is it wrong to feel hungry after the huge lunch we had?

‘Possibly wrong, but not unusual for you.’

Seth looked around. ‘Should we grab Sinbad?’

‘Food, Sinbad!’ called Izzy and laughed as he came running. ‘Maybe we should rename him Seth.’

Seth shot her an amused glance. ‘That remark counts as another forfeit.’

Seth couldn’t help feeling their peaceful evening was the calm before the storm. He hadn’t actually spoken with Jonno since he and Izzy had left for Sussex, so who knew how he’d be feeling now? He really hoped he’d turn up. Zach was supposedly driving them both down, so he’d know pretty soon in the morning whether Jonno was a no show or not – it seemed Zach hadn’t heard from him in over a week either.

They sat outside in the garden with glasses of wine and watched Sinbad race around after a very territorial robin who hopped from branch to branch of the apple tree chattering down at him.

‘If he makes just one mistake, Sinbad will grab him.’ Izzy looked worried.

‘Nah, he won’t make a mistake,’ said Seth. ‘Old hand at cat worrying that one.’

‘How do you know it’s the same robin?’

‘I just do.’

Izzy smiled at him. ‘I hope you’re right.’

‘Do you think Jonno will actually turn up?’ Seth couldn’t help but voice his thoughts.

‘Are you worried he won’t?’

Seth frowned. *Am I worried? Yeah, probably.* 'A bit,' he said eventually.

'I think he'll come.'

Seth twisted in his chair so he could see her properly. 'What makes you so sure?'

Izzy shrugged. 'A kind of gut feeling. He's desperate for his track to be included on the next album, and then the next tour. So … he has to come and work on it with you guys. If he doesn't, then he's got no chance.'

Seth drank some wine thoughtfully. 'All true, but Jon's always been a bit of a law unto himself, so to speak.'

'By not coming, he'd have to wave bye bye to the track once and for all.'

'That he would.' For the umpteenth time that evening, Seth scrolled through his phone messages, spotting one from Zach.

Should be with you about twelve. All good so far. Z.

Seth typed in a reply. *You think he'll turn up?*

Yes.

'Zach seems confident,' he mentioned to Izzy.

'There you go then.' She gave him a reassuring smile. 'Want to watch a silly movie?'

'Sure.' Picking up the bottle and their glasses, he stood up and led the way back to the house.

Chapter Twenty-Four

For the second morning running, Seth was up early. He felt too on edge to stay in bed. Sinbad came running to meet him in the kitchen with delighted mews, slipping on the flagstone floor as he ran, and wound himself in and out of Seth's legs with his usual greeting.

Seth looked down at the tiny kitten. 'Yep. I get it, matey – you want breakfast.' He laughed as Sinbad miaowed and purred and wound through his legs again. 'And you're in luck 'cos I know where the stash is kept now.'

Green eyes stared up at him hopefully.

'Go get your bowls then.'

Sinbad yawned.

'Down to me then, I suppose. I don't usually do washing up – I'm a rock star.'

Sinbad looked unimpressed.

'Okay, fair cop. I'll get the food.'

The September sun shone in through the windows, making the kitchen feel warm and welcoming. Well, it looked like a good day for it, whatever "it" turned out to be.

With Sinbad happily hoovering up every morsel in his bowl, Seth turned his attention to the coffee machine.

Izzy came out of the bathroom, towelling her hair and thinking about dates. Very important monthly dates, and the fact that she couldn't remember *ever* being even a few days late before, let alone a whole week. She'd been doing her best to explain it away to herself – all the stress about starting her new course, the whirlwind jet-setting experience of the past few months – but now whenever she thought about it, her stomach gave a panicky lurch.

Seth came into the bedroom at that moment carrying a mug of coffee, and she hurriedly pulled herself together.

'Just to prove I can not only feed kittens, I can work the space-age coffee machine too.' He put the mug down and glanced across at her. 'Anything wrong?'

'No,' said Izzy hastily. 'Just thinking.'

'You want to be careful of that,' said Seth. 'Does you no good.'

'So I'm told.'

'I'm making my very famous breakfast this morning, which I will not be making when the others are here,' Seth informed her.

'Which is?'

'Bacon and eggs.'

'Sounds fabulous, very exotic. I'm in.' Izzy smiled, pushing the niggling worry to the back of her mind for now. 'This I have to see.'

Promptly at twelve, Zach buzzed from the entry phone at the gate and Seth pressed the button to let him in. Seconds later he drove round and parked next to Seth's Audi.

Izzy looked up from putting out bowls of crisps and pretzels on the big garden table and waved, feeling relieved to see both Zach and Jonno get out of the car. She poked her head round the kitchen door. 'Both here,' she called. Seth gave her a thumbs up and picked up his phone to order food. Izzy had offered to do a buffet, but it would have meant shopping and Seth had vetoed that. Anyone would think he didn't want to be left alone while he waited for Zach and Jonno. *Fancy that. Big famous rock star and all.*

'Hey Iz, how's it going?' called Zach, hauling out a big holdall from the boot and handing it to Jonno.

'Good,' she called back. 'How are you guys?'

'Hungry,' said Jonno with a grin. 'And hot!'

'Everyone's heading for the coast today as if it's the last chance saloon of good weather.' said Zach. 'Motorway's like a bloody car park.'

Seth appeared in the doorway. 'Food's on its way,' he announced. 'Wine? Beer?'

Everyone except Izzy opted for cold beer. She decided to go for fruit juice and soda ... *just in case* ... and followed Seth into the kitchen to help herself, leaving him to sort out the beers.

They sat in the shade of the fruit trees and clinked beer bottles together. Izzy hoped Seth was too preoccupied with his guests to notice she'd gone teetotal all of a sudden. Unfortunately, it appeared Zach wasn't ...

'No beer today, Iz?' he asked.

'Too hot for alcohol,' said Izzy with a smile. 'This fruit juice is fantastic with soda and ice.' She sipped at her drink, then set the glass back on the table slightly shakily, and prayed someone would change the subject.

'I'd forgotten how peaceful this place is,' commented Jonno, looking around. 'It was a good find, mate.'

'That it was,' agreed Seth. 'No neighbours for a few miles, top security, horses, a swimming pool, and now – of course – a gorgeous woman.'

'I'd forgotten you had a pool,' said Izzy.

'Too busy riding horses.' Seth laughed.

'Could do with a dip now ...' Zach raised his eyebrows in Seth's direction.

'You know where it is,' said Seth.

The "quick" dip turned into an hour, by which time the food had arrived, and that quickly disappeared as if by magic. Before long everyone was ensconced in the studio. Everyone, that is, who wasn't Izzy. She could have sat in on the session if she'd wanted to, which Seth had made very clear, but she felt she'd only be in the way, and, if she was honest, even a little bit bored. So she'd opted to clean tack. She desperately needed something normal to distract her from her manic thoughts anyway.

The kittens were playing out in the yard and Sinbad had deigned to join them, whilst Willow kept a watchful eye on them all from the shade of a lavender bush.

It's certainly hot for September, Izzy thought as she soaped the bridles. The stables were quiet without their usual inhabitants, who were enjoying being outside under the oak trees in their shady field. The only sound was the drone of bees in the lavender and the occasional indignant squeak from a kitten when one of its siblings played a bit too rough.

Suddenly, light footsteps sounded outside on the gravel, and Izzy looked up towards the open door, expecting to see Sarah. But the person who was standing in the doorway, silhouetted against the afternoon sun, was slight, much smaller than Sarah, and very definitely blonde.

'Can I help?' asked Izzy, wondering how – whoever the woman was – had actually managed to get through the gates.

'I want to see my husband.'

That wasn't the answer Izzy had expected, and her first thought was that Sheryl had come back. *Paranoia be gone.* She stood up from her seat on the straw bale and walked towards the person. The voice had sounded vaguely familiar.

'And he would be?'

As Izzy's eyes adjusted to the glare of the sunlight outside, she realised the woman was Sophie and not Sheryl at all.

Yet Sophie appeared different to how Izzy remembered her from their last meeting. Less brash, less confident altogether, and with an air of vulnerability about her which almost made Izzy feel sorry for her.

'Ah Sophie, I couldn't see who you were with the sun in my eyes.'

'I want to see my Jonno.'

Okay, maybe not that sorry.

'They're in the studio, so they can't be disturbed at the moment, but they should be out in an hour or so for a break.'

Sophie went to say something but obviously thought better of it, biting her bottom lip.

'You're welcome to share my straw bale though.' Izzy attempted to inject some humour into the conversation.

Sophie glanced over at the straw bale and flared her nostrils. 'Is it clean?'

Izzy shrugged. 'As clean as straw gets, I imagine.' She walked back, sat down again and picked up the bridle she'd been soaping. 'How did you get in?'

'Someone in the house opened the gates. I thought it was you.'

Izzy thought Seth might need to have a word with Sarah about letting random women in through his main gates; if she'd been in charge up at the house, she would definitely never have let Sophie in. Then she remembered Sophie had said *husband.*

'So ... did you two go off and get married then?'

Sophie nodded. 'Last week. My dad's furious … that's why I came down here.'

'Threaten to disinherit you, did he?' Izzy sounded sarcastic even to herself.

'Not for the first time.' Sophie smiled, and Izzy suddenly saw a different girl.

She grinned back. 'For heaven's sake, sit down! You're making my neck hurt.'

Sophie walked gingerly into the tack room on her customary skyscraper heels before perching daintily on the straw bale.

'Are there rats?' she almost whispered.

'Almost certainly,' agreed Izzy. 'But there are also loads of cats.'

Right on cue, Sinbad appeared with a furry donation, and Sophie leapt up again with a squeal. Dropping it at Izzy's feet, he turned and left again.

'Er … thanks, Sinbad,' said Izzy. She held the large rodent up by its tail. 'Well, that's dinner sorted.'

Sophie looked pale.

Izzy's phone buzzed with a message and she glanced down. 'Guys are out for a break,' she said. 'Let's go and get a drink with them.'

She quickly replied to Seth, warning him Sophie was here. Hanging the, now gleaming, bridle back on its hook, she carried the rat outside, put it in the bin by the door, then washed her hands thoroughly at the outside tap.

'The joys of country living.' She grimaced at Sophie.

'I remember,' replied Sophie with a shudder. She definitely looked queasy.

They walked slowly together back towards the house – Sophie none too steadily. Izzy couldn't help wondering how Seth would take Sophie's arrival. She hoped he wouldn't throw her out, because it appeared her father had already done that.

The session had gone pretty well so far. Jonno was enthusiastic and receptive to Seth's suggestions. They'd made some definite improvements to the track already, and with Zach's talent at mixing, Seth felt sure they could whip it into something pretty decent. But he was more than ready for a break. They all trooped into the kitchen, and Seth headed straight for the fridge. His phone buzzed.

He glanced at Izzy's message and frowned. 'It would appear your missus has arrived mate,' he said to Jonno carefully.

Jonno had the grace to look embarrassed. 'Ah, sorry … I meant to warn you she might appear. Big fall out with her dad.'

Seth raised his eyebrows. 'Because …?'

'Because she married me.'

'She did? *You* did?' Seth felt flabbergasted. 'When?'

'Last Wednesday.'

'Where?'

'Marylebone Town Hall,' Jonno said. 'The Paddington Room – very swishy.' He smiled, but looked really uncomfortable and still pretty embarrassed. Clearly he was expecting a sudden backlash from Seth. 'We got engaged on holiday. Soph flew out to meet me.' He added by way of an explanation.

Seth remembered the blonde he'd seen at the end of tour party. *So I was right.*

Zach joined them. 'Erm … and you travelled down with me this morning without saying a word?'

'Yeah, sorry man, I wanted to tell you both together. Soph … she's … well she's sorry for all the trouble she caused. Truly.'

'But why go and get secretly *married*?' Seth still felt the breath had been knocked out of his body. 'Let's grab some beers and get some air.' He opened the fridge door and started pulling out bottles of assorted beers. Handing a bunch of bottles to Zach, he led the way out of the kitchen to the gardens. They were just sitting down when Izzy and Sophie came through the garden gate followed by an eager Sinbad, who probably thought it was supper time. The girls appeared to be chatting easily enough together, although personally Seth felt that if someone couldn't talk to Izzy, there must be something seriously wrong with them.

'Hey girls, come and get a beer,' he called. Turning back to Jonno, he said, 'So you two not only made up, you went and got hitched? Should we have a party or something?'

Jonno's face lit up in delight. 'That would be awesome – thanks Seth … really. We're flying out to California middle of next week on honeymoon, but I would really love to celebrate with the band.'

'Saturday here then?' Seth looked over at Zach and raised his eyebrows.

'I'll call Anna,' he said. 'If anyone can make it happen on Saturday, she can.'

Grabbing a beer, he left the table and went back into the kitchen.

Sophie sat on the seat next to Jonno and he put his arm around her.

'Congratulations,' said Izzy, raising her newly replenished glass of fruit juice to them in salute.

'I want to apologise …' Sophie faltered, looking straight at Seth. 'I behaved like …'

'Like a spoilt rich kid,' said Seth helpfully.

'I guess so ...' Sophie agreed somewhat reluctantly. She pouted perfectly made-up lips, then clearly remembered she was a changed person, and smiled instead.

'Bit harsh, Seth,' said Izzy, sitting down on a chair next to him.

'Well, let's hope you don't go running off to the tabloids every time there's a row within the band.' Seth still looked stern. 'Or try to get your dad to buy out our label.'

Sophie flushed. 'That was awful of me, and I *am* really sorry.'

'You can make it up to us all by partying with us on Saturday if Anna can get it arranged in time.'

'Specially for us.' Jonno smiled at her. 'To celebrate.'

'Best bibs and tuckers.' Seth grinned suddenly, and felt relieved when Sophie smiled tentatively back.

Zach came back giving a double thumbs up. 'Party's a go-er.'

Jonno and Sophie left on Thursday in her car to get different clothes for the party. Izzy almost welcomed the distraction of wondering what to wear herself, although she suddenly felt unsure about the clothes she had with her. But she really didn't fancy driving back to London just to get some random dress she'd probably decide not to wear anyway on the day.

Asking Seth's advice on clothes was pointless because he'd just laugh and tease her, and turn up himself in jeans and a T-shirt looking like a million dollars. She supposed you either had it or you didn't, and she really didn't.

'Looking thoughtful, Iz.' His voice brought her back to earth with a bump.

'Thinking about clothes.'

He looked amused. 'That must be riveting.'

'For the party.'

'Is that a girl thing?'

'Of course. This is the first party with all the band for me.' She gave him a look to stop him saying anything. 'And after show parties don't count.'

He took hold of her hand in both of his. 'It's a party here in my house – well, hopefully in the garden – and I just want everyone to have fun. And I want to be with you. I don't give a damn what you wear; you always look perfect to me.'

'You always know what to say …'

'But?'

'But I don't have the same kind of clothes that Sophie or the other girls wear.'

'Iz, you don't need them. Trust me, the girls wear the classy gear for gigs, it's work stuff if you like, but they'll turn up for the party in jeans or shorts.'

'I don't want to let the side down …'

He did laugh then. 'Isabelle Grant, I never thought I'd hear you stressing about what to wear to an informal party here.'

'You said "best bibs and tuckers"…'

'It was a joke.'

'Jonno and Sophie have taken it seriously.'

'Only because the party is kind of in their honour.'

'I guess …'

'A lot of people will end up in the pool if it stays as warm as this.' He smiled and stroked a gentle hand down her hair. 'And I *know* how good you look in a pool.' He wiggled his eyebrows at her, making her giggle.

Izzy appreciated the joke. 'Thanks.'

'Anna has managed to organise a whole bunch of chefs to barbecue for us too.'

'She's amazing.'

'She is.'

Friday morning saw Zach heading to the station to pick up his amazing Anna, and Izzy upstairs sorting through a mound of black tops she'd strewn across the bed, that would potentially look good with either jeans or shorts. Maybe she'd ask Anna's advice later. She idly picked up two of the black tops – they looked tiny – how long would they continue to fit her *if ...?* And what the hell would she do if she actually *was* ...? There was no way she'd be able to tell Seth, that's for sure. He'd just think she was doing a Sheryl on him. What on earth *could* she do? *Worry about it when it's an actual fact*, she told herself. *Now, time to put a smile on your face and go downstairs.*

Sarah had risen to the challenge of preparing two more rooms for guests and changed the sheets on everyone else's beds. Izzy toyed with the idea of offering to help and made the mistake of mentioning it to Seth when he came upstairs to find her. He'd said a very definite no.

'She'd be insulted,' he said firmly. 'Honestly, Iz, she gets well paid and I'm not here a lot of the time. She and Ted could be having raving orgies here for all I know.'

'You don't think ...' Izzy began and then laughed at his expression. 'Another joke. I get it.'

Zach's voice called from downstairs, and Izzy went down to greet Anna.

'Might need a fork lift to get Anna's suitcase upstairs,' said Zach with a grimace.

'Ah, the very important bricks,' said Seth with a grin at Izzy.

Zach looked puzzled. 'Bricks?'

'Because it's heavy,' said Anna, rolling her eyes at Seth. 'Hey, Iz.'

Izzy stepped forward and hugged her. 'So good to see you,' she said. 'I really need your advice ... sorry to bombard you when you've just got here ... but *what* are you wearing tomorrow?'

'Jeans,' said Anna. 'Unless it's hot, then shorts.'

Seth gave her a smug "told you so" grin, and started handing out beers.

'There's a whole bunch of stuff in the fridge for lunch,' he said, waving at it. 'Shout when you're hungry.'

'I could eat something,' said Zach hopefully.

'Me too,' said Anna.

Izzy started getting out cheeses, cold cuts of meat, dips and salads from the fridge, and putting everything on to serving plates.

'Seth usually eats all this on his own,' she said with a laugh.

'Oh, we know.' Anna laughed too.

'Help yourselves,' said Izzy, putting cutlery and plates on the breakfast bar before fetching the fresh bread from the bread bin.

Plates were soon piled high and everyone trooped out to the garden to eat.

It felt good to be just the four of them, and Izzy relaxed in the friendly atmosphere.

Her worry about what to wear almost gone, she enjoyed listening to the banter between Seth and Zach. Although her busy brain kept hopping back to the bigger and much more serious niggle. *What if …?* But no … it really didn't seem likely ... did it? *But then why …?*

Anna had certainly managed to get everything organised in a very short time. She was up and about early the next day, supervising the party people who were decorating the garden with thousands of tiny white fairy lights. Luckily, the weather was still dry and warm, so it looked good for the barbecue.

Izzy took mugs of coffee out for them both. There was no sign of the boys yet so, as far as she knew, they were both still asleep.

Anna looked up from her check list. 'So how was the girlfriend from hell?' she asked.

'I'd say contrite, eager to get on with everyone, and now, happily married.'

'Zach said she apologised to Seth. Did he buy it?'

Izzy thought for a moment. 'Not sure,' she said. 'Hard to tell.'

'Did you?'

'She seemed genuine enough,' admitted Izzy. 'But time will tell.'

'Good call,' said Anna. 'I think we play it by ear … and maybe don't trust her for a second.'

Izzy nodded. 'Sounds like a plan. They'll be here after lunch sometime.' She looked around at all the lights in the trees. 'It's going to look fantastic out here when it's dark.'

'It will.' Anna looked pleased. 'You like tuna steaks, right?'

'Yes – not for breakfast though.'

Anna laughed. 'Don't get cheeky, missy, or I'll force feed you a beefburger.'

Seth wandered out, followed by Sinbad. 'Is there coffee?' he asked, running his hands through his shower damp hair and yawning.

'In the usual place.' Izzy made a pushing motion with her forefinger. 'Just press the button.'

He gave a thumbs up and wandered back into the kitchen.

Anna watched him go. 'Not really a morning person, is he?'

'He'll be fine once he's had his caffeine hit,' said Izzy. 'Then he'll be hungry.'

'He's always hungry.'

'True.'

After breakfast, Seth and Zach excused themselves and disappeared to the studio. Izzy wondered aloud why Sophie and Jonno had opted to come later in the day.

'She's never had a reason to get up early in her life, I imagine,' muttered Anna tartly. 'Probably never worked a day in her spoilt existence.'

'You really don't like her at all, do you?' Izzy grinned.

Anna looked ashamed. 'Sorry, I know I'm being unfair, but I've always looked on Seth as a big brother, known him for ages, and she really did cause a lot of trouble.'

'Did you ever know Sheryl?' Izzy asked suddenly. She realised she needed to know. Unfortunately, Sheryl was more on her mind than ever at the moment.

Anna gave her a shrewd look. 'No, they were divorced way before I started working for Seth. I have met her though.'

'And …?'

Anna pulled a face. 'Makes Sophie look like Mother Teresa.'

Izzy laughed. 'That makes me feel better.'

Anna put her arm through Izzy's. 'Good. Now let's see if the decorating guys have put some pretty lights around the pool, shall we?'

The rest of the band turned up in time for lunch, and Seth felt relieved they'd agreed to come. He'd been worried Gina and Caz would refuse and persuade their men not to attend either but, according to Caz, as long as Sophie didn't want to sing, she was "cool with the whole marriage gig".

Everyone decided to take advantage of the unseasonably warm weather and make use of the pool. A noisy and hilarious game with a basketball was in full swing when Jonno and Sophie arrived. Jonno instantly went into the pool house to change and jumped in to join the game, but Sophie declined, saying she'd just had her hair done. She sat on one of the sun-loungers in the shade instead, watching the game from a safe distance behind her flashy-looking designer sunglasses.

Seth hauled himself up to sit on the side of the pool. He loved having everyone together. He watched as Izzy streaked through the water after the ball, and laughed when Zach ducked her under the water so he could take it from her.

'Hey! No drowning my woman!' he yelled.

Izzy re-emerged spluttering. 'You are so dead.' She took off after Zach, only to have Micky and Joe head her off. She beckoned to Seth. 'Boys are ganging up on me.'

Seth jumped back in the pool and headed for Izzy. Not that he was going to help – perish the thought. But he fancied causing some trouble.

The caterers arrived mid-afternoon, when everyone had dried off and changed. Seth had been right in his assumption of the girls' dress code. Gina and Caz were in cut-off jeans and off-the-shoulder tops, Anna was in shorts and a loose silky shirt, and Izzy had opted for her favourite cut-offs with a black top. He felt pleased to see she'd added the silver pendant he'd bought her. She looked so lovely, and she'd caught the sun since they'd been out riding most days, which had topped up her Hawaiian holiday tan. She came over to him with her special Izzy smile and he pulled her in close.

'You look fantastic,' he murmured against her hair. 'Gorgeous.'

'Why Mr Roberts, are you hitting on me?' She looked up at him, her green eyes sparkling.

'Bloody right I am,' he said. 'And don't you forget it.'

'Oh thank goodness,' she said. 'I was worried I'd have to do all the running again.'

Seth laughed. 'Let's get a drink.'

Two barmen had set up a bar under the apple trees in the garden, and one was busy mixing up Pimm's. Seth wasn't at all sure how the evening would go if everyone started on those too early, and steered Izzy towards the safer beers and soft drinks.

Anna and Zach were already sitting at the table, both drinking coffee.

'Not tempted by a cocktail or six then?' Seth sat down and took a swig of beer.

'Pacing ourselves,' said Zach.

'The caterers have brought a cake,' Anna chipped in. 'When I first asked them, they were a bit iffy – but they did it.'

'Cake?' Seth raised his eyebrows.

'Wedding cake.'

'They made one in a few days?'

'They did, and it looks good.'

The smell of meat being grilled on several barbecues filled the early evening air, luring Seth to go and inspect the food. Izzy felt sure he couldn't be hungry again already, but Anna assured her he really could.

When she found him at the third grill, he'd wangled a hot dog from the chef and was happily chowing his way through it.

'Are you going to eat all evening?' She eyed the rapidly disappearing hot dog with interest.

'I hope so.' He grinned as he finished it. He gave a nod of approval to the chef. 'Thanks, that was great.'

'I hope you leave enough for everyone else.' She laughed.

A burst of laughter made them both turn around to see Micky attempting to balance an empty beer bottle on his nose. He managed a full thirty seconds before it toppled off and he caught it deftly.

'It's gonna get messy,' Seth said. 'I hope Anna's remembered to book a clean-up crew for tomorrow.'

He hooked an arm around Izzy's shoulders as they watched Jonno attempting to beat Micky's time. He only managed twenty seconds but, as he pointed out, he did have a much smaller nose.

The chants of 'Seth, Seth, Seth' accompanied by slow hand claps encouraged Seth to try his luck. Izzy took a few hilarious photos at his attempts. He beat Jonno but Micky was still in the lead.

Pushing up imaginary sleeves, Caz gestured for someone to hand over the bottle.

'You're all rubbish,' she said, and promptly balanced the bottle on her pert little nose with an experienced flourish. She managed a full minute to rapturous applause and took a triumphant bow.

The food was a huge success, the Pimm's, beers and wine flowed, and even Sophie appeared to be relaxed and happy. When the wedding cake was brought out, the look on her face was one of wonder.

Seth stood up and everyone fell silent. 'In the absence of any blood relatives,' he began. 'I feel it's my duty to make a speech for the happy couple.' Enthusiastic applause greeted his statement. 'But I'm actually pretty rubbish at making speeches, so I'm just gonna say – congrats you two, be happy, make babies and don't forget we're starting work on the new album in a few weeks.' More applause. 'Now cut the cake, it looks fantastic!' *Actually, this marriage malarkey is looking and sounding cooler by the day*, he thought.

Chapter Twenty-Five

The lecturer from Izzy's course had emailed asking for a meeting before term started. She'd tried to get the date moved nearer to the start of term, but it wasn't possible, so she had to make a special trip to London.

Seth and Zach were going through potential new tracks in the studio, Jonno and Sophie had flown out to California and everyone else had gone back to town, so Izzy supposed it was a good time to make her trip.

'Stay over at the flat, Iz,' advised Seth. 'Drive back the next day.'

It sounded like good advice to Izzy, who hated driving on motorways in the dark. They were better driven on during daylight hours in her opinion.

She left in the morning and joined the M23 to head for London. Having started out after the initial rush hour, she found it wasn't too bad now the holiday season was well and truly drawing to a close. Fewer caravans and trailers anyway, which was a huge relief.

Unfortunately, time alone meant the recurring niggling worry she'd been burying for a while kept popping back up. She couldn't ignore it any more, and the only person she felt she could talk to was Jo. She'd arranged to have dinner with her friend that evening, and although she knew what advice she'd give, she still wished the worry would just go the hell away.

'Have you taken a test?' Jo was practical as ever.

Izzy shook her head. 'I think I'm too scared to.'

'Well, that's rubbish.' Jo cut up the garlic bread. 'That's the very first thing you should do.'

'I told you about his first wife, didn't I? Pretending she was pregnant ...?' Izzy couldn't actually remember telling Jo the whole story.

'I'm not sure if you mentioned that part ... but Iz, you aren't her; he knows that.'

'But it might seem like history repeating itself.'

'Take a test first.'

'I suppose …' Izzy chewed on a bit of garlic bread. 'I just don't want him to hate me.'

'And that's nonsense too.' Jo gave her an exasperated look. 'The man is smitten. Any idiot can tell that.'

'But—'

'Take a test,' Jo said firmly. 'Then you can take it from there.'

'I know you're right.' Izzy finished her bread and looked across the table at Jo. 'It's the most sensible thing to do, but I can't think how it happened—'

'Why? Have you been sleeping in separate rooms or something?' Jo asked sarcastically. 'It can always happen, Iz. You know some birth control doesn't always work.' She took a sip of her wine. 'And you might just have forgotten—?'

'Okay! I'll take the test,' Izzy nodded quickly. 'You're right, of course.'

'Thank heavens for that,' Jo rolled her eyes. 'Get the answer first, and then worry about what to do. The chemist down the road stays open until ten. We'll go and get a test from there on the way home.'

'Okay.'

'Good.'

With the test duly bought and the instructions followed, Izzy now sat alone in Seth's beautiful bathroom, waiting the allotted time before she would know once and for all. If it was positive, what would she do? Would she tell him? *Could* she tell him? More importantly, would he think she was trying to force him into marriage just like his first wife did?

After trying unsuccessfully to make Izzy take her back to the apartment with her, Jo then made her promise to call the moment she had the result. Izzy felt grateful to her friend for that, but assured her she really needed to be alone. *What if …?* Would Seth really think she was pushing him into a second marriage? Or *worse* ... would he simply not believe her?

A part of her still felt he could have proposed on holiday if he'd really wanted to marry her, but he hadn't, even though they'd been in one of the most romantic places in the world. She wondered if he would ever want to marry anyone again after his first experience. *What on earth will I do if I am …? Will he hate me?* She didn't think she could bear that.

She checked her watch. *Nearly time.*

Her phone rang in the bedroom and she rushed to answer it.

'Hey gorgeous, how you doing?' Seth's voice sounded so close.

'Missing you,' she replied.

'Good.'

'How's the recording going?'

'Still in the very early stages. Are you coming home tomorrow?'

Home. Her heart skipped a beat. After checking the test, he might never say that to her again.

'Yes.'

'Meeting go okay?'

'I think so. I'm sure it could have waited, but apparently he's seeing every MA student before term starts.'

'Zach's going back to town in the morning. What time will you be back?'

'I'll text before I leave.'

'Do that. Drive carefully.'

'Says the man who thinks he's Lewis Hamilton.'

'Who do you think taught him?'

Izzy didn't reply, her mind on the test sitting on the bathroom shelf.

'Night, Iz.'

'Night.'

Seth finished the call and frowned. It wasn't his imagination, Izzy had definitely sounded a bit strange. Just preoccupied perhaps? He didn't think so, but something was off. He just knew it. He tried to think whether anyone could have upset her.

For the life of him, he couldn't think of a thing. But he needed to find out …

Izzy took a deep breath and looked at the test result. *Negative.* She didn't know how she felt. She didn't feel ready to start a family yet, but the thing that worried her the most was the fact she hadn't felt she could talk to Seth about it. She'd gone running to Jo. Shouldn't she be able to discuss any problem with Seth if they were going to continue as an item? And would he ever actually discuss having a baby after his previous experience with Sheryl?

So many questions. She decided then that she'd stay in London another day and take some time to get her head back in order …

Chapter Twenty-Six

Midday, and Seth couldn't help thinking that Izzy should have texted or called by now. He felt a worrying nag in the pit of his stomach. This wasn't like her at all. Not his Izzy. He was wary of calling her in case she was driving and lost concentration. Even if he texted, the alert could distract her.

Carrying a large mug of espresso, he went outside and sat at the table. It was strange without her, especially now all the guys had gone too. Zach had left quite early and the place was quiet and peaceful, apart from Sinbad chasing butterflies round the garden.

So where was she? He wondered whether she'd dropped in on her parents on the way, but didn't dare call them in case she hadn't and they started to worry too. He'd call Anna first, and then maybe Jo; he still had her number.

He pressed the call button for Anna, who, true to form, answered straight away.

'Hi Seth, what do you need?'

'Anna, hi, have you heard from Izzy?'

'Isn't she with you?'

'She went to town for a meeting, but she should have been back by now.'

'You're worried?'

'Little bit, yeah …'

'I'll give her a call. Have you tried calling?'

Seth felt a bit of an idiot. 'No, I thought she'd be driving.'

'Dingbat,' said Anna kindly. 'I'll call her.'

A few minutes later, his phone rang. Anna was back.

'Sorry, Seth. It goes straight to voicemail.'

'Thanks. I'll WhatsApp her, and then call Jo.'

'Let me know.'

'Sure.'

He wrote a message, deleted it, then wrote and deleted two more messages before he finally sent …

Iz, is everything okay? Have you left yet? S xxx

He hoped it didn't make him sound like a clucky hen. The guys in the band would probably hoot with laughter at him. He certainly wouldn't live it down for a while.

Finishing his coffee, he scrolled through his log of calls and eventually found Jo's number. She answered quickly with a distracted-sounding, 'Hello?'

'Jo, sorry to bother you. It's Seth.'

'Oh … hi, what's up?'

'I –er – can't get hold of Iz. And I know it sounds a bit lame, but I'm worried.'

'Worried because …?'

'She should have been back down here by now.'

'When did you last speak to her?'

'Last night.'

'How did she sound?'

'Odd. Distracted.'

'Ah.'

'Do you know something I don't?'

There was silence.

'Jo?'

'You need to speak to Izzy, Seth. She is worried about something but I can't tell you. It has to come from her.'

The pit in Seth's stomach grew larger and he felt cold in spite of the warm sunshine.

'Has she found someone else?' He almost felt disloyal asking the question.

'Don't be an idiot.' Jo laughed. 'As if. Look, if you want my advice … do you want my advice?'

'Of course I do, I'm bloody drowning here.'

'Get your butt up to London and talk to her face to face.'

'I did think of that, but I thought we might pass each other on the motorway.'

'Knowing her, she's still in your flat, sitting there like a stuffed wombat, thinking.'

'Do wombats think?' Seth felt this conversation had taken a turn for the weird.

'Now you sound like her.'

'So she had no intention of coming here today?'

'Why don't you just go and see her? What are *your* intentions anyway?'

'You think she wants me to spell it out for her?'

'I think it will help, yes.'

'Fair enough.'

'But you didn't get any of this from me – okay?'

'Thanks.'

'Take her flowers or something.'

'Relationships are such a bloody minefield.'

'Are you still here?'

For the first time that day Seth laughed. 'I'm gone. Cheers, Jo.'

Seth reached Finchley by late afternoon. He parked his car and felt relieved to see Izzy's car still there, plus a few hopeful fans lurking outside. He gave them a cheery wave and sprinted into the building.

He had no idea what he was going to say to Izzy; his track record wasn't brilliant with serious relationships after all, but he knew he wasn't letting Izzy go without a fight. Especially when he had no idea what was wrong. They'd had a great time at the barbecue and an even better time before everyone turned up. He wondered whether Sophie had turned malicious again and targeted Izzy, although he doubted it; things appeared to be calm on the Sophie front now, and she and Jonno were still on honeymoon as far as he knew. Unless the Sophie She-Monster had resurfaced and they'd split up again. He knew he was being a little unkind, but she had been a nightmare ever since she'd arrived on the scene, and he still didn't quite trust her. Once bitten and all that ...

Letting himself into the building, Seth took a deep breath and then strode to the lift.

He hoped she was in. He felt like a besotted teenager, for heaven's sake. Seth Roberts, the internationally famous singer for Scarlet Gryphon with a legion of fans, worrying about – well, who knew what the hell he was worrying about? – all because his girl hadn't turned up when she said she would. Pathetic. *Yeah, that's a good ploy, Seth. Get annoyed, that will solve everything.* Not.

He took another deep breath and let himself into the flat.

Izzy felt so guilty for not answering Seth's message – even in a WhatsApp he'd sounded worried. Was she being totally ridiculous here? She'd spoken to Jo at length on the phone after reading the result, and she'd been sympathetic to a point, but had also told Izzy she was being silly. Then she'd made things a whole lot worse by not driving back down to Sussex when she said she would. The busy Izzy brain had got her all befuddled for no reason and now she'd no doubt upset Seth, which she wouldn't have done for the world. She sighed. She had no idea what to do next; Jo had told her to sleep on it and then see how she felt. Well, she'd slept on it – kind of – been up for hours now, and still didn't know how she felt. Perhaps some more coffee would help.

Izzy went downstairs to the kitchen and turned on the coffee machine. This one made more noise than the newer version in Sussex, which probably explained why she didn't hear the key in the lock.

'I hope there's enough for two brewing in there.'

She spun around to see the man himself standing in the doorway. He looked serious, his bright eyes holding her gaze intently.

'Do you want to tell me what's on your mind?'

'I … erm … yes …' She busied herself pouring two coffees and handed one to Seth. 'I will.'

He gestured to the stools at the breakfast bar. 'I feel this might be a kitchen kind of conversation, don't you?'

'I don't know …' Izzy wasn't sure whether he was serious or teasing, but he looked deadly serious.

He sat on the nearest stool, his expression now cool and calm, and started sipping at his coffee. 'You have to start talking, Iz,' he said. 'Because I have no damn idea what the hell is going on unless you talk to me.'

Izzy sat on the stool nearest to him, cradling the coffee mug in both hands. She looked at his lovely face. Whatever she said now would probably sound ridiculous, but how to start?

'You remember telling me about Sheryl, and how she pretended to be pregnant?'

He nodded. 'Sure, but why would that upset you?'

Izzy looked down into the depths of her coffee, hoping a halfway intelligent answer would swim to the surface, but it didn't. She looked back up at Seth. 'I thought *I* was pregnant,' she said finally.

'You *did*?' He stared at her, looking totally flummoxed.

'I couldn't tell you in case you thought I was the same as her …'

Seth swore, put his mug down and, taking Izzy's from her, put that down too. He took hold of her hands in his. His eyes appeared as deep as any ocean.

'You can always tell me anything, you know that,' he said. 'Are you completely insane?'

'That's kind of what Jo said, except with more swearing,' admitted Izzy quietly.

'Iz, I hardly know what to say without bloody swearing,' he said. 'I love you more than anything, more than I have ever loved anyone. If you are pregnant, I'll be over the moon happy, and if you aren't, well – we have plenty of time for kids. What's the problem?'

'You wouldn't mind?'

'*Mind?* Why the hell would I mind?'

'But she … lied about it … to get you to marry her ...'

'And you are not her.'

Tears trickled down Izzy's cheeks. She couldn't help it. The tension of the last few days had really taken its toll. With a muttered oath, Seth got off the stool and pulled her into his arms.

'You are the most infuriatingly complicated woman I know,' he said. 'Wherever did you get this stupid idea that you couldn't talk to me? Did you take a test?'

Izzy nodded against his broad shoulder. He pushed her away so he could see her face.

'And?'

'Negative.' More tears fell.

Seth pushed a frustrated hand through his wild tangle of hair. 'So … are you upset because you *thought* you were, or because you *aren't*?'

'I don't think I know …'

'Thank god you didn't drive today, that's all I can say.' He grinned down at her and gently brushed the tears away. 'Don't you ever do anything like this again.'

'Or?'

'Or I'll hunt you down …'

'I think you already did that.'

Chapter Twenty-Seven

Izzy was still asleep when Seth crept downstairs to make a few early morning phone calls. He'd thought long and hard in the early hours, and he knew what he wanted to do. He had a plan and everything was arranged, thanks to Anna's help as usual.

It was late morning when Seth drove them both back to the farm. It was drizzling, which hadn't been part of the plan but, according to the weather forecast, it would be brighter and warmer later in the afternoon.

Sure enough, by the time the farm gates loomed into view, a watery September sun was breaking through the clouds. *Great timing*, thought Seth, *couldn't be better*. He drove round to the back of the house and parked in his usual spot. Unbuckling his seat belt, he turned to face Izzy.

'Welcome home, Izzy,' he whispered, tracing the backs of his fingers down her soft cheek.

She smiled.

He leaned forward and kissed her. 'Let's get your stuff inside.'

Izzy felt so happy to be back at the farm. The atmosphere was peaceful and welcoming. Seth unlocked the kitchen door and a joyful Sinbad shot out, wriggled under the garden gate and hurtled off in the direction of the stables and playmates.

'Hello to you too,' muttered Izzy as the kitten darted past her, before following Seth inside.

With Izzy's holdall dumped in the bedroom, they opted to sit in the garden now the sun had decided to show its face properly.

Seth took hold of Izzy's left hand and grinned his mischievous grin. 'I was going to do this by the book,' he said. 'Big romantic stuff, I'd planned everything, I was all geared up to do the perfect proposal in Hawaii, but then I kind of chickened out somehow. And when we were here together, we ended up talking about Sheryl, and I know you thought I was anti doing the whole marriage thing again ... which I will admit, I was for a while. But *you* changed all that. Iz ... wonderful, gorgeous *you* ... and then I got to thinking ...'

'Oh heavens, *you* were *thinking*?' Izzy wasn't at all sure where he was going with this. *Is this actually a real proposal? From Mr Once Bitten?*

'Yeah, I know ... anyway, I'm asking you for real now, hours earlier than I'd planned. Even though I sort of did arrange to propose properly over a candlelit dinner tonight – you know, the whole shebang – but because I think that's kinda cheesy, which isn't me really – and probably isn't you either – *and* because I can't wait until the food arrives, I'm asking you now. Please marry me, Iz.'

Izzy stared into his serious blue eyes. '*What?*'

'Don't make me say it all again.'

Izzy took a deep breath. *Wow ... this is really happening ... he's actually proposing! Jo would be proud of him*, she thought to herself with a smile. He'd even said "please". But she had to be sure ... 'Is it definitely what you want?'

'I wasn't sure what I wanted for a while, and I didn't know how you felt about the whole marriage thing either. Then I thought you'd gone and found someone else, and there was no way I was going to lose you.' Sincere blue eyes met hers. 'I really panicked a bit then, so I asked Jo.'

'Someone *els*e? Are you mad?' Izzy stared at him. '*Wait* ... you asked *Jo*?'

He looked really embarrassed now. 'Well, I didn't know what to think. Like I said, I'm pretty crap at putting the seriously romantic stuff into words – well, saying it out loud anyway. But all I know is that I always want to be with you – *only* you – and I want us to be together forever … and I love you shedloads too, of course.'

'Me too.'

'I'm pretty clueless about rings and all that stuff too – particularly the kind of designs you might like best – but I found a few I really liked when we were in Aus, and got Anna to go and buy them ... secretly ... then I've been kind of hanging on for the right moment … whenever the hell *that* is. Since then, I've been carrying them from country to country, to be honest ...' He gave an apologetic grin. 'Then Jonno made up with Sophie and *they* went off and got hitched ... so it's all been going well, huh? Then you go to London and don't come back ... but one thing I *am* sure of is that this proposal won't be like in the movies where the ring always fits perfectly, and there are shmaltzy violins playing in the background ...' He paused for a moment, miming playing a violin. 'Although I could always get my guitar out ... but please just say yes, Izzy. Then you can choose the ring you love the most and we'll get it to fit. But if you hate them all, we'll send them back and start again.'

Izzy burst out laughing. She'd never heard Seth babble quite so much. Mr Cool and Confident was apparently having a mini meltdown. Over her. And she'd never loved him more than she did at that precise moment.

Seth set half a dozen expensive-looking ring boxes tentatively on the table. 'Anna helped a lot.'

'In that case, they'll probably all fit.'

'Good point. We'll keep them all. So what's the verdict?'

Izzy leaned forward to kiss him. 'Seth Roberts, you are definitely the most incredible man I've ever met. Totally bonkers of course – but incredible. And the answer's yes – a really big fat YES.'

'Are you sure I'm better than the best man?'

'You *are* my best man.' Izzy wound her arms around his neck and smiled. 'But who will be yours?'

* The End *

Thank You

Thank you so much for reading *It's Only Rock and Roll* – and thank you Mick Jagger and Keith Richards for inventing the title all those years ago ... it fits the book perfectly!

Several readers became very fond of Seth and Izzy in *Izzy's Christmas Star*, the first book of the series, and they wanted to know how their story would progress. So this book shows another glimpse into the crazy world of rock music, the world tours and the travel, with a bit of jealousy and angst thrown in. I'm also very aware how much everyone wants a wedding – I won't let you down, I promise.

It's always important for me to know the readers are happy, and I'd be thrilled if you could find the time to write a quick review either on Goodreads or the website from which you bought the book. Please let me know if you enjoyed *It's Only Rock and Roll.*

If you'd like to write to me, you can find me on Facebook and Twitter – please see the details on my 'About the Author' page, next. You can also always contact me via my publisher, Choc Lit. I'd love to hear from you.

I hope 2022 brings you health and happiness.

With love

Berni

x

About the Author

Berni Stevens lives in a four-hundred-year-old cottage in Hertfordshire, England, with her husband and black cat. She trained in graphic design and has worked as a book cover designer for more than twenty years.
Books and art remain her passion, and her love of the paranormal began when she first read Bram Stoker's Dracula, aged fourteen. She is now on both the committee and the book panel of the Dracula Society, a society for fans of gothic literature and film.

For more information on Berni visit:

Twitter: www.twitter.com/Berni_Stevens1
Facebook: www.facebook.com/BerniStevens1620Author

More Choc Lit
from
Berni Stevens

Izzy's Christmas Star
Book 1 – Izzy

You don't only find stars on top of the Christmas tree ...
Student and Zumba instructor Izzy Grant leads a pretty normal life, but in the run-up to Christmas an unusual encounter with a friendly Santa paves the way for the most wonderful and star-studded Christmas she's ever experienced.

Because at almost exactly the same time, Izzy also meets Seth Roberts – as in the Seth Roberts, bona fide rock star and lead singer of Scarlet Gryphon. As their connection grows, Izzy's Christmas countdown becomes a glittering whirlwind of after-show parties and classy restaurants – and does she have her mystery Santa to thank?

Visit www.choc-lit.com for more details.

Laughing All the Way on the Jingle Bells Express

If you received a mysterious invitation for a fun-filled festive train ride the week before Christmas, would you go? When teacher Dee Nicholls receives her invitation, she isn't sure what to make of it. Surely it's some kind of joke to get her out of bed early on a weekend? Perhaps a clever festive marketing ploy?

But as the Christmas countdown begins, it becomes clear that Dee isn't the only "Jingle Bells Express" invitee. There are other people out there who have received the same invitation: Tom the intern, Rachel the aspiring writer, Dylan the musician and his dog Muttley – and they're not the only ones!

Could the unusual festive journey they eventually take together show them all the true meaning of Christmas, and also that happiness is sometimes right in front of you – if you just take the time to *look*?

Visit www.choc-lit.com for more details.

One Magical Christmas

Christmas magic doesn't really exist – does it?
When Annie Berry collides with Nik Knoll in a car park on the day of her sister's wedding, it feels like all of Nik's Christmases have come at once. Annie seems like just the sort of woman he'd like to get to know, and the chance nature of their encounter is almost like, well … Christmas magic.

But Nik has a secret, and he has to be sure that he can trust Annie before he tells her. The problem is that this secret has a Christmas deadline, and time is running out …

Visit www.choc-lit.com for more details.

Revenge is Sweet
Book 2 - The Immortals of London series

Hell hath no fury like a vampire seeking revenge ...
Life hasn't been exactly normal for Ellie since she became a vampire. Although joining the legion of the undead was always going to take some getting used to, even if you are the partner of Will Austen, the Elder of London.

But when Daniel, a fifteen-year-old fledgling vampire, unexpectedly turns up at Ellie's and Will's Highgate home, things start getting very strange – and more than a little scary.

Events take a devastating turn as a mystery troublemaker leaves behind a trail of carnage – and it soon becomes clear they will stop at nothing to get the Elder's attention, even if it involves hurting the person he cherishes the most …
But when it comes to Ellie, Will Austen is the wrong vampire to mess with.

Visit www.choc-lit.com for more details.

Printed in Great Britain
by Amazon

35010531R00148